RANDALL LOMBARDI

The Ascension

To everyone cheering me on throughout this journey.
Thank you!

Contents

1

Tera-Sue

The world was spiraling to a slow halt until soft fingers brushed my forearm and brought me back to it.

I snapped my eyes open, sat up straight, and inhaled slowly through my nostrils. I'd been dozing off during English again. This time, my melatonin-laced sermon was dedicated to The Crucible. Thankfully, the teacher was too focused on pushing through their last lecture of the day to notice me on the verge of snoring.

I glanced over to my right to find Ben nestled in his desk. I could still feel the ghost of his touch. He gave me a soft smile and a wink before turning his attention back to the teacher. His jaw tensed and relaxed as he fought to keep his focus on the front of the classroom. After two years of dating, I would still catch him staring at me like it was the first time he'd seen me.

I couldn't blame him. Whenever I saw him, every butterfly in North Carolina held a conference in my stomach. When I was little, I always said I'd marry a dark and mysterious man. Of course, I'd ended up in love with the human version of a golden retriever, complete with sandy blond hair and soft brown eyes.

I pulled my gaze from Ben and focused back on the front of the classroom just as the teacher announced our exit ticket for the class. The girl in front of me passed me a half sheet of paper.

There was only one question: what drove the townspeople to murder? The only thing I could say for certain was that the answer wasn't witchcraft.

A pen tapped the left side of my desk in two quick, soft beats. I made a face at my sister, Selene, and then took the pen from her. She glanced down at her paper before fixing her gaze back on the clock.

Selene was my identical twin sister. While we shared the same raven-colored hair and emerald-green eyes, she couldn't have been any more different from me. When it came to academics, Selene was a genius, easily at the top of our class. I focused more on the social aspects of high school; sports and clubs were where I shined. Thankfully, we always had each other's back.

I did my best to glance down at Selene's answer without drawing any attention; she had written a whole paragraph. She was great at doing too much.

I scribbled down one word: hate.

By the time the bell rang, some students had already lined up at the door. Selene packed her bag slowly, and I stood and slung mine over my shoulder the moment I'd passed my paper forward.

"I've got to get to the field early today," Ben said as he stood. "Coach wants me to run the warm-ups and drills."

"Okay, I'll see you when I get out there." I grabbed his hand and gave it a gentle squeeze. He gave the back of my hand a gentle kiss before letting go and leaving the classroom.

"Don't people usually save the PDA for the hall?" Selene mocked as she stood from her desk.

I laughed. Selene wasn't wrong, though. The hallways were always flooded after the last bell with students, some rushing to their buses, others to after-school activities, and others taking up space to be PDA sideshows. We slipped and shoved our way through the masses until we reached our locker.

"Are you going home?" I asked.

"No, I was planning to do some homework in the library. Aunt Jules is staying late anyway," Selene said.

Jules was the school librarian, our aunt, and our legal guardian. Sometimes, she let us stay after school to use the computers and get ahead on our homework before she drove us home. Our uncle Dan refused to let us drive to school. He claimed we should take the bus and help the environment. Jules didn't care what he said and drove us to school most days, anyway. Uncle Dan was our dad's brother, and Jules was our mom's sister. Jules called the shots most of the time. On rare occasions, she let Uncle Dan think he made decisions. Thus, we weren't allowed to drive his car to school.

She opened the locker and pulled out a couple of books. "Do you have practice today?"

"Yeah, but I think it's going to end early. Rumor has it that Coach has a family thing later today."

I slipped my backpack off and hung it on the designated hook at the back of the locker. Selene was in charge of organizing the locker, and I was in charge of decorating it. The inside of the locker door was sprinkled with photos: one of me and Selene in a photo booth last summer, one of us with Jules and Uncle Dan, two of us and our best friend Ashlyn, and one of Ben and me in front of the Ferris wheel.

"Tera, don't stunt today," Selene said.

"Huh?"

"Stay on the ground. Don't stunt. I've been having a bad feeling that I can't seem to shake," she said.

I nodded.

When Selene had a feeling, I listened. Selene had feelings before bad things happened—like our dog dying or Uncle Dan getting in a bad car accident—and she'd never been wrong. I always said she was psychic, but she didn't tell anyone else after she tried to tell Uncle Dan, and he didn't believe her. It didn't matter what anyone else believed because I sure as hell always believed her.

"Hey," Ashlyn said as she came up beside me. She pulled us both in for a half-hug and then leaned against the wall beside our locker. Her blonde and pink box braids smelled of cotton candy. "Are you two making plans for tomorrow without me?"

"The only plans we have so far for tomorrow are the ones you're already included in," Selene said.

"Well, that's no fun," Ashlyn said with a sigh. "You only turn eighteen once. I mean, you two should be making a bigger deal out of this."

"We turn every age once," I said as I pulled my gym bag from the top shelf of the locker. "Besides, what else do I need to do? I'm already going to be spending the day with my favorite people."

"That was so cheesy." Ashlyn laughed. "Are you ready for practice?"

"I was just telling Selene that I'm not feeling too good." Selene closed our locker.

"Does that mean you aren't coming?" she asked with a raised eyebrow.

"I'm still going. Just going to take it easy."

"Boo. That sucks. I was hoping you'd stunt with me," Ashlyn said.

I looked at Selene and made a face. We couldn't let Ashlyn stunt, but I knew Selene was not comfortable just telling her the truth about why she couldn't stunt today. Knowing Ashlyn, she would just do it, anyway. I stared at her, trying to think of something to tell her, but my mind was blank. Selene waved for Ashlyn to come closer and whispered something in her ear. Ashlyn stepped back and grabbed my hands.

"We won't stunt this week, but next week, you're gonna do it with me," she said.

"Uh, yeah, of course," I said as I shot Selene a look. She nodded.

"All right, I'll meet you in the gym," she said before turning to Selene. "And I want to see you in the bleachers giving us all of your support."

"I'll be there," Selene said with a smile.

As quickly as she had appeared, Ashlyn was gone.

"What did you say to her?" I asked.

"I told her that your stomach is really bothering you and that you've been on the toilet all day," she said with a giggle.

"Wonderful," I said as I rolled my eyes.

Ashlyn was sitting on the gym's indoor bleachers when I finished changing, texting a storm. Given her expression, something intense was going on. Coach always told us to dress comfortably for practice, so for me, that meant sweatpants and a tank top. Ashlyn's definition of comfortable was a crop top and leggings. Her high ponytail swayed back and forth as her narrowed eyes traced side-to-side across her phone screen. With a forceful push of her thumb, the swish of a text sending sounded. Then, she walked over to me with a huff.

"How are you feeling?" she asked.

"I'm okay, just a little uncomfortable," I lied. "How are you?"

"I'm fine," she said. "Douchebag is not answering my texts, but other than that, fine."

"What was his name again? Jared, Jack, Josh, or something?" I asked in a mocking tone.

"Not funny," she said with a smirk.

"Why are you wasting your time with that douche? You can do so much better."

"I know I can, but not all of us can find 'the one' the first time around. He's just entertainment for now. I mean, once we graduate, I won't remember his name." She pushed the door to the field open. "Speaking of devils, how is your boo?"

"Ben is fine. He left early so he could run practice." I held down my vomit at her use of the word "boo."

"I'm sure he'll text you later all apologetic like, 'Hey, baby, sorry I couldn't walk with you to practice today. I just wanted to tell you how fine you are,'" she said as she deepened her voice to mimic him.

"Oh god, is that what you think he sounds like?" I asked, laughing.

"That's what all men sound like when they're trying to seduce you," she said, wiggling her eyebrows.

We reached the field laughing as we always did. The team was already stretching in a circle by the time we arrived. On a normal day, Coach would have been waiting to jump down our throats for being late, but we got lucky, and she wasn't. Ashlyn and I stepped into the circle and followed the girl leading the warmups.

Other teams practiced on the field with us: football, women's lacrosse, and men's soccer.

Bingo, I thought. I could see Ben towering over the others as he ran through drills. The butterflies in my stomach danced as I watched him. He caught me looking and flashed me a quick, bright smile. I smiled at him and nodded back.

"Okay, ladies and gentlemen! Let's get to it!" Coach's raspy voice snapped my attention back to our practice. "Get in formation. I want some new volunteers to fly today. Let's see some hands."

Ashlyn and I looked at each other. A couple of freshman girls volunteered, eager to get the practice in. Part of me wanted to tell them not to. Another part of me hoped that Selene had been wrong. Her feelings could be wrong, couldn't they? We all fell into our positions for one of our simpler routines.

Coach counted as we went. I could feel the hairs on the back of my neck stand up. One, two, three, four, one, two, three. We grew closer to the part of the routine where the flyers went up. I fought to keep my focus on what I was doing, but I could hear my heartbeat in my ears.

The flyers went up. Then, as if on cue, someone sneezed. I whirled my head around to see one of the flyers coming back down as the back spot began to have a sneezing fit.

The girl hit the ground. I could have sworn I heard a crack.

Coach was beside the girl instantly, one hand raised to tell everyone else to freeze. "Everyone, give her some space. Ashlyn, run to the nurse's office. Tell them to come quick."

Ashlyn nodded before sprinting back toward the school. The rest of the team just stood around, watching the scene unfold. Coach talked to the injured girl. She tried to get information out of her about where the pain was. The girl was beet red and heaving as she spoke. The back spot was hysterical, like she was the one who fell. The other teams on the field seemed to notice the commotion and started to walk over.

I looked to the bleachers to see Selene standing at the bottom. Her expression was unreadable. We locked eyes briefly before her attention was drawn to Ashlyn and the nurse coming onto the field.

The nurse had a bag with him. He knelt beside the girl and started to speak to her. I read his lips. The girl's arm was broken. Coach talked to the other coaches on the field when the nurse entered their huddle. Ashlyn made her way over to me.

"Thank god for your weak bowels," she said. "That could have been one of us."

"Yeah, thank god." I couldn't keep myself from looking back toward the bleachers. Jules was there, talking to Selene. *Selene is psychic,* I thought.

"All right, folks, we're going to have to cancel the rest of practices today," one of the other coaches announced. "Please head back to the locker rooms and go home."

No one complained. No one said much of anything as we left the field. The only sounds that filled the air were the crunching of turf beneath shoes and the sobs of a girl in pain. I waved goodbye to Ashlyn as I went toward the bleachers.

"Are you all right?" Jules asked.

"Yeah, I'm fine."

"Are you ready to go home?" she asked. "I'll drive you."

"I have to change and get my backpack out of my locker."

"Okay, we'll meet you in the car. Take care of your business," she said.

"Thank you, Aunt Jules," I said before heading back into the school.

I pushed my gym bag back on the top shelf of the locker and unhooked my backpack. I had everything I needed for the weekend. I took all the books out of my backpack and put them into the locker. I didn't plan on doing any schoolwork. I zipped up the almost empty bag and put it on. I looked in the mirror at the back of the locker and pulled my headband off.

Just as I was about to close the door, I caught a glimpse of someone behind me in the mirror. I whipped around to see Ben standing behind me with a goofy smile.

"Scare you?" he chuckled.

"Yes, creeper."

"Sorry, I wanted to make sure I saw you before you left." He pulled me in for a hug.

He was warm and smelt of spice and burning wood. I let myself relax in his arms. We stayed there for a few moments.

"I have to go; Jules and Selene are waiting for me."

"Okay," he said. I didn't pull away. I just hugged him tighter. He laughed. "I'll see you tomorrow, right?"

"Yeah, we're supposed to go to lunch with Selene and Ashlyn at the cafe," I said, still not lifting my head from his chest.

"My dad is in town," he said. I felt myself tense as he said it. Even after two years of dating, I hadn't met Ben's dad. Ben always said his dad traveled a lot for work. I sensed that Ben didn't want me to meet the guy. He avoided the subject. "He wants to have dinner with us while he's here."

"Okay, just tell me when."

We stayed quiet for a few more moments. I ached to know what he was thinking. I always did.

"You better go before Jules comes in here and kills me," Ben said, breaking the silence.

"She would," I said. I gave him one last squeeze before pulling away.

"See you tomorrow," he said and kissed me on the forehead.

With one last smile, I locked my locker and headed out to the parking lot.

I opened the back door of Jules's gray sedan and noticed a small lavender bag on the seat. I picked it up and looked at Jules, who was in the driver's seat. She looked back at me with a smile.

"I know it's not until tomorrow, but I just couldn't wait," she said. "Happy birthday."

"Thank you," I said as I climbed into the car.

"You can open them now that you're together," she said. Selene, in the passenger seat, had a similar bag on her lap.

I pulled the tissue paper out of the bag and reached inside. Something cold and metallic brushed against the pads of my fingers. I grasped it and lifted it from the bag.

A necklace. The metal chain was dark, and the charm was made of a similar metal in the shape of the sun. In the charm's center was a crystal, a shimmering, translucent gem with accents of orange and green. I could have sworn the flecks of color danced as the necklace dangled in my hand.

"You didn't have to do this," Selene said. She held hers by the chain above her palm: a moon set in front of a different crystal.

"It's the least I could do for you girls," Jules said. "I'd give you the world if it'd let me. And I wanted to make sure I gave you these early. That way, you can wear them tomorrow."

I pulled my hair into a high ponytail using a scrunchie I pulled out of my backpack. I fiddled with the clasp on my necklace, unhooked it, and slipped the chain around my neck. The charm sat over my heart, the metal cold against my skin. I swore I could feel something warm stirring inside me as it settled against my skin. Part of me felt giddy. I was starting to get excited about my birthday.

"Come on. Let's get home before I have to hear Dan's mouth," Jules laughed. She pushed the CD button on the radio and turned the volume up: the throwback 2000s mix we'd made in elementary school.

It was undoubtedly the best throwback mix ever made. The three of us sang our hearts out as we drove home with the windows down.

2

Selene

I stood at the foot of my bed, staring at the two outfits I had laid out. On a normal day, it wouldn't matter which one I picked. However, it was not just any other day. It was my eighteenth birthday.

Ashlyn was right; this was a milestone in my life that I wouldn't get back. I would be an adult, at least in some minuscule sense. Aunt Jules said it was supposed to be a full moon too, which meant it was supposed to be a day of high energy. I didn't always grasp the things Aunt Jules told me about energies. There was a time when she tried to tell me something about vibrations, but I tuned it out. I wasn't about to go through that talk with Aunt Jules after what I had seen in my health class.

I checked my phone. It was already eleven thirty. I should make sure Tera was up. I left my room and walked across the hall to knock on her door.

When I heard her groaning from inside, I banged louder.

"Tera! Get up. We have to go to the cafe soon," I shouted through the door.

We didn't have to be at the cafe for a few more hours, but it would take Tera at least that long to get ready, maybe even longer, because Ben would be there. I returned to my room and looked down at the two outfits again. Black turtleneck, burgundy skirt, black tights, and boots. That was the outfit I felt most pulled to. That was more than enough to base my decision on.

After I finished getting ready, I looked in the mirror. It was time for the finishing touch. I gingerly clipped on the necklace Aunt Jules had given me the day before. It sat perfectly in the center of my shirt: a crescent moon over a circular crystal. The crystal was green, with stripes and swirls of lighter and darker green throughout it. It was impossible to tell which green was the stone's true color. It mesmerized me every time I looked at it.

I pulled myself away from my mirror and left my room. I pressed my ear against Tera's door. I could hear her shuffling through her drawers. I had done my job.

I made my way downstairs to the kitchen. The warm scent of pancakes met me at the bottom of the stairs. The island in the center of the kitchen was stacked with food. Uncle Dan stood in front of the sink, scrubbing some pans. He wore a navy blue shirt, jeans, and a hot pink apron that said, "Kiss the cook."

"Are you cooking for an army?" I asked. Uncle Dan must have bought every fruit at the store.

"Oh, you're up," he said as he turned the faucet off and wiped his hands on the apron. He hugged me. "Happy birthday."

"Thank you."

"I made breakfast." He began pointing to the items on the table. "Pancakes, chocolate chip and plain, fruit, eggs, bacon, toast, and home fries."

"There are only three of us, though."

He laughed. "I know, but I have to work later tonight, so we are going to have breakfast and cake this morning. I wanted to go all out.

I closed the shop until two today, so I invited Tati to join us too."

Uncle Dan owned a convenience store in town. He ran the store four days a week but was there every day for shipments. The other three days of the week, Tati ran it. She had worked in the store for as long as I could remember. Uncle Dan's boyfriend, Liam, also worked there while he was completing his bachelor's. He went to school at the local community college. Tera and I helped sometimes, working an occasional weekend shift or filling in when someone was sick.

"Where is Aunt Jules?" I asked.

Uncle Dan inhaled through his nose.

"She said she can't make it. Something about working with the historical society? She said she'd be here when you got home."

"Oh, okay." Aunt Jules was a busybody, always working on several projects at a time. I wasn't surprised she was busy. She always made it up to us later.

I pulled out a chair at the island and sat down as Uncle Dan took off his apron and hung it over the oven's handle. He grabbed a stack of plates from the cabinet, placed them on the counter, and handed me one from the top of the stack.

"Go ahead, serve yourself. Everyone else should be back soon."

I took the plate and surveyed the table. I grabbed some strawberries and kiwi from the fruit platter and a fork from the stack at the center of the table. Then, I pulled two pancakes onto my plate with the fork. I could hear the front door opening as I took a bite of one of my strawberries.

It was cold on my teeth and sent a chill through my whole body. Liam came into the kitchen. He had shopping bags on both shoulders, which he dropped off in the dining room. Then, he approached me and gave me a side hug.

"Happy birthday," he said.

"Thanks."

Uncle Dan handed him a plate. He didn't wait for a blessing to ravage the table's contents. Liam shoved a pancake into his mouth before putting anything onto his plate. He looked at me and squinted.

"Where's the other wonder twin?" he asked with a mouth full of half-chewed food.

"She's upstairs," I said as I pushed my plate away.

"Is she still sleeping? That girl is such a bum," a voice from behind me said.

I turned to see Tati standing in the kitchen doorway with a white bakery box in her right hand. She put the cake on the island next to me and looked at me with a tilted head. I stood up and gave her a hug, which she returned, squeezing twice as tight as I had. Her tight black curls smelled of coconut.

"Hi, Tati."

"Happy birthday, baby," she said. Her presence always filled me with warmth.

"Let me go upstairs and say hello to the other birthday girl," she said. "Everything looks delicious, Dan."

"Thank you, Tabitha," Uncle Dan said. He pulled the island seat out next to me and put his plate on the table. It was piled almost as high as Liam's. He looked at me with a sly smile.

"Why are you looking at me like that?" I asked him.

"Just looking at my niece," he said. "What are your plans for today?"

"We're supposed to meet Ashlyn and Ben at the cafe later today." He made a face at Ben's name. He hated the idea that Tera had a boyfriend.

"How's Ashlyn doing? It's been a while since we've seen her," Liam asked from the other side of the island. Uncle Dan took a bite of some bacon and nodded along at this question. They loved Ashlyn. She would gossip with them about almost anything.

"She's all right, I guess. She spends more time thinking about graduation than she does focusing on school."

Ashlyn had been mine and Tera's friend since kindergarten, but I always felt she was closer to Tera. That didn't change in high school. Once Tera started dating Ben, all Ashlyn wanted to discuss was boys. Boys were a fine enough topic for some conversations, but there were only so many times I could listen to her go on about her flings. I couldn't relate to Ashlyn's desire to always be in some sort of entanglement. I had more important things to focus on. I was of the mind that if it were meant to happen, it would just happen.

"Looks like she woke up all on her own," Liam said, looking toward the stairs.

"I don't know about that one. When I got up there, she was video chatting with a very handsome young man," Tati said as she followed Tera down the stairs.

Tera wore a white sundress with a denim jacket, and she had curled her hair. She wasn't wearing the necklace Aunt Jules had given her. I wondered if she would try to sneak it on later before we saw her. Uncle Dan and Liam greeted her with birthday wishes and hugs just as they'd greeted me. Then, she looked at me with a smile.

"We're gonna have to leave soon if we want to make it on time," she said. I held in a laugh. Tera was never on time anywhere. She was probably more worried about the thirty-minute walk ahead of us.

"I'm ready whenever you are."

"Whoa, you girls can't leave yet. We haven't had cake," Uncle Dan said.

"Or done presents," Liam added.

"But we'll be late," Tera said.

"No, you won't. I'll drive, honey," Tati said.

"It's settled! We'll do cake now," Uncle Dan said. "Come to the dining room."

He led the trail of people into the dining room. He placed the cake in the center of the oval table and opened the box. It was a white frosted cake with fondant flowers and little balloons sticking out of it.

He ushered Tera and me to the side of the table closest to the wall. We sat beside each other on the bench like we had every birthday. The cake had our names written on it—Tera-Sue and Selene—in tiny font, so they fit on the same line. Tati put a bunch of candles into the cake and lit them in one motion. Everyone else gathered around the table and sang.

Something about the air in the room started to feel thin. As the singing came to an end, Tera nodded to me. We leaned forward and blew out the candles together, as we did year after year. I couldn't make a wish. Something hollowed inside of my chest. My stomach sank. Something horrible would happen. Everyone in the room clapped.

"We should get going," Tera said. "We can eat cake when we get home." I nodded as she spoke.

"All right, let's go get in the car," Tati said. She motioned for us to follow.

Once outside, we were met with a white car parked in front of the house, a giant red bow on it. Tera shouted in disbelief.

"You didn't!"

"We did," Uncle Dan said. He held a set of keys.

"Oh my god," she shouted before wrapping her arms around him. "Thank you."

While the gift was amazing, I couldn't bring myself to feel the same sense of excitement as Tera. The pit in my chest felt even more hollow as I looked at the car. I forced a smile and attempted to push through the feeling.

"Thank you, Uncle Dan."

"I'm driving," she said, dangling the keys at me as she strutted, triumphant, to the car.

"With the bow on the hood?" I asked as I followed her.

"Oh yeah," Tera said. She pressed the key fob and unlocked the door.

I pulled open the passenger door and climbed inside. Tera was already in and buckled up. She checked all the mirrors and adjusted them one by one. I put my seatbelt on and folded my hands into my lap. I made a circle on the back of my left hand with my right thumb, something that Aunt Jules had taught me to do to ground myself. Tera pulled away from the curb.

"What's wrong?" she asked.

"Nothing. Just thinking." I kept my gaze out the window. As we came to the stop sign at the end of our block, I could see Tera turning to look at me.

"What's wrong?" she repeated.

She wouldn't settle for an "I'm fine," just like I wouldn't have. I didn't want to tell her about the pit in my chest, not today of all days, and especially not after everything that had happened at practice yesterday. She always trusted my intuition, even when I couldn't. I got these feelings, and I knew they meant something bad would happen. However, I could never really tell how bad or exactly when. I could make guesses, like with the cheerleading practice, but they were just that: guesses. I didn't want to risk ruining the day for her over something small.

So, I told her a half-truth. "I'm just thinking about mom."

Her expression softened. "I was thinking about her this morning too," she said. I had always wondered if Tera thought about her as much as I had.

I nodded as I felt a part of me screaming. I had played the dead mom card. "We should keep driving, or we're going to be late."

"Yeah," she said with a nod.

The rest of the car ride was silent. We pulled into the parking lot of The Grind and parked across from the doors. I exited the car and stretched. I took a deep breath. It smelt of coffee and chocolate. Tera got out of the car.

"I was thinking that maybe we should see her," Tera said.

"See who?" I asked.

"Mom," she said. "You know, like, to see her grave. Bring some flowers or something."

I was shocked that Tera had said that. She hadn't been to Mom's grave in years. I went at least once a month just to talk. The idea of going there made me feel a bit better.

"Yeah, we should."

"Come on, they're already inside," Tera said. She locked the car with the key fob.

We walked into The Grind and saw Ashlyn and Ben at a booth against the right wall. The Grind had been a diner before it was a cafe, so it was still set up like one. It had checkered tile floors and purple accents, like the furniture and bar top.

Tera sat next to Ben, and I sat next to Ashlyn, who was typing a thousand letters per minute on her phone. Ben greeted us with a smile that showed his perfect white teeth. I tried to remember if he ever had braces. Honestly, I had never paid him much attention before he started dating Tera.

"Happy birthday," he said to me with a nod before kissing Tera on the cheek.

"Yeah, happy birthday," Ashlyn said without looking up from her phone. Tera and I exchanged glances.

"Ashlyn."

She didn't respond. Tera snapped a few times. No reaction.

"She's been like that since I got here," Ben said.

"Hello," I said, waving my hand in front of her phone screen. That broke her laser focus.

"Oh, sorry," she said, locking her phone.

"Is everything all right?" Tera asked.

"Yeah, douchebag is being…well, a douchebag," she said. Tera looked at me, but I averted my eyes.

"What did he do this time?" she asked, taking the bait. I thought I saw a glint of pain in Ben's eyes.

"He dumped me," she said.

"Oh, Ashlyn, that's horrible." Tera grabbed her hand from across the table. "I'm so sorry."

"It's whatever," she said. "I'm just pissed he dumped me first."

A server approached our table. She was an older woman with a dyed-black pixie cut. I could see the dye stains on her skin behind her ear and around the back of her head. Her name tag read "Lucy." She must've been new. She had a sweet smile. My breathing grew shallow.

I tried to focus on the air flowing in and out of my lungs, but they felt like they were being pressed shut.

"What can I get y'all?" she said. Her voice was soft, but I could barely hear her over the ringing in my ears.

"I'll have a water and a chocolate chip muffin," Tera said. The server scribbled onto her notepad. I wanted to scream for her not to get anything. I wanted to get up and run out of the cafe, but I was frozen. Petrified.

"Could I get a turkey club and a black coffee?" Ben said.

"You sure can, sweetie," the server said. "Are chips good for that?"

"Yes, ma'am," he said. She turned to look at Ashlyn.

"I'll have a strawberry milkshake with extra whip and the half-portion avocado BLT without the bacon," Ashlyn said, not looking up from the menu once.

"And what about you, honey?" she said.

I could barely form words. "Just a tea."

"All righty. I'll be back with your drinks in a few minutes," Lucy said as she slipped her notepad into her apron.

The moment she walked away, a little of my discomfort lifted. My breathing felt normal again, but the hollow in my chest grew deeper than it had ever felt. I looked at my hands in my lap. They were shaking.

I stood from the table.

"I'm just gonna run to the restroom. I'll be right back." I walked away before any of them could respond.

I walked to the back of the cafe and into the bathroom. I closed the door behind me and locked it. My breathing sped up as I approached the sink and turned it on.

I splashed some water onto my face. It was cold and stung my warm skin, but I could feel myself starting to relax. I looked at myself in the mirror. I felt like I was losing my mind.

The glint of my necklace caught my eye. I wrapped my hand around it and closed my eyes. I traced a clockwise circle around the stone and moon charm with my thumb.

I thought of Aunt Jules. Part of me wanted to call her for help, but I had never told her about my feelings. I feared she would look at me the way Uncle Dan had when I told him. It was just before his accident. I told him I'd felt like something bad would happen. When we went to see him in the hospital, he looked at me like he was scared, like I was a monster. After that, I never told anyone other than Tera.

I opened my eyes and let go of my necklace. I pulled some paper towels off the roll beside the sink and used them to dry my face. I looked in the mirror to make sure it wasn't noticeable that I was having a breakdown in the bathroom and nearly jumped out of my skin. In the mirror, I saw a glass of water sitting on a table, as though I was looking out of a window. My reflection was an afterthought in the image. I reached out to touch the mirror, and the image changed. It was a full moon; I pulled my hand back.

"What the hell."

The rustling of leaves and heavy breaths filled the room. It was less of a breath and more of a pant, like a dog's. The image shifted again; barren and twisted trees filled the mirror. I took a step closer and squinted, trying to make out the image better. That was when a wolf's head lunged toward me from inside the mirror. I could hear its teeth snapping as I squealed and jumped back. The mirror flooded with flames for an instant before it cracked.

I stood there for a moment, just staring at myself in the shattered mirror. I must've been hallucinating. Normal people didn't see things in mirrors while in a cafe's bathroom. I approached the mirror and ran my fingers over it, feeling the cracks. My hands were shaking again, even worse than when I had stood up from the table. I jumped again at a knock on the bathroom door.

"Are you all right in there?" Ashlyn called from the other side of the door.

"Uh, yeah. It was just a spider," I lied, putting my hands on top of my head. "I'll be out in a minute."

"Gross," she said.

I took a deep breath and flicked the light switch off in the bathroom before opening the door and stepping back into the cafe. I must be sleep-deprived. That was the only logical explanation. Yeah, I was just really tired. I walked back to our booth and sat down. I took a deep breath.

"You good?" Tera asked.

"Yeah, just a spider in the bathroom, that's all."

"Since when are you scared of spiders?" she asked. I could tell she was becoming suspicious.

"It was a really gigantic spider." I was still shaking, so perhaps that helped sell the lie. "So, what did I miss?" I asked.

"Ben was just telling us about his dad's beach house in Surf City," Ashlyn said. "I actually think he was just getting ready to invite us there next weekend."

"Oh, was he now?" I asked, looking at Ben. He was biting into his sandwich, but he raised his eyebrow.

"I was?" he said after swallowing with a large gulp.

"Oh, totally," Ashlyn said. "We need a beach trip. It's been so long since I got to wear one of my good bikinis."

"I mean, why not," he said. "My dad is home from work right now, so I can ask him."

"Perfect," Ashlyn said. "He's definitely a keeper, Tera."

"It's a good idea in theory. But our aunt and uncle would never let us go without some sort of supervision."

"You're right. But maybe we could invite Tati," Tera said.

"Oh yes, invite Tati. She'll let us do anything we want," Ashlyn said. "And that will also help get my mom on board."

"Then it's settled. We're going to Surf City next weekend," Tera said.

I watched Tera lift the glass to her lips and take the water into her mouth. She swallowed the water and wiped the side of her mouth with her thumb. She placed the water on the table in front of her. I was hit with a wave of sickness. The first image from the mirror flashed into my mind. A chill crawled up my spine, and all the hairs on my arms stood upright. I could hear that they were still talking around me, but it was muffled. My heart's thumping filled my ears.

"Selene? Are you paying attention?" Tera said, snapping in front of my face.

"No, I wasn't. Sorry," I said as the world around me came back into focus. They were all staring at me. "I was zoning out," I lied again.

"Well, we were talking about going to the movies later tonight," Ashlyn said.

I could feel their eyes analyzing me, like I was a glass tower that could crumble at any moment. Part of me wanted to blurt out what had happened, but a larger part of me was terrified they'd think I was crazy. I thought I was crazy. I just had to make it through the rest of the day.

"What movie?" I tried to act natural. Which I was sure made me seem even more awkward.

"*Just One Bite,*" Tera said. "It's the Snow-White retelling about the Evil Queen."

"That sounds interesting."

"Yeah, supposedly she poisoned Snow White because Snow White stole her man," Ashlyn chuckled.

"You want to go see it?" Tera asked.

"Sure." I could get some sleep at the movie theater.

"You coming?" Tera asked as she rested her head on Ben's shoulder.

"I can't," he said. "It's after my curfew."

"Lame," Ashlyn snorted.

"Wait, when's this movie?" I asked.

"Midnight," Ashlyn said.

Just my luck.

For the rest of the time at the cafe, I was half paying attention to the conversation and half looking for the woman who had served us. I hadn't seen Lucy since she took our order, but everything was at the table when I got out of the bathroom, so she must've come back. I didn't touch the tea.

After a while, the others noticed she hadn't returned with the check. Tera went to the cash register and called into the kitchen. The cook emerged and checked us out, but he didn't seem to know where our server had gone, either. We left the cafe and said our goodbyes in the parking lot. Ben and Tera hugged for what felt like ten minutes before they shared a goodbye kiss.

"I'll call you later," Tera said as she finally separated from him.

"Okay," he said. "Happy birthday again," he called back to us as he climbed into his truck.

"Eleven-forty at the movie theater?" Ashlyn asked.

"Sounds good to me," Tera said, looking back at me. I nodded in agreement.

"Don't be late," she said. She pulled Tera in for a hug and then waved for me to join them. She squeezed us together. "See you bitches later," she said as she let us go and walked to her car.

Tera and I climbed back into our car. The soft seat felt like a cloud under me. I hadn't realized how stiff my muscles were until then. Tera looked at me with concern in her eyes.

"Are you sure you're okay?" she asked again.

"Yeah, I'm just feeling tired."

"Okay," she said. "You can nap when we get home."

"I was planning on it. I'd be lucky not to pass out on the car ride there."

"You better not. We have to go to the graveyard first. And the florist."

"To the what?" I asked.

"The graveyard. We're going to visit Mom," she said as she pulled out of the parking lot.

I had forgotten Tera wanted to do that. We didn't talk much for the rest of the car ride to the florist except to argue about what flowers to get, orchids or roses. I was persuasive enough to convince her that roses were tacky. Once we pulled up to the cemetery, we parked outside the gates. *Maybe I'll see Mom's ghost, and she can tell me that I am, in fact, crazy,* I thought as we walked through the gates and past the rows of graves. The sun was almost set, and the sky was filled with vibrant oranges and reds. I could see Mom's willow at the far end of the lot, a few feet from the trees at the cemetery's edge.

According to Aunt Jules, Mom didn't want a tombstone; she wanted a tree, and her tree was the most beautiful of them all. It stood proud and prominent, almost defiant, on the cemetery's property and away from the trees of the woods beside it. Its branches extended high above the ground, but its green tears hung low. Some of them touched the ground. Whenever I went to the cemetery, the walk to Mom's willow filled me with what-ifs that made me want to smile and cry at the same time.

We followed the paved path and then made our way to the bench that was against its trunk and hidden in the foliage of the willow's weeping. I looked up at the intertwined branches above us. Every branch seemed to touch each other at some point. I was like looking at an abstract painting in a museum.

"You remember when Aunt Jules used to give us a card from her every year?" Tera asked.

"Yeah, she said when she found out that she wasn't going to make it, she wrote us as many cards as she could."

"I guess she only got to our tenth birthday," Tera said.

I could hear the sadness in her voice.

"Aunt Jules used to bring us here every year to give them to us."

"I never wanted to come back here after the last card," Tera said. "I blamed her for leaving us."

I looked over at her and saw the tears slipping down her cheek.

"Do you think she'd forgive me for staying away?" she asked.

I grabbed her hand and squeezed it. I could feel my own eyes starting to fill up. "I think she'd be happy you're here now. She wouldn't blame you for feeling hurt. We're gonna graduate soon and go off to college. She's probably proud."

"Yeah," she said, leaning her head onto my shoulder. She sniffled.

"I mean, you'll probably be getting married to that tall soccer player that Aunt Jules said Mom would've tried to hit on," I said with a smile.

"Oh god," she chuckled. "She probably could have stolen him from me."

"Oh, totally. I have no doubt that we'd be calling him dad if she'd had the chance."

"Ew," she said. "I don't think I'll ever be able to look at him the same again now."

"Probably not," I chuckled.

We sat there for a while longer, in silence, until the graveyard became dark after the sun disappeared beneath the horizon. I stood from the bench and walked over to the tree, running my fingers over the bark. It was coarse under the pads of my fingers, but the tree was warm to the touch. It was the kind of warmth that felt like a light flowed into my body, filling my core with joy and love. Stepping back from the tree was like breaking away from a comforting hug. It left my shoulders cold but raised higher than before.

"We should get going."

"All right, just let me put these down," Tera said, gesturing to the flowers in her lap. She stood from the bench and stumbled forward a bit. The bouquet fell at her feet with a soft thud.

"Whoa, are you okay?" I asked.

"Yeah," she said with a shake of her head. "Just a little lightheaded, I guess." She took another step before hunching over in pain. She let out a gasp like all the oxygen had been sucked away from her.

"What's wrong?" I said, rushing to her. I could feel the panic set in as my heart thumped against my chest, and the hollow feeling returned.

"My skin feels like it's on fire," she said. Her face was red and hot to the touch. A sickening crack rang out, like bones being crushed. Tera screamed as she collapsed to the ground.

"Tera, what's happening?" I asked. Nausea washed over me.

"I don't know." She coughed. "I can barely breathe." She screamed again as another crack echoed through the empty graveyard.

"What can I do?" I asked. I knelt beside her and tried to hold her still. In her thrashing, she knocked me onto my backside.

I pushed myself up into a sitting position. Tera shifted onto her knees. She was hunched over, covering her face like she was sobbing. When I moved to reach for her, she began dragging her hands down her face. Blood poured down her face from large gashes where her fingers traced. Her nails were like claws as she scratched at the skin on her face and neck. I inched myself away from her until my back slammed against the willow.

I couldn't stop watching. Tera tore away at herself, ripping the clothes and skin underneath off her body. Blood was spewing out of her and onto the grass beneath her. Her breathing was rapid, and she was heaving like an animal fighting to survive.

I tore my gaze away. I closed my eyes as tight as I could. I remained still as she sloshed around in her blood and skin for what felt like hours until, finally, Tera's breathing steadied.

I opened my eyes and scanned the massacre. It took everything in me to hold back my urge to vomit. I could see Tera curled up into a ball in the center of all the blood. Her shoulders were moving with each breath she took. I couldn't make out anything else about her in the darkness, but something still felt wrong.

"Tera?"

She froze. The figure stood up, taller than Tera ever could have. It would have towered over any person I had met. Its muscles looked like rocks.

I stopped breathing as the creature's face came into view. It had the head of a dire wolf with fangs longer than kitchen knives. Its claws were like machetes dangling at its side. The most striking feature was its eyes, one electric blue and the other ruby red, both devoid of any humanity.

The creature crouched down as if preparing to lunge at me. It would have cleared the distance between us in an instant. I raised my hands to protect myself and squealed as I closed my eyes. There was a sudden burst of warmth, and I saw a light beneath my eyelids. The creature whimpered loudly.

I opened my eyes. A ring of fire had erupted around the willow like a barrier between me and the creature. It cowered away from the flames. It gave me one last glare and then fled into the nearby woods.

I sat there staring at the flames, trying to process what had just happened. *This must be a dream,* I thought. *That didn't just happen. I'm crazy and...and sleep-deprived.*

Then, I thought back to the sight of Tera clawing away at herself. I sobbed. *I need to get help. Who's going to believe me, though? Aunt Jules, she'll believe me. I hope. Is Tera even alive?*

I forced myself to get up and go. As I walked toward the fire, it died out. *What is going on?* I thought as I kept walking. I looked at the blood and carnage as I walked past. Tera's jacket lay in the mess of gore, tattered. *Fuck.* The keys were in her coat. I gagged as I picked up her coat and dug into the pocket for the keys. Once I had them, I started walking to the car.

When I heard a howl, the walk turned into a run.

3

Tera-Sue

The sun burned against my skin, and something stung around my neck. It was like I had a shock collar chained on, and it was cranked to the highest setting. My vision was blurry, but it refocused steadily. The pavement underneath me was caked with drying blood. All my muscles ached, and I was drained of all my energy. I could barely lift my head off the road to look at the rest of my body. I was naked and covered in crusted blood.

What happened? I thought as I looked around, trying to take in more of my surroundings. There was a blue truck on its side in the middle of the road with a trail of blood leading to me. *Was I in a car accident? Whose truck is that?* I tried to piece together the night, but everything was blank after I stood up from the bench at the graveyard. I pushed myself up, but the world spun, and I collapsed back onto the ground. My vision was blurry again. I could hear someone shouting.

"I found her. She's over here," a woman said as she approached me. I couldn't make out who it was until she got closer. "Tera, are you okay? Tera?"

"Jules," was all I could get out before I passed out.

The next thing I knew, I was running through the woods. I didn't know why; I just knew I needed to keep running. All my hair was standing on end. My heart was thumping in my ears. It grew harder to breathe. I couldn't stop. I was being hunted. There was a deep huffing behind me. A tree root hand snagged a hold of my foot. I crashed to the ground. I tried to get up. I was not quick enough. I could hear the thundering footsteps of my pursuer come to a halt.

The darkest shadow I had ever seen loomed over me. I turned to face it. An even blacker mass, the living epitome of darkness, no features but two glowing eyes. One blue and one red. That was when the burning sensation around my neck returned. A tingle jolted throughout my whole body. I snapped out of my sleeping nightmare and back to what would become a real one.

I sat up, soaked in my own sweat, screaming in pain. Selene was sitting next to the bed. She jumped up almost as fast as I had jumped awake. She grabbed me by the shoulders and squeezed me. Her grip was the only thing that could ground me in reality then. I took a deep breath as she guided me back down onto the bed.

"Tera, it's okay. You're safe now," she said.

"Where are we?" I asked.

"We're at the house in the basement. Aunt Jules! She's awake!" Selene shouted. Her eyes were red and puffy.

"What happened?" I asked. I pushed myself up so my back was against the wall.

"How are you feeling? Are you in pain?" Selene asked. She adjusted the pillows so that they supported my back.

"I'm sore, but I'll live," I said. "What happened, Selene?"

She sat on the bed beside my feet. Her cheeks became even redder, and her eyes turned to glass. Something horrible had happened. She opened her mouth to speak but stopped when she heard Jules come down the stairs. Jules had her usual stoic look. Her expression was always like steel when she was serious. Even through that I could still see the worry in her eyes.

"Hey, kiddo, how are you feeling?" Jules asked. She pulled a chair up beside the bed.

"I'm just confused. What's going on?" I focused my question on Jules.

"Well, um…" Her voice cracked as it trailed off. She closed her eyes and took a deep breath. When they opened again, all the worry that was there earlier was now replaced with anger. "Something happened last night. It's going to sound crazy, unbelievable even, but I need you to understand that what I am about to tell you is very serious and very real."

"Okay," I said with a slow nod. I could feel my eyes filling with water as my nerves began to tremble. My expression must have reflected the fear that crept along my skin because once Jules met my eyes, her resolve was shattered.

"Tera, I—" Jules paused. I could see her desperate search for words to tell me what had happened. Selene stood up from the bed and began to pace.

"What is it? What happened?" I asked again. My fear was starting to turn to frustration.

Jules looked at me blankly. Selene was still pacing, refusing to even glance in my direction.

"What happened? Just tell me!" I shouted. My skin became hot as frustration boiled into rage inside of me. A sudden jolt of pain flashed through me as quickly as my anger had. I gripped at the necklace around my neck. It burned to the touch.

"You turned into a giant wolf-monster thing! And then you killed a man!" Selene snapped, tears streaming down her cheeks.

The room fell silent. I looked back and forth between them, waiting for one of them to crack a smile. They both stared back at me with pain-filled expressions. It had to be a joke. It had to.

I kept flashing back to the nightmare I had. *That thing that was hunting me...was that me?* I thought. Panic and realization set in all at once. *The blood, oh god, that blood wasn't mine. The truck. It wasn't an accident. I did that.* I could feel myself beginning to hyperventilate. Jules started to rub my back.

"This has to be a bad dream," I said. "I must've hit my head when I fell."

"Tera, you aren't dreaming," Selene said as she sat back on the bed beside me. I could try to deny what happened, but I could not deny the fear in my sister's eyes.

"Why are you so calm?" I asked, looking at Jules.

"Because I've been trying to prevent this your whole life," she said.

"You knew this was going to happen?" Disgust filled my voice as I pulled away from her touch.

"I didn't know that this specifically would happen, but I've been trying to protect you from this," Jules said with a sigh.

"What are you talking about?" Selene asked.

"It's time I started telling you both the truth," Jules said. She looked at us both before continuing. "You girls come from a long line of witches. O—"

"What?" Selene cut her off. "Witches?"

"Yes, witches," Jules said. "Not just ordinary witches, either. Witches from a powerful group known as the Original Covens."

"What does that even mean? This sounds even crazier th—" Selene's voice came to an abrupt halt. Jules held her hand out, and in her palm danced a small flame.

The warmth caressed my cheeks like we were sitting at a campfire. The way the light lit up Jules's face made her seem more beautiful than I'd ever realized, and the soft smile spread across her lips was the most magical part. The flame bubbled into the shape of a heart before she closed her hand into a fist, and it went out.

"Can I continue?" she asked.

I nodded for her to continue. I gave Selene a genial nudge with my foot, and she nodded too.

"There are twelve Original Covens, each of which was blessed by a goddess known as All-mother. To the covens, she is known as the mother of witchcraft. It is from her that each of the covens was given power. It is her power that flows through us now. That is why only witches from the Original Covens can manifest her divine gifts." Jules paused for a moment. She took a deep breath and took a hand from both Selene and me.

"There are a lot of politics that go into being a witch from one of the Original Covens. Your mother broke a vow made by our coven by falling in love with a man who wasn't from another original coven. Because of that, a witch from another coven came to seek revenge on her." Jules wiped a tear that had streamed down her cheek.

"While your mother was pregnant with you, a witch came after her. The witch killed your father and tried to curse you both. I had cast a protection spell earlier that ended up being only strong enough to protect one of you. In order to protect the other, we had to do a powerful spell that would break the curse. We did, and that is why Tera was born without any magic. It was part of the price paid for her protection. I've been trying to hide and protect you ever since, but I failed." Jules's voice was hollow with defeat.

"Is that why you didn't tell us? To protect us?" Selene asked.

"There was still a chance that you would manifest one of the divine gifts, which you did, and it would've brought us at risk for exposure," Jules said.

"Why would that bring us exposure?" I asked, gripping her hand tighter.

"When a witch manifests at least one of the divine gifts, they must go through a series of trials to determine the extent of their power. It is known as The Ascension," Aunt Jules said.

"And I'll have to go through this?" Selene asked. I thought I heard her voice trembling.

"Right now, don't worry about that. Let's just focus on Tera. You and I will talk more about it later," Jules said. Selene was slow to nod. "How are you feeling?"

"I feel hot, and my necklace burns." The burning had gone down to just a sting, but it was still there.

"That is because I had to enchant it to suppress your werewolf side. The burning means it is actively fighting to keep you human," Jules said.

"Why is it burning her now, then? I thought werewolves only came out during the full moon. It's daytime," Selene said.

"The full moon sends werewolves into a ravenous frenzy that can't be controlled. If the moon is full for three nights, the moon's hold over the werewolf will last from the first night until the last night, including while the sun is present. However, werewolves can shift at any time. With practice, some werewolves can function as normal members of society if they can keep their anger under control," Jules said.

"Their anger?" I asked.

"Yes, anger is the trigger for the curse. If they become too enraged, they will change, and most of them cannot control themselves after the change," Jules said. "That is why you won't be taking off the necklace until you're cured. So you can stay under control."

"Cured?" Selene asked.

"Wonderful, you got me a shock collar," I sighed.

"Of course, we're going to find a cure. We are not leaving her like this," Jules said, ignoring my quip.

"How are we going to do that?" Selene asked.

"With magic, of course," Jules said. "The Ascension will bring enough witches here that we should be able to find some answers."

"Ascension," Selene repeated.

"It seems we've come full circle then…"

Their conversation faded into the background as I tried to remember as much as I could about last night. I slipped out of Jules's grasp and looked at my shaking hands. *Am I really a monster?* I thought. No memories from the night came back to me.

"I killed someone," I blurted out. Selene and Jules looked at me. Selene's eyes grew wide.

"It wasn't your fault," Jules said as she grabbed my hand again. "You weren't yourself."

"That doesn't matter. If I weren't this monster, that man would still be alive," I said as tears filled my eyes. There was a pit in my stomach.

"Tera, you're a victim too," Selene said. "You're not to blame."

"Who was it?" I asked.

"You don—" I cut Jules off before she could finish.

"Who was it?" I shouted.

"It was Maggie Fera's dad," Selene said.

That was the straw that broke me. Every emotion that wasn't anger flowed out of me. I began sobbing and wailing like I was in pain, but the only thing I had broken was my own heart. I did not know Maggie that well, but nobody deserved to lose their dad like that. No one deserved to die because of me.

My tears made my cheeks burn. I curled up on the bed into a ball. Selene curled up next to me so that we were facing each other. She had tears of her own slipping down her cheeks. Jules hugged me from behind. *I don't deserve to have them here comforting me. I ended someone's life. I am a monster.*

I spent the rest of the weekend and the beginning half of the week in that bed, hoping I would just wither away. Praying I would slip into the nothingness I so desired. I didn't eat; I didn't move. I willed myself to be catatonic so that I could never hurt anyone again. The thought of confessing to what I had done had crossed my mind more than once, but that would only put more people in danger. It would raise too many questions, and Selene or Jules could get hurt. Uncle Dan would probably implode.

Selene entered the room with a bag of clothes that she plopped down on the bed. She ripped the blankets off the bed. I looked at her like she had four heads.

"What are you doing?" I asked. I could feel my annoyance bubbling. I had made it clear I was never leaving this bed again.

"I'm taking you out of this house," she said.

"I'm not leaving," I said and rolled my back to her.

"Yes, you are," she said. "We are going to Mr. Fera's funeral."

My muscles became stone at her words. "What?"

"You heard me."

"You want me to go to the funeral of the man that I murdered?" I whispered.

"Maggie does."

My heart deflated when I heard her name. If I had any left, tears would have filled my eyes. "What are you talking about?"

"She asked about you today," Selene said as she pulled clothes out of the bag. "Just like everyone else at school, they are all worried about you."

"They wouldn't be worried if they knew the truth."

"No one would blame you if they knew the truth," Selene said. She grabbed my hands and pulled me up.

With her guidance, I scooted to the edge of the bed and put my feet on the ground. The concrete was cold under my feet. I wiggled my toes as I stood and started looking through the bag of clothes. The least I could do for Maggie was attend her father's funeral.

"We're leaving in thirty minutes," Selene said as she started up the stairs. "You should definitely shower."

I touched my necklace and tapped on the crystal in it as I picked out a black dress. I hadn't worn it before. It still had the tags. The necklace had stopped burning after the third night of the full moon. *How am I gonna face his family? How am I gonna face myself?*

37

4

Selene

"Do you think…" My voice trailed off before I could finish my question. Aunt Jules knew exactly what I would ask, though.

"Eventually, she will be. Right now, she's just going to need us to help her through it," she said. She wrapped her hand around my waist and pulled me closer to her on the porch. "She'll be back to normal once we find the cure."

Aunt Jules seemed so sure that we would cure Tera, but I could feel the fear and doubt twirling around inside me. "Is there even a cure to find?"

"There has to be," she said. For the first time since the night Tera turned, I could feel Aunt Jules's resolve waver. It was just for a fleeting moment, but that brief second scared me more than anything. It scared me more than watching Tera turn into that terrible monster. "If there isn't one already, we'll make it."

Just like that, her determination was back. Aunt Jules was convinced that The Ascension was the key to curing Tera. Not because it would give me some big power boost, but because it would give her access to witches from all the Original Covens. With that many witches in one place, someone was bound to know something. The Ascension was apparently a big deal, and every witch from the Original Covens would attend. That probably included the witch who had cursed Tera.

I never realized I could hate a person I'd never met. The thought of them filled my heart with hatred and longing for everything stolen from Tera. From everything stolen from me. Aunt Jules was still tight-lipped about the details of The Ascension. She could tell I was on the fence about participating. She probably wanted to give me time to process what was happening, but she told me it was so we could focus on Tera.

"Magic comes from the world around us. It is an energy that exists in everything from the grass to the breeze. It is nature's greatest force, and nature always has a way of balancing itself out," Aunt Jules said. It felt like she could read my mind. "We will find a way to help Tera."

Uncle Dan stumbled out of the house, fighting with his tie like it was a snake trying to devour him. I couldn't help but laugh at how helpless he looked.

"Dammit, Jules. Do I have to wear this stupid thing?" He huffed as he threw the tie to the ground.

"Yes, Daniel. You have to wear it," she chuckled as she picked it up off the floor. She looped the tie around his neck, and in seconds, she had it knotted and ready to go.

"Show off," Uncle Dan said. He rolled his eyes and patted the wrinkles out of his shirt.

"Where is Liam? Will he be joining us?" she asked.

"No, Liam is helping Tati run the store today. One of the cashiers quit yesterday," he said. "I'll get the car started."

Uncle Dan left the porch, went to his old, beat-up red pickup, and started it. The sound of the engine struggling to life was hard to listen to. Even with no car expertise, I knew it was time to put that truck out of commission. Aunt Jules and Uncle Dan had a weird relationship.

They never talked much beyond things they needed to do for us. It was obvious that the only reason they even tolerated each other was because of us. I had begun to think it was because Uncle Dan knew that there was something he didn't know about Aunt Jules—something he didn't know about us and something he didn't know about his own brother.

Aunt Jules tried to engage in small talk here and there, but usually, Uncle Dan shut it down with bland responses. I wondered if she'd ever thought about telling him the truth. If she'd ever thought about telling anyone the truth.

The door creaked as Tera pulled it closed behind her. She hadn't left the house in days but somehow pulled herself together in minutes. Her sense of fashion and skill with a makeup brush left me looking like a hermit. She looked at us, and something seemed different about her. She almost looked eager to leave.

"Ready?" Aunt Jules said with a smile to her.

"Ready as I'll ever be," she said as she breezed past us and down the porch stairs.

"You take shotgun," Aunt Jules told her as we walked to the car.

I climbed into the back seat. I caught a glimpse of my necklace in the window as I did. I rubbed the charm between my fingers. *Aunt Jules had enchanted Tera's necklace. Did she do that to mine too?* I thought. The crystal was smooth and comforting to rub. It made it easy for me to zone out during the car ride.

The parking lot of the funeral home was packed with cars. Everyone in the town must have come to pay their respects. I had known Maggie since middle school. We'd had a few classes together here and there. I never thought of her as more than an acquaintance, so I was surprised when she asked if Tera and I were going to the funeral. I understood after seeing how many people had packed into the funeral home. Maggie wanted to see some familiar faces. Tera and I just happened to have the same one.

Inside the building, there was no path to walk along. We had to fight through people to go in any direction. Tera had begun to do just that. I thought she had spotted Ben or Ashlyn, but once we neared the front of the room, I realized she was going straight toward Maggie.

Maggie was a short girl with thick glasses and pink hair. She had always looked so frail to me; the wind could've just swept her away. That day, she looked stronger. She was smiling at the guests and chatting with the people who came up to her. I wouldn't have picked her out of the crowd as the daughter of the man who had just passed if I didn't know better. Once it was Tera's turn to speak to Maggie, she didn't. The two just looked at each other before Tera pulled her in for a hug.

Then, Maggie's smile broke, and she sobbed. *They barely know each other,* I thought as I stopped in my tracks and watched the scene unfold. Maggie excused herself from the hug and ran to the restroom.

Tera found her way back to me. Aunt Jules had pulled a disappearing act while I was in shock. Uncle Dan was talking to Mrs. Fera at the other end of the room.

"What was that?" I whispered to her.

"Her eyes were just screaming, 'I'm only pretending to be okay,' and I knew exactly how she felt," Tera said, her gaze fixated on the coffin at the front of the room. Sadness washed over me.

"Tera," I said, putting my hand on her shoulder. "You're not alone in this. We're right here with you."

"No, you aren't. You just found out you have this deep connection to our family line. I just found out I turn into a monster who eats people," she whispered. She wouldn't meet my gaze.

"That doesn't mean you are alone in this."

"For the first time in our lives, I think I am," she said.

I wanted to scream—scream bloody murder and shake Tera back to reality. I wanted Tera to know that she wasn't fighting this alone. I was right there with her. I couldn't, though; how could I understand what she was feeling? I was still having nightmares about what I had seen in the graveyard. I couldn't even imagine what she was going through. I clenched my fists at my side as I tried to stop myself from crying out of frustration. That was when Ashlyn slithered her way over to us.

"Where have you been?" she said, glaring at Tera. Her tone was fierce.

"I've been really sick," Tera said without looking up from the ground.

"Oh, you poor baby," Ashlyn said as she pulled Tera into a hug. All of her anger melted into worry. She clenched Tera's head against her chest, looked at me, and mouthed, "What's wrong with her?"

I just shook my head in response. It was the only response I could think of. Ashlyn must have sensed that we were serious about Tera not being well because, after that, she kept a death grip locked around Tera's arm. She was a guard dog ready to snap at anyone who put their hand to close.

"I hope you are doing everything you can to get better," Ashlyn said. "We are still going to Surf City this weekend."

"Ashlyn, I don't know if that's the best id—" Tera started to say.

"Nonsense! You are going," Aunt Jules had materialized beside me and cut Tera off.

"Perfect," Ashlyn said with a wide smile. "It will be good for you to be out and in the sun."

I laughed. Tera snapped a fierce glare at me. "Vitamin D is important."

"There won't be anyone to chaperon us," Tera said.

"Don't be silly. If you need someone to chaperon, we can make it happen," Aunt Jules said. "I'll ask Tati to go with you."

Tera pushed the air out of her nose in frustration.

"How is Ben?" Ashlyn asked. It was times like this that I was glad she had the attention span of a goldfish.

"I don't know," Tera said. Her voice was so low and soft that I was afraid she would burst out sobbing.

"Oh god, you must really be sick. You haven't even talked to prince charming," Ashlyn said.

"Yeah," Tera said before breaking from Ashlyn's grip. "I'm going to go get some air."

Before any of us could respond to her, she disappeared into the crowd of people. *You're not alone,* I thought as I watched her walk away. I could feel my cheeks warming as I thought about what Tera had said earlier. I needed to get to a less crowded place.

"I'm going to go to the restroom and wash my face."

"Oh, I'll go with you," Ashlyn said.

"No, it's okay," I said before pushing through the crowd. I didn't wait for her to protest or try to follow me.

Once I had made it to the hallway where the bathrooms were, it was clear of people. Most of the guests probably stayed in the lobby and showing room. I had narrowed my focus on making it to the ladies' room when someone came out of the men's room and slammed into me. The moment our bodies collided, a tingle shot through my body. The deafening sound of a gunshot rang out, and a flash of the woods filled my vision. I was pulled back to reality when the man grabbed my shoulders.

"Are you okay?" he asked.

"Yeah, sorry." He was tall with silver hair and soft blue eyes. He had a warm smile. I couldn't shake the feeling that something was wrong with him.

"Wait a minute," he said. "I think you might be my son's girlfriend. We haven't met, but I've seen pictures of you. It's nice to meet you."

I looked at him with confusion before it clicked. "You're Ben's father."

"Yes, I am," he said with a chuckle. "You're Tera, right?"

"No, I'm actually her sister, Selene."

"Oh." He looked mortified. "I'm sorry. Ben never told me he was dating a twin."

"It's okay. People always mix us up. It's almost like we have the same face or something."

"Did you know Ted Fera?" he asked. The joke was lost on him.

"Not personally, but I know his daughter, Maggie," I said. "Did you know him?"

"Yeah, he was a coworker of mine," he said. "Such a tragedy. They're saying it was an animal attack."

"That's horrible." The thing I found the saddest is that his family would never know the truth. I wondered how the police had come up with the story of an animal attack. I'd never seen an animal that could flip a truck like that. *Maybe it's better that way.*

"Well, anyway," he said. "It was nice to meet you. I better go find my son."

I nodded at him before going into the ladies' room. I went to the sink and turned it on. I refused to look in the mirror. *What just happened? Was that a vision?* I thought as I splashed water onto my face. *I need to talk to Aunt Jules about these visions.* I hadn't gotten the chance to talk to Aunt Jules about what being a witch meant. She didn't even know I was having these visions. She'd been so focused on Tera she left me high and dry with news I didn't understand.

I dried my face and left the restroom. I stopped to look at the crowd in the doorway of the viewing room. *Maybe Tera had the right idea about going outside.* I looked around for a back exit to avoid fighting through the crowd. Once I had found my way out the back door, I decided to walk around the building to the front. I stopped myself from going around the side of the building when I heard two people talking. It sounded like the start of a very intimate conversation. I was about to go the other way when I recognized one of the voices as Tera's. I stopped moving and put my back against the building.

"Ben…I-I have to tell you something," Tera said. Her voice was timid. Tera was never timid. My heart started beating twice as hard as I wondered what she was about to tell him.

"What's wrong, Tera?" Ben asked.

"I just can't do this anymore," Tera croaked before sobbing. I fought the urge to blow my cover and go to her. *What is she doing?* I thought.

"Tera, what are you talking about?" Ben said. He sounded so scared. "What happened?"

Tera was silent. Was she sobbing into her hands, or was she looking at him with tears streaming down her cheeks? Ben had never seen Tera cry before that moment. *Is she about to tell him the truth?* I thought. The truth would've been kinder.

"I'm talking about us," Tera said. It sounded so cold that goosebumps spread across my skin. I covered my mouth to stop the gasp from escaping.

"What? What do you mean?"

"I can't do this anymore. We're over, Ben."

"Tera, can't we work through this? Did I do something wrong?" His voice was breaking as he struggled to get out more words. "I'm sorry."

"No," Tera said. "It's not you. I just don't love you. I never will."

Tera, why? I tried to wrap my head around her lie to him. *Why would she say that to him?* A year ago, she was planning the best way to tell him she loved him. I spent hours brainstorming with her. She wanted it to be perfect. It was one of the most important things in the world to her. She had planned out an entire day for them at the fair, where she would tell him at the top of the Ferris wheel. She came home with a glow brighter than the sun's. She recited the story to me four times that night. It was one story that never got old because each time she told it, it was like she was reliving it, and joy radiated off her.

"Tera, please don't do this," Ben said. He was crying now.

"I'm sorry, Ben. I'm becoming a different person, and I don't think you'll ever be able to understand why," Tera said. That was when I was hit with a realization. *She's doing this because of the curse. I can't let this be her life.* Tera was willing to give up one of the people she loved the most to protect him. I had doubts about being able to cure Tera, doubts driven by fear of the person who'd cursed her—a person I'd never even seen. *How selfish,* I thought. *Tera is suffering. I have to do whatever it takes to make it stop.*

I went to find Aunt Jules before the end of Tera and Ben's conversation. She was leaning on the tailgate of her, swiping through her phone. Uncle Dan must've still been inside. She looked up when she heard my footsteps approaching her in the gravel parking lot.

"There you are. I've been looking for you and Tera," she said.

"I need to be ready to complete The Ascension."

"What?" she looked shocked.

"We can't let Tera go through this. *I* can't let Tera go through this, not when I have the power to help her. We need to break the curse."

"I was worried you'd be too afraid of who might be there," Aunt Jules said.

"Not anymore. There's too much at stake to be scared."

"I'll put out the word that we are holding the next Ascension here. There are a lot of things we will need to do for us to prepare. You will have to go through a lot of intense training," Aunt Jules said.

"Whatever it takes."

5

Tera-Sue

Returning to school was the only semblance of normal I had. However, even that was different. Selene had started missing school to prepare for The Ascension. I was going in alone. I didn't meet Ben at his locker before the first period or after lunch. I quit the cheerleading team; Ashlyn did the same. She claimed she wanted to do it in solidarity. Ashlyn was attached to my hip at every chance she had. She thought I was dying, and I wasn't entirely sure I was living. The only thing that felt the same was my classes. My same boring classes.

During our lunch period, Maggie Fera started to sit with us. A week before our table had been filled, Ben, Selene, and some of the cheerleaders sat with us. It was just Ashlyn, Maggie, and me since I returned to school. Seeing Maggie every day made my chest tight with guilt. *Killer. Monster.* The words echoed in my head, but I pushed back the thoughts. Jules and Selene had been adamant in assuring me. *"It wasn't your fault."* It felt like my fault, though.

Jules and Selene seemed convinced that they would be able to break the curse. The confidence they had and the time Selene was putting into it gave me hope—hope that I could go back to the way things were before. Though in the darkest parts of my mind, there was doubt. I felt like a stranger in my own life, like my skin wasn't my own. I was fighting so hard for it to fit. How much longer could I fight? The possibility that they couldn't break the curse was scary, but the chance I couldn't hold on long enough for them to try was scarier.

"Hello? Are you ignoring me?" Ashlyn asked. She smacked her hand down on the lunch table in front of me. I jumped.

"Sorry, I was zoning out," I said. "What were you saying?"

"I was saying that I talked to Ben yesterday. He still wants us to go to his dad's beach house tomorrow," she said. I had told Ashlyn that I had dumped Ben the night it happened. She tried to convince me it was temporary. If only she knew that, I might not be.

"I don't think that's a good idea." The thought of seeing Ben churned my stomach. The broken image of his face at the funeral was burned into my mind. If I'd listened close enough, I could've heard his heart shatter. I would've heard my own shatter too.

"Oh, you're going. You can't avoid him forever. How else are you gonna get back together?" she asked.

"I think that's the point, Ashlyn," Maggie said. "I don't think she wants to get back together with him."

Oh, I do. I want to, but I can't. "Maggie's right, I don't."

"Fine, but you can be his friend, right? We need a friend with a beach house, Tera," Ashlyn said. "How else will we pick up the beach boys?"

I laughed. Ashlyn had been the only person who made me smile during that time. "Fine, I'll go. I can try being just friends, but you need to make that clear to him."

"Done," Ashlyn said.

"And Maggie's going to come because Selene can't."

"What?" Maggie asked, shocked.

"Selene isn't coming?" Ashlyn asked, her eyebrows knitted in frustration.

"She'll be helping Jules with something." I could see Maggie wasn't on board with my sudden shift in plans. "Come on, Maggie. It will be fun."

"Oh, you're coming, Maggie. It will be our first trip as a trio," Ashlyn said.

"I guess I can ask," Maggie said.

"Your Aunt Jules and Selene have been missing a lot of school lately," Ashlyn said.

"Yeah." I sighed. It was filled with enough sadness that no one asked anything further on the topic. We sat in silence for a few seconds before Ashlyn pulled out her phone and showed us a picture of her in a red bikini.

"What about this one?" she asked.

The rest of lunch was spent helping Ashlyn decide which of her many bikinis she would wear. I owned many clothes, but Ashlyn's collection rivaled a department store. The end of the school day went by in a blur. I was either lost in my thoughts or fighting off sleep.

After the last bell, I went to the locker room to change into a white and green striped polo, the uniform Uncle Dan had picked out for the store. I thought it was ugly. On a good day, I would not be caught dead in one, but Uncle Dan needed me to cover a shift that day, and I didn't have the motivation to fight it. I left the school with my head down, not looking up again until I was in my car. It was easier to look at my feet than the other students walking the halls.

As I entered the store, a bell jingled above my head. Tati was behind the counter, moving boxes of supplies. She saw me coming down the aisle. Her face lit up with a smile. Joy filled me. Tati's happiness was infectious.

"Hey, baby! How are you doing?" she said. She came around the counter and gave me a big hug.

"I'm good, Tati. How are you?" I asked, melting in her arms.

"I'm doing well. Happy to be alive and healthy," she said. "How's your sister?"

"She's good." I pictured Selene buried in the pile of books Jules had given her to read. She would've been done with all of them in no time.

"What can I help with?" I asked.

"Could you refill the candy aisle?" she said. She put a box on the counter.

I nodded and took a handful of small boxes. I walked down the snack aisle and stocked the shelves. I enjoyed working at the store; it helped to keep me busy. The busier I was, the less my mind wondered. I returned to the counter to grab more candy, and Tati was filling up the scratch-offs. I paused to watch her work.

"Have you ever played one of these?" she asked. She looked over her shoulder at me.

"No. Uncle Dan doesn't like gambling, so he never lets us."

"Life is just one big gamble. We have to take risks to get the things we want," she said. "If you are afraid to gamble, then you're afraid to chase your dreams. You can't be afraid to chase your dreams. If you fight hard enough, they'll come true. Sometimes, you need to take a chance."

I grabbed my necklace and moved the charm between my fingers. "How do you know if it's worth it?"

"Sometimes, you don't. You just have to go with your gut," she said. Tati yanked one of the scratch-offs out of the bunch and a penny from the dish on the counter. She rubbed the penny across it and smiled. "And you never know when a single moment can change everything."

She handed me the scratch-off. It was a winner, fifty dollars. "What if that change isn't a good thing?" I asked.

"Honey, you should embrace every change, even if it doesn't look good at first. People grow from facing the tough times, not the easy ones. The universe won't throw anything at us that we aren't ready to deal with," she said. She seemed so sure in her words. I began to question what I was afraid of.

"Thanks, Tati," I said as I handed her the scratch-off back.

"Oh no, baby, you keep that. It was meant for you," she said.

"Are you busy tomorrow?" I asked.

"Yes, I am. I have plans."

"Oh, okay."

"I am going to the beach tomorrow with a beautiful young lady and her friends," she said with a chuckle. I blinked in confusion. "Your auntie already called me and asked me to go with you.

"I wasn't sure she'd remember. She's been really busy lately."

"In all the years I've known her, Jules has never forgotten anything," Tati said with a laugh.

I grabbed the rest of the candy boxes from the counter and finished restocking the aisle.

The ride to Surf City was three hours—three hours of being crammed into Tati's minivan. Three hours with a snoring Ashlyn, a silent Maggie, and a starring Ben. Tati was singing along to the radio while I pushed my headphones as deep into my ears as they would go. It was bad enough that I was going to the beach with Ben, but being trapped in the car with him was like a timeless hell. Every part of me wanted to talk to him. Every part of me wanted to tell him the truth. Whenever I looked at him, *monster* echoed through my head. I caught him glancing at me through the rear-view mirror often. I ignored it by opting to look out the window over Ashlyn. I still couldn't look at Maggie for too long without feeling like I was about to cry. The more time I spent with her, the easier it became, but having Ben there made it feel worse. Every time I looked at Ben, I reminded myself of the happiness I was depriving myself of, the happiness I was depriving him of. Looking into his eyes was like being transported to the best moment of my life.

It was a night of winning carnival games and eating funnel cake that all came to a culmination on top of the Ferris wheel. We'd been dating for six months, and I knew that I was unmistakably in love with him. I'd spent every hour of the entire week planning every moment of the night because I knew that would be the night I told him I loved him. Jules and Selene had listened to my plan at least a hundred times a day. I knew it so well that I could've done it in my sleep. Ashlyn and I even went to the fair the night before so that I could do a practice run with her. It was the only thing I ever wanted to be perfect. Of course, though, it wasn't exactly perfect.

My nose was red from how cold it was that night. The air was nipping at all of my exposed skin. Ben had given me his varsity jacket to keep me warm. This was part of my plan, of course. I knew Ben was a gentleman and would give me his jacket even if I thought about being cold. As we got on the Ferris wheel, I could feel the butterflies fill my stomach with their dancing. Ben was unusually quiet, though. I was worried he'd vomit when I told him, or he'd dump me in response, but I wasn't abandoning my plan. As the Ferris wheel ticked its way along and we neared the top, I noticed how small the people looked below us. The entire fair just looked like a little flea circus as we entered the ozone layer. The stars above us turned brighter and bolder, but so did I. Finally, when the ride jerked to a stop and was at the top, I turned to Ben, and he turned to me. We looked at each other for a few moments in silence. He smiled widely. His perfect white teeth joined the stars as he leaned close to my ear and whispered.

"I love you." The butterflies inside me explode into fireworks of joy. He ruined my plan in the most perfect way possible.

I kissed him on the cheek and whispered back into his ear. "I love you too."

Our lips met, and we kissed for a few more moments until the Ferris wheel jolted back to life and made me nearly jump out of my skin. We laughed the rest of our way down to earth. It was my fondest memory, and it had become a ghost of sorrow to haunt me.

This was a horrible idea. I hoped that Selene was having a better time. She had fully immersed herself in her witchy training. It made me feel even more alone. Selene and I had always been connected, but I hadn't spoken more than a few words to her since the funeral. She had this thing that connected her even more to Jules and our family. I had something that alienated me from everyone. Some people would probably kill to have something that made them different, but I missed being ordinary. I felt like a bomb that could explode any second, and the only thing keeping me from going off was a necklace. So much had changed, and I couldn't risk letting my guard down.

I looked up into the rear-view mirror, hoping to catch Ben looking at me again, but this time, Tati looked at me with a smile. Something in me felt clearer at that moment. *Maybe I should try embracing this change a little more.*

I unclipped my necklace and put it into my backpack. It felt like a weight had been lifted off my shoulders. I felt freer, more awake. I closed my eyes and took a deep breath through my nose. I could smell more than I could a second ago. I caught the scent of flowers from outside the car, peanut butter from Maggie's lunch, and the crisp scent of Ben's cologne. He smelt like a campfire in the middle of the cold woods. I opened my eyes. It was like everything was moving slower than before. I could hear everyone's heartbeat. I could hear their lungs expand and compress. If I focused hard enough, I could hear the blood rushing through their veins. I was on a sensory overload. It was all new to me, but I was comfortable for the first time since I'd changed. I spent the rest of the car ride letting myself adjust to all the new things I was experiencing.

The beach house was massive—three stories, with more glass than wood. I knew that Ben's dad was well off. I hadn't realized how well off. There was a black motorcycle in the driveway. Ashlyn walked to it and ran her fingers over its smooth paint. It squeaked softly.

"This bike belongs to a bad boy," Ashlyn said.

"What is that even supposed to mean?" I said. I closed the van door behind me.

"It means that there's a fresh victim here for me," she said.

Maggie looked at me with a concerned face. "Ashlyn considers herself a man-eater," I laughed.

"I am, and the one that owns that bike better be on his guard because I want to devour him," Ashlyn said.

"That's my brother's," Ben said from the other side of the van.

"Pray for your brother, sweetie," Tati said. She put her sunglasses on and grabbed her folding chair out of the trunk. Her beautiful black curls danced with every step she took. "Why don't we head down to the beach and pick out a nice spot? We'll leave the girls to carry the stuff into the house."

Ben made a face that looked as though he was questioning our capability. "We've got it," I snapped. My tone even took me off guard. It was more aggressive than I intended.

"I'll go with you," Maggie said. She seemed eager to get down to the water ever since we got in the van that morning.

The three of them walked down a path beside the house that led down to the beach. That left Ashlyn and me to bring in the bags and cooler. I smiled at her.

"I'll grab the bags. You grab the cooler." I grabbed everyone's bags out of the trunk and my backpack out of the backseat.

"Fine. It will be lighter anyway," she said. She huffed as she fought the cooler out of the trunk.

The stairs leading to the front door were an entire flight. Inside the house, another staircase led up to the main floor. I found my way up both sets with ease. I made my way to the kitchen, where I left the bags on the floor. The house had an open layout, allowing the kitchen and living room to be connected. An entire wall on this floor was made of windows overlooking the beach. I gasped at the view. I went to the windows to get a better look.

The beach was filled with hundreds of people, all spread out, enjoying the sun and water. The water was sparkling like a thousand little diamonds dancing in the sun's light. It was like I could see the world curving in the distance. I could hear the waves crashing against the shore and the laughter of children running and splashing each other.

Bare feet slapped against the tile coming toward me. I listened for a heartbeat. It was calm and well-paced. I didn't look away from the window; I just kept listening as the person crossed the room until they were a few feet behind me.

"You must be one of Ben's little friends," a man's voice said. I could smell soap.

"Yeah," I said, "We are just dropping a few things off in here before heading down to the beach."

"I'm surprised I didn't startle you," he said.

"I heard you coming."

I turned around to look at him. He was a few inches shorter than Ben. His hair was buzzed short, and he was covered in tattoos. His arms, neck, chest, and stomach had ink. It was like several pieces of independent art reflected on both sides of his body. His chest and abs were wet, and he was only wrapped in a towel on his bottom half. I had to force myself to look away from him. I could hear my own heart rate increasing. I could hear his heart beating faster, too. He was looking at me as intensely as I was at him. He licked his lips before parting them. They glistened.

"Were you trying to sneak up on me?" I asked.

He laughed, deep and hearty. Warmth prickled across my skin. "Not exactly."

My heart was now beating outside of my chest. I was fighting the urge to leap across the room and grab him. *Control yourself, Tera. You don't even know him. Why are you acting like this?* My thoughts raced as I tried to think about anything but the water slipping down his chest.

"So, you're Ben's brother," Ashlyn said as she dropped the cooler in the kitchen. I caught my breath the moment she spoke. I hadn't even noticed her coming up the stairs.

"Um, yeah," he said. He shot her a look like she was bothering him. "I'm Will."

"Pleasure to meet you." Ashlyn held her hand out for him to shake. "I'm Ashlyn."

He shook her hand and glanced over at me. "Oh, sorry, I'm Tera."

"Are you ready to head down to the beach?" Ashlyn asked.

"Uh, yeah, let me just run to the bathroom."

"It's down the hall and to the left," Will said.

"Thanks," I said. I almost ran out of the room to go find it. I could hear Ashlyn talking to him.

"You should come with us," she said. She was trying to coax him.

"Maybe I will," he said. I could hear the smile in his voice. A tinge of jealousy tingled in my chest.

Why am I jealous? I love his brother.

I made it into the bathroom and closed the door. The bathroom was massive, with a shower stall and a jacuzzi tub. It had to be bigger than my bedroom. I went over to the sink and turned on the cold water. I was burning up as if my blood was lava. I was hot and bothered by Will and jealous that Ashlyn was hitting on him. I splashed water on my face. I tried to pull my mind off it. *Cold thoughts, ice, snowmen, winter.* I tried to think of anything that would help me get control over my emotions.

The last thing I needed was to wolf out.

I thought of my necklace in my bag. I could feel where it lay on my neck as if it had left a mark. *I shouldn't have taken it off. I took much of a risk. I put everyone in danger. What if I hurt someone? Just like I hurt Mr. Fera.* The thought of Maggie's dad made a wave of despair and guilt wash over me. I didn't feel hot anymore, but I couldn't stand to look at myself in the mirror any longer.

I opened the bathroom and rushed into the hallway, slamming into someone as I did. It was Will. I imagined it would have felt better if I slammed into the wall. I thought it would have been like I had walked into a stack of bricks, but it wasn't. He crumpled back as we collided, as if I was the one built of bricks. He grunted and gasped for air. He grabbed onto my shoulders.

"Jeez," he coughed as he tried to catch his breath. "Are you okay?"

"I'm fine. Are you okay?"

"Oh, uh, yeah, I'm fine. Just slow down, killer, and watch where you're going," he said. *Killer* rang through my head. I just looked at him, trying to find words to speak, but I had none. "Are you sure you're okay?" he asked.

"Um, yeah, sorry," I said, shaking my head. "I should go." I went to move, but he didn't release my shoulders. He just kept looking at me. I could feel myself turning red.

"Your friend is waiting for you," he said. He let go of my shoulders. His gaze felt so invasive, like he was trying to read into my soul.

"Yeah, she is," I said, walking past him and down the hallway into the kitchen. Ashlyn looked up from her phone as I entered the room.

"What's wrong? Why do you look like that?" she asked.

"Nothing. Let's just go down to the beach." I tried to shake his creepiness off me.

"Did he say something to you?" she asked with a clenched fist.

"No, he just gave me a weird vibe."

"He's a jerk," she said. She linked her arm with mine. "He called me childish and told me to go build a sandcastle."

I laughed. "What happened to devouring him?"

"Definitely not happening. I would stab him, though."

On the beach, Tati was laid out on her towel, her dark skin sparkling like a gem. She looked so peaceful. Ashlyn and I decided not to bother her. Ben and Maggie were in the water, talking and laughing. Ben's laugh was so kind and full of life it made me smile.

"What are you smiling at?" Ashlyn asked.

"Don't you hear them laughing?" I asked.

"No, I don't. How can you hear them over everyone else?" she asked.

I hadn't even picked up on all the other sounds on the beach until she said something. I was so focused on Ben and Maggie that they were the only people I heard.

"I guess my hearing is just really good."

"Yeah, like supersonic," Ashlyn said.

Once we were at the waterline, Maggie and Ben gave each other a devious look. In unison, they both reached down and splashed water at us. It was like it was happening in slow motion. The individual water droplets were flying toward me. I slipped out of Ashlyn's grip and leaped to the side, avoiding the water, while Ashlyn was left to be slapped with both waves. She squealed.

"That's freezing," she cried. Ben and Maggie laughed. Ashlyn and I shared a look and a nod. Without speaking, we both began splashing them.

Maggie squeaked as the first wave hit her right in the face. Ben tried valiantly to fight off our assault, but he was left spitting out seawater when we were finished. Ashlyn and I laughed and high-fived.

"That's why you don't start a battle you can't finish," Ashlyn said. She stuck her tongue out at Ben.

"Oh, that's it," Ben said. He stood from the water and grabbed Ashlyn in a bear hug.

She wiggled in protest, trying to get out of his arms. I couldn't help but laugh at her, knowing what would happen. Ben swung her high into the air and let her go.

"No! Ben, my hair!" she shouted as she hit the water with a splash and sank. A few seconds later, she resurfaced, shaking her head like a dog. She started splashing at Ben.

I stepped further into the water, grabbed Maggie's arm, and whispered, "Girl code." She frowned and looked at Ben, like she was sad to betray him, but then she looked at me with a smirk.

Maggie started splashing Ben from the side. He splashed back at the two of them, trying to fight off their assault from two sides. I took this opportunity to sneak up behind him. I leaped onto his back. I forced his shoulders and head down and under the water. I slid off him and let him out of the water. He gasped for air. He turned to me, wrapped his arms around my waist, and lifted me.

"No!" I shouted, knowing what he was planning to do. I locked my fingers behind his neck and squeezed, pulling him closer to me. He grunted as I squeezed him. "Don't stop splashing!" I shouted.

Maggie and Ashlyn unleashed a flurry of waves that soaked Ben and me. It was impossible to see. Ben tried to throw me, but my grip on him was too tight, and I brought him down into the water with me. The water was cold, and my teeth were chattering underneath it.

Ben put one arm behind my legs and one behind my back. He lifted me out of the water. We locked gazes. His doughy brown eyes melted me, locks of wet hair dangled down his forehead, and his lips separated. I could feel his body against mine. Everywhere our skin touched, a thousand fireworks detonated. It felt like gravity was pulling us closer together. For a moment, we were the only two people in the entire world.

Ashlyn coughed and brought me back to reality. It looked like it brought Ben back as well. He let me down from his arms. I didn't look at him, but I could feel his eyes on me. I could hear his heart racing; I could hear my heart racing. Ben sloshed out of the water and up the beach without a word to any of us. I wanted to scream for him to stop, but I didn't. I could feel anger bubbling up inside me. I gritted my teeth as I watched him. He walked to the house and disappeared around its side. The temperature inside my body had risen, like I had a fever.

Why am I mad? I'm not mad at Ben.

I tried to figure out what was triggering my anger. Jules had told me that anger triggered the curse, but she never told me my emotions would feel so out of control. *What am I angry at?* I thought, and that was when it hit me. I was angry at myself for pushing Ben away and even more for becoming this monster. That realization did not quell my anger. It was like waving a match over gunpowder.

A sharp pain in my gut caused me to wrench over. I screamed. Ashlyn and Maggie rushed to me. Tati sat up from her relaxed position. It took a moment for her to process that I had screamed. Fear spread across her face. I looked around to see many people around me staring at me. *Oh no, it's happening,* I thought as another pain stabbed into me.

I pushed away from Ashlyn and Maggie and sprinted out of the water, through my pain, past Tati, who was rushing to me and into the house. I cleared the distance with inhuman speed because I wasn't human anymore. I rushed up the stairs and into the kitchen. Ben was sitting at the table when I came stumbling in.

"Tera? What's wrong?" he asked as he stood up.

I didn't look at him. I grabbed my backpack from the ground, ran down the hallway, and crashed into the bathroom. I slammed and locked the door behind me. Each breath I took was painful, and my fingers were burning.

I looked in the mirror. My eyes had changed colors; one was red, and the other blue. I didn't have much time to stare as another pain stabbed into my abdomen, this time accompanied by a sickening crack. I reeled in pain as I threw my backpack onto the bathroom counter. I went to unzip it when I saw my fingers had sprouted talons.

"No, no, no," I whispered as I struggled to unzip my bag. There was a knock at the door.

"Are you okay in there?" It was Ben. Hearing him made me panic, making it harder to open the bag. Another crack echoed throughout me, sending a shooting pain up my spine. I screamed again. Ben started banging on the door. "Tera!" he shouted as he slammed against the door.

I was running out of time. I ripped open my bag with brute force and fumbled through the things inside. I grabbed my necklace. The metal burned in my hands, but I pushed through the pain and clipped it around my neck. Tingling shot through my body like I had stuck my finger in an electrical socket. I watched my hands as the talons receded underneath the skin. I looked in the mirror, and my eyes had returned to their natural green.

A wave of relief washed over me as my vision began to blur. I collapsed onto the floor and lost consciousness just as Ben came crashing in.

6

Selene

"How many more of these books do I have to read before I can do something real?" I asked Aunt Jules as I looked up from the copy of the *Encyclopedia of North America Herbs* she'd been forcing me to read.

"You'll never be done reading books," she said without looking up from her own book. "As witches, we should always be learning and absorbing new information. Witchcraft has existed for thousands of years and major for thousands more. We can only hope to truly understand a fraction of it in our natural lifetimes."

"That didn't answer my question." I closed my book.

"When I feel you are ready, I will tell you."

"Aunt Jules, The Ascension is coming sooner rather than later, and I will not be prepared for it by just reading books. I don't have the advantage of years to practice like the other witches who will be there."

She looked up at me and closed her book. "You're right."

"I am? I am," I said, processing how that plan succeeded. I had been trying to get Aunt Jules to skip the research stuff for days, but she hadn't budged.

"Yes, I think it's time we talk about what the trials for The Ascension are," she said.

"I'm ready." Part of me was excited to get started, and the other part of me was excited that this was real and I wasn't crazy. I hid my excitement, though. Aunt Jules wanted me to take this seriously, so I had to try.

"The Ascension will have three parts to it. Each trial tests your inherent strength and releases any latent power you might have. The Ascension is also used to determine the hierarchy of the Original Covens. The covens with the most promising young witches hold the highest status. The three trials reflect the All-Mother's three children. The Trial of the Sun, the Trial of the Moon, and the Trial of Creation."

"Her children?" I asked.

"You didn't read our family's journal, did you?" Aunt Jules said and glared at me.

"It was next on my to-do list," I said with a nervous laugh.

Aunt Jules sighed heftily. "The All-Mother is the creator of witchcraft, that I already told you. Long ago, it was said that she was the only being who could harness any magic. She shared her magic with mortals, the Original Covens. She had three children. They helped guide the covens in mastering magic. The All-Mother is the only goddess that the Original Coven worshiped. Her children are the only ones who have seen her for centuries, though."

"Wait, they're like real? This isn't some myth?" I asked.

"Are you really surprised? You watched your sister turn into a monster."

"That's a good point. What about other gods? Like Athena and Ra?"

"They're out there. They are worshiped by pagans and witches outside of the Original Covens. The magic those witches harness is not as potent because they require help from forces outside themselves, like ancestors or gods. Our magic comes directly from our blood. Don't ever underestimate any witch, though, Original Coven or not."

"That may have confused me more than I already was."

"You'll understand over time," she said.

"So, what exactly are the trials?"

"The Trial of the Sun is a test to prove that you belong to an Original Coven. The Trial of the Moon requires you to perform a ritual that comes from one of the All-Mother's legends. The Trial of the Creator asks you to create a spell or potion, but you are not told what kind until during the trial," Aunt Jules explained.

"So far, I'm not exactly quaking in my boots."

"Good," she said. "Then we can start getting ready for them. We'll start with the Trial of the Sun. Meet me in the backyard in ten minutes. I have to get some things together."

I jumped up from my chair, eager to get started. I left the encyclopedia behind and made my way outside. The sun's rays sent streaks through the green tree's leaves, creating shadow puppets on the grass that danced when the breeze came. I stood in the sun, closing my eyes as I absorbed the heat. I wiggled my toes against the blades of grass. The air was crisp with each breath I took. I thought of Tera at the beach with our friends and felt a tinge of joy. It was good to know she was doing normal things because once I broke the curse, everything would be normal for her. Breaking the curse had taken center stage in my attention; I wanted to give Tera her life back. I would've done anything to do it. I didn't know how much being a witch would change my life, but I didn't care. I only cared that I could give Tera a chance to live with hers.

Aunt Jules came out of the house with an old leather-bound book in her hand. She opened it to one page and handed it to me.

"What is this?" I asked.

"That is my journal from when it was time for my Ascension. You will use it as your cheat sheet and guide for now," she said. The book smelt of dust, and its pages were stained yellow with time.

I looked at the page and saw a list of names. Dilton Dyer, Lacy Novak, Tabitha Valentine, Pax Aradia—with a heart next to it—Elena Aradia, and Mary Boleyn. I looked at Aunt Jules with a raised eyebrow.

"What's this?" I asked.

"Those are the other witches who did The Ascension with me," she said.

"How many will be doing it this time?" I asked.

"I have received word that so far, three other witches will go through The Ascension with you," she said.

"What does that mean?" I asked.

"It doesn't really mean much. You will all just be doing it together," she said.

"So, it's not a competition or anything?" I asked.

"Oh, it is. The witch who proves to be the promising will receive a gift from one of the All-Mother's three children," she said with a devious smile.

"Oh, I'm so gonna win that gift." There wasn't a ghost of a chance that I would let myself lose. I was competitive, and I always won.

"What matters is curing Tera. A gift from one of the All-Mother's children could help us do that. Winning will also place our coven at the top of the hierarchy, meaning another coven wouldn't dare attack any of us again," she said.

Winning can help save Tera and protect us. I won't lose, I thought as I looked over the list again.

"Who's Pax Aradia?" I asked with a smirk. I traced my finger over the little heart.

"Nobody," Aunt Jules said, turning red. I chuckled.

"Wait a minute. Tabitha Valentine. Why does that name sound so familiar?" I asked.

"Probably because you know her." Aunt Jules was the one smirking now.

"Tabitha, Tabitha." Then, it hit me. "That's Tati! Tati's a witch?"

"Yes, she is. We've been best friends since our Ascension," Aunt Jules said.

"This whole time, I never realized that anyone but you knew the secret."

"Tati is the only other one who knows," she said.

"I can't wait to tell Tera."

"We're getting sidetracked," Aunt Jules said. "Flip to the next page."

The next page was decorated with fancy handwriting on the top that read, "The Trial of the Sun." Below the header was a smaller subheading that read: "The All-Mother's Eleven Gifts," "Pyrokinesis," "Future Sight," "Telekinesis," "Time Manipulation," "Electrokinesis," "Illusionary Manifestation," "Breath of Life," "Necrokinesis," "Tempest," "Transmogrification (Shapeshifting)," and "Suggestion."

"That is a list of the divine gifts that the All-Mother passed down to the Original Covens. Every witch of the bloodlines will manifest at least one of them. It is rare for witches to manifest more than one, but possible, especially for the more powerful ones," Aunt Jules said.

"What if you don't have one of these?" I asked.

"Then you are not considered a witch of the Original Covens," Aunt Jules said. "This is why the Trial of the Sun exists. Witches who are not a part of the Original Covens cannot complete The Ascension."

"Which one do you have?" I asked.

"I have manifested two. Telekinesis was the first and the one I used during my Ascension. Later in life, I manifested Pyrokinesis, like you have," she said.

"Is that what I did in the woods?" I asked. I flashed back to the wall of fire that had erupted between Tera's beast and me.

"From what you told me, I believe so. Do you think that you've shown any signs of others?" she asked.

My eyes were stuck on the words "Future Sight." I thought of my experience in the bathroom mirror and the flash I had when running into Ben's dad. "I think I have future sight. I saw a vision in the mirror before Tera turned. I didn't understand what was happening, though." I thought I was crazy.

"Selene, I am sorry I hid this all from you," Aunt Jules said. Her voice was soft. "I was just trying to protect you both."

"I know," I said, choking back tears.

Aunt Jules cleared her throat. "For the Trial of the Sun, we will stick to pyrokinesis. It will be easier to prove and train."

"How do we get started?" I asked and put the journal down on the ground beside me.

"We will start with a fire that is already lit," Aunt Jules said. She waved her hand, and a flame erupted between us. "You will need to focus on the flames, feel the warmth entering you and spreading. The key to understanding fire is in your breathing. Fire breathes just like we do. Breathe your energy into the fire, and it will grow. Suck it out, and it will die down. Now, try to grow the flame."

I put my focus on the flames. They swayed back and forth as I reached out to them. With each inhale, I let myself feel the warmth entering my body, connecting me to it. The fire grew taller with each breath I took. I could feel the energy flowing through me the more I focused on the fire. I waved my hand upwardly, and the flames sputtered before growing taller. The fire was now a few feet tall. It was the largest fire I had seen, but it was also the calmest. It didn't spread from its origin; it didn't even seem to have the desire to. It was completely under my command.

"Very good," Aunt Jules said. "Now move it."

I nodded. I tried to feed the fire more of my energy with the focus of spreading instead of growing. The fire ate up more of the grass around it as it grew in circumference. The fire became more agitated. It was embracing its destructive nature as it spread.

"No," Aunt Jules said. "You do not need to put more energy into it to command it to move. You must manipulate the energy that you have already given it. If you feed too much into it, you will lose control. The larger the fire, the harder it is to manipulate."

I nodded again. If it was easier to manipulate a smaller flame, then that was what I'd do. I focused on my connection to the fire. I inhaled slowly, pulling energy away from the fire and into myself. The flames receded to their original size. I then commanded the fire into a line between myself and Aunt Jules. The flames slid across the grass, slowly scorching the ground beneath them. My command was precise and focused, so the line was straight with no unwanted curves or bumps.

"Now, extinguish it," Aunt Jules said.

I inhaled sharply and pulled more energy away from the fire. It hugged close to the ground and fought to stay lit. A tinge of sadness grew inside me as I watched the flame struggling to stay alive. I pulled the last of the energy away from it, and I clenched my hand into a fist. The fire went out with a puff of smoke. I could feel sweat slip down my forehead. It was more work to concentrate on than I realized.

"Well, it seems like the basics came pretty easy to you. Do you think you're ready to start with some more advanced stuff, or would you like to get some rest?" Aunt Jules asked.

"No, I'm ready. Let's keep going." *I need to do this now. I don't have time to waste.*

"All right. Next, you're going to create a fire," Aunt Jules said as she moved to stand beside me. "You will need to create the element using only your own magic and energy. Stay focused on your intention. Be careful not to exhaust yourself."

"I've got this."

I stared at the scorch marks on the grass and tried to replicate the feeling I had when I was connected to the living fire. The warmth reignited inside me as I felt the energy swimming around inside me.

The fire was there, but I could not get it to spark to life on the grass as it had before. I could feel myself growing frustrated as I struggled to get the fire to ignite.

"I can feel it inside of me, but I can't get it out," I said through gritted teeth.

"It can be hard to manifest your will in the physical world. Sometimes, you need a trigger to help you. When I was a young witch, I used a snap to ignite my pyrokinesis. Think of it as giving yourself a spark," Aunt Jules said.

I brought my hand up and followed Aunt Jules's suggestion. I snapped. The moment the sound echoed through the air, flames erupted to life. I took a deep breath. I could feel fatigue coming over me, but I pushed through it.

"You won't need to snap once you have more experience and come into the rest of your power," she said.

"What's next?" I asked. My breathing was becoming heavy.

"I think that should be it for today," she said.

"No, we need to keep going." I kept my eyes trained on the flames that danced before me. "I'll need to be a lot stronger if we can even hope to break Tera's curse."

Aunt Jules nodded. "Let the flame grow. Then, try to control it. You won't need to feed it any energy to make it grow. Release your control over it and let it run rampant for a few moments. I will tell you when to take control back."

I let go of my focus on the fire, and the connection I had to it was severed. The warmth inside of me vanished as my control over it did. The flames' calmness also dissipated as they consumed more of the surrounding grass. It was like watching a monster rampaging through a city. The flames didn't care what was destroyed; they just kept expanding—twigs, grass, flowers, insects, anything that could burn did. Aunt Jules and I took a step back as the flames came closer to us.

"Now," Aunt Jules said.

I stared at the flames and their destructive power and tried to reform the connection I had severed. The warmth of the flame felt different from before; it felt stronger and more aggressive. The flames themselves spat and hissed at me as I tried to force my influence over them. I was forced to step back again as they got closer to me.

"Selene," Aunt Jules said.

"I'm trying." I shook my head as I refocused on the flames. I pulled the warmth into me. I could feel the rage that existed inside of the flames. It was unlike any anger I had felt before. I funneled my energy into the flames, but that only made them grow taller. The fatigue set in harsher as I tried to force my will onto the flames.

"Magic comes from the world around us." Aunt Jules's words from the other day popped into my head. I focused on the worlds around me outside of the flames and took another deep breath. I could feel the energy flowing into me. My fatigue vanished. I put my attention back to the flames.

I began slowing my breathing, embracing the anger that the element felt as I did. The flames began responding to the commands I was giving. They stopped spreading. I pulled energy away from the fire with each breath. The flames shrunk in size and pulled themselves tighter together.

"I did it. Now what?" I said.

"Put it out," Aunt Jules said.

I focused on snuffing the flames, but something stopped me. The flames began to sputter and hiss again. I watched in confusion as the flames folded into one another. I looked at Aunt Jules, who seemed just as confused. The flames morphed into two silhouettes dancing, a man and a woman. They were dancing some sort of ballroom routine. He dipped and spun her. As they moved, their embrace was close, but the flames didn't blend into one another. They remained two distinct shapes. The two separated before the man's flame sputtered out. The woman fell to her knees and screamed. The flames burst into a larger flame. I jumped back and covered my face. The skin on my arm stung as frigid air rushed to it. The flame had died out, and the silhouette of the woman was gone. I looked at Aunt Jules. She had a side smile.

"That has to be the strongest future sight I've ever seen. Most witches cannot share their visions with others like that," she said and grabbed my hand to look at my arm.

"That was my future sight?" I said.

"Yes, it was." She looked at my arm. "You're gonna need to rub some ointment on that burn. It's only minor, but better safe than sorry."

"Aunt Jules, what does that even mean?" I said as I gestured to where the fire had been dancing.

"I'm not too sure. I've never seen future sight this powerful before," she said.

"How do I learn to control it?"

"You can use traditional means of divination to help focus it, but future sight is the only of the All-Mother's gifts that can never be truly controlled. Some say that the visions are given directly to you from the All-Mother. Others say they come from somewhere more primordial. It is one of her least understood gifts because of how rare it is," she said.

"Great, so I'll always be susceptible to seeing the future in the bathroom mirror." I let out a frustrated sigh.

"I'm not saying that," Aunt Jules said. She picked the journal up off of the floor. She put an arm around my shoulder and started leading me into the house. "Using tools to divine the future can help to focus your energy to reach out to the visions. Doing that is a way to prevent your future sight from building up inside of you until it explodes like that."

"We don't have enough time for this. I don't have enough time to be prepared for The Ascension. How am I going to learn to control this power, too?" I asked. I sat down at the kitchen table.

"I know you didn't get a head start on witch life, but don't kick yourself in the ass just yet. Your future sight might just be a lucky break," Aunt Jules said as she pulled a tube of ointment out of her medicine cabinet.

"What do you mean?"

"Put this on your burn. I have to grab some things, then I'll explain," she said. She put the ointment on the table with the journal.

I opened the tube of ointment and smeared some of its icy contents onto the burn on my forearm. It stung. I clenched my teeth and opened the journal; it was filled with notes in the margins of the pages. There were notes about everything she did to prepare, on the powers of the other witches present, and even notes on what the weather was like on the day of The Ascension. Aunt Jules wrote every detail that she observed, as if she knew this journal would be used to guide future generations.

I flipped through the pages, looking for the next trial. I found a page had been ripped out of the journal just before The Trial of the Moon page. I ran my finger over the jagged edges that poked out of the book's spine. Aunt Jules returned to the kitchen with something wrapped in a black cloth. She sat down at the table across from me.

"You started reading ahead. Good," she said with an eager smile.

"I only just opened the book."

"That's fine. I don't think you'll need to do much reading for the next trial," she said. She laid the cloth on the table and unfolded it, revealing an obsidian hand mirror. She flattened the cloth before picking up the mirror.

"What's that for?" I asked.

"For the Trial of the Moon, you must replicate a ritual that the All-Mother did before the birth of the first witches. One of those rituals is performing an act of divination," she said, "With your future sight, this trial will be easy for you, and we can use it as an opportunity to train you to manipulate when the visions come."

"Okay, but what's with the mirror?"

"There are many forms of divination. Tarot cards, reading flames, tea leaves, and scrying are the most common. Scrying is using a reflective surface to help you peer beyond the veil of our world. It's like wiping the fog off a mirror to see what's behind it," she said. She laid the mirror on the cloth in front of me.

"Okay, so how do I do it?" I asked.

"I've never really been much of a Diviner myself," Aunt Jules said as she stood up and walked to one of the kitchen drawers. "But your mother and grandmother were."

"They had future sight?"

"No, but you don't need it to do divination rituals." Aunt Jules pulled another old book from the drawer and brought it to the table.

"I think I might vomit if I see another book."

"This isn't just any book. This is our family grimoire; it's been in our family since the birth of witchcraft."

The book was bound in a cracked black leather that almost looked burnt with age. I traced my finger over the insignia on the cover, a serpent wrapped through a human skull. It felt like electricity was coursing through the book—like it was charged with energy. Something about it felt alive. If I hadn't known better, I would've said it was breathing.

The book soon enchanted me. I wanted to grab hold of it and read every word inside it. The desire was so intrusive that it felt hypnotic. I wanted to know every secret. Aunt Jules snapped her fingers, and the feeling left my body, like I had just been awoken from a trance.

"What was that?" I asked.

"The book has a powerful protection magic on it that will affect anyone who hasn't bonded with it. It seduces them into opening it where our family's spirit guardian, the fierce snake, will strike them. Its venom is powerful enough to kill a hundred full-grown men. This protection spell makes our family's grimoire the deadliest of them all," Aunt Jules explained.

"I feel like that can't be safe to have around, and you just kept it in the kitchen drawer?" I asked.

"Once bonded with the grimoire, you have full command over its protector. The book is no threat to anyone who we allow near it. And yes, I keep it in the kitchen. No one in this house has ever even touched a dish beside me," she said. She wasn't wrong. Usually, Aunt Jules never let anyone touch anything in the kitchen. I could only imagine her reaction to the aftermath of Uncle Dan's birthday breakfast.

"How do I bond with it?" I asked.

Aunt Jules held out her hand. I put my hand inside of hers. She pulled a needle out of her pocket and pricked my finger. I sucked air through my teeth as she did. She squeezed my finger until a drop of blood came out. She then pressed my finger onto the snake's head in the book's crest and held it there.

"Now what?" I whispered.

"Now we wait to see if the snake appears to strike you," she said.

"What!" I shouted.

"Don't worry. If the book wants to bond with you, the snake won't strike. Only our family's blood will keep the snake from striking," she said. "Whatever you do, just don't move your finger off the crest."

A low hissing filled the kitchen. The book moved as a snake slithered out from the pages. Its cold, slimy scales brushed against my skin as it coiled on top of the book's cover and over and around my hand. I kept my finger pressed tight to the crest. The snake raised its head to look me in the eye. Its tongue flicked in and out of its mouth as it inched closer to my face. It was brown with a yellow underbelly and a black head. Its eyes were scanning my every atom. It could probably hear the thumping in my chest that flooded my ears. The snake's coil tightened as it folded the upper part of its body into a tight S shape. It was preparing to strike. I looked past the snake to Aunt Jules, who was nodding to me, trying to be supportive, but I could still see the worry in her eyes. I swallowed the lump in my throat as I switched my gaze back to the snake. It hissed before loosening its coil and slithering back into the pages of the closed book. I sighed.

"I feel like I'm going to throw up," I said as I pulled my hand off the book.

"You and the grimoire are now bonded, which means we can prepare for the Trial of the Moon," Aunt Jules said. She filled a cup with some water and handed it to me.

"Was it like that when you bonded with the book too?" I asked and took a sip of the water.

"No, when your mother and I did it, the snake didn't prepare to strike like that. It almost looked scared of you," Aunt Jules said.

"If that's what it looks like scared, I don't want to see it angry."

"I've never seen it acting like that before. I'll have to do some more research into it. Maybe I'll c—" She was cut off by the sound of her phone ringing. She pulled it out of her pocket and pulled her glasses down from her hair to read the message. "I have to go," she said.

"What is it?" I asked.

"Your sister almost turned the beach into an all-you-can-eat wolf buffet," she said.

7

Tera-Sue

I woke up in the backseat of a moving car. The smell of clean linen invaded my nostrils. I sat up. I didn't even get to take in my surroundings before the interrogation began.

"What were you thinking?" Jules snapped.

"I was trying to see what it would be like to embrace the change. Live without the collar."

"Embrace the change?" she asked. "Tera, this isn't like you got a new job! And it's not a collar. It's meant to stop things like that from happening."

"You mean it's meant to keep me under control?"

"To keep the curse under control, to protect you. To protect the people around you," she said.

"I can't just wear this thing forever."

"You won't have to. Once Selene and I break the curse, y—"

I cut her off. "You're not listening to me! What if you can't break the curse? What if there isn't a cure? What then?" I snapped.

Jules was silent. I stared into the rear-view mirror, but she didn't look back at me. I didn't understand why I was fighting with Jules. I only knew how much wearing the necklace weighed me down. I thought about when I first took it off. Everything felt so much more vibrant. I liked the feeling; it was the first time that I wasn't burdened by what had happened to me. I wanted to embrace that feeling, even if it was selfish and put everyone around me at risk. I wanted to feel okay being myself. I needed to feel okay being myself.

"I don't want to live my life scared of what I am. If I can learn how to control what I am, then maybe I can live a normal life. I don't want to feel like a monster anymore." I could feel tears flooding my eyes. I could feel the necklace burning around my neck.

"I understand," Jules said.

"What?" My voice cracked. I could see tears slipping down her cheeks.

"You can't risk your entire life on something that might not happen. We need to have a backup plan, something else you can rely on. I'm taking you to see a friend of mine," she said. She reached into the passenger seat and grabbed a plastic bag. She handed it back to me. "Here are some clothes to put over your bathing suit."

"How did you know what happened?" I asked.

"Tati texted me," she said.

"Tati? What did she tell you happened?"

"Tati knows exactly what happened because she knows the truth."

I was shocked, but Tati wasn't the one I was worried about. "What about everyone else? What do they think happened?"

"We told them you've been very ill for the past few weeks, and sometimes you have episodes of pain."

"They believed that?"

"Ashlyn and Maggie did. Ben took a little more convincing, but your sister handled that. The only one who didn't seem satisfied with that excuse was Ben's brother," she said with her brows furrowed. "I don't like him. There is something off."

"I agree. He was giving me creepy vibes. It felt like he knew there was something different about me. He looked at me like he knew everything."

"I'll have to keep a closer eye on him," Jules said.

"Do you ever feel bad for lying to so many people?" I asked. I did, and I would've bet Selene did too.

"It's a necessary evil. I'd rather lie and keep my family safe than tell the truth and risk them being hurt," she said.

"Yeah." I couldn't argue with that logic. I didn't want anyone to get hurt because I couldn't keep my mouth shut.

"Your sister doesn't agree. She was set on telling Ashlyn and Ben the truth. She stopped herself when she saw Maggie and Will."

"Is it even possible to tell them the truth? What kind of life would we live after that?"

"I don't know; I've never thought about telling a human the truth before."

"Never? Aunt Jules, you've never wanted to tell someone you loved that you're a witch?"

"The only man I've ever loved was also a witch, so I didn't have that problem."

"That's why I broke up with Ben."

"You broke up with him?" she asked. Her voice was sad, and she looked back at me through the mirror.

"Yeah. I didn't want to drag him into this world, and one lie now would protect him from a hundred lies later if we stayed together."

"Does your sister know?"

"No, I've only told Ashlyn and Maggie."

"I'm so sorry," she said.

"It's okay. It's for the best." The best hurt, and I hated it. I changed the topic. "Where is Selene?"

"She is with Tati. She has a lot of work to still do," she said.

"How hard is The Ascension?"

"The trials themselves are not hard. There is a lot more that goes into The Ascension that worries me. Sometimes, witches change after The Ascension. That's what scares me most," Jules said.

"Come on, it's Selene. She is the strongest person I know. She can handle it." I could see the worry on her face. "Right?"

Jules was silent. I waited for a response I knew wasn't coming. I looked for my phone, but it wasn't there to help distract me from the awkwardness. I must've left it in with my bag at the beach house. Thinking about Ben and his beach house filled me with a tinge of guilt. I hated lying to my friends, but it couldn't be helped. I was living a lie, pretending to be a normal girl, pretending I wasn't a killer and that it would all go away soon.

We drove for a while on empty roads before we turned off down a dirt road that led us through a heavily wooded area. Jules parked the car and got out. I followed her lead as she walked into the brush. It felt like a bad horror movie where a masked killer could get us at any time. I could feel the hair on my arms standing up and a chill creeping down my spine. Even though I was the scariest thing in those woods, I still picked up my pace. The closer I was to Jules, the safer I felt.

We came to a grove with a large rock in the center. There wasn't much there but a rock and light that slipped in through the gap between the treetops. I was about to ask Jules what was happening when a twig snapped on the other side of the grove. I jumped closer to her, and I clutched onto her arm. She chuckled.

A wolf stepped into the grove. It glared at us. Its yellow eyes were piercing, and its gray coat shined in the light. Awe washed over me as I watched it stalk about the other side of the grove. The wolf let out a ghastly howl before it moved behind the rock and out of sight. A bright yellow light flashed through the grove from behind the rock. I put my hand out to protect my eyes. When the light died, I dropped my hand and looked around the grove. Nothing happened.

"What was that?" I whispered.

"That was a showoff," Jules said.

"That wasn't showing off. You know I have much better tricks than that," a man said as he emerged from behind the rock. He was buttoning up a pair of jeans and held a shirt in his hand.

"Some things never change, huh, Pax?" Jules said. She went and hugged the man.

"Hey, Jules," he said with a smile as they embraced. I had never seen Jules's smile so bright. Their embrace was long. I coughed to remind them I was still there.

"Pax, this is my niece, Tera," Jules said as she broke away from his grasp.

"Nice to meet you, Pax." I reached out to shake his hand. His grasp was firm, but his hands were soft like silk. I couldn't help but stare at his biceps as he shook my hand. I glanced toward Aunt Jules out of the corner of my eye, who was turning red.

"You look a lot like your mom," Pax said. I didn't know what to say. Selene and I had only ever seen one picture of our mother. It was a picture of her and Jules from their childhood. I just smiled and nodded.

"Right, um. Tera, Pax, is going to try to help you. He has some experience with changing his shape," Jules said.

"Something tells me that his transformation might be a little different from mine." I thought of the flash of light and how painless it seemed to him. My change was excruciating and not smooth or clean.

"You're right," Pax said. "But I have some experience working with your curse."

"You do?" I asked.

"My daughter had the curse too," he said. Jules looked at him with sad eyes. There was clearly something more to their relationship than just being friends. Whatever it was, she trusted him enough to tell him about what happened. I knew I could trust him too.

"Well, where do we start?" I asked. He chuckled. I could see Jules fighting off her smile.

"We start off nice and easy. With meditation," he said.

"Meditation?" I echoed.

"Yes, but it won't be so simple. You'll need to take off your necklace."

I looked at Jules, who nodded to me. I unhooked the necklace and balled it up into my hand. Pax took the necklace from me. I let the chain slip through my fingers as I handed it to him. He pushed the necklace down into his jeans pocket. I was worried that something would happen and I wouldn't be able to get to the necklace. *What if I hurt him or Jules?* I thought. I inhaled deeply through my nose and closed my eyes. *Everything will be fine. Jules can handle herself. She's a badass witch, and I'm sure she could rescue Pax too.* I tried to convince myself.

I took in more of my surroundings now that the necklace no longer suppressed my senses. The scent of honeysuckles filled my nostrils. I didn't remember seeing any as we came in. They must've been hidden somewhere in the woods around the grove. I could hear squirrels rustling in treetops and deer drinking from a stream. The stream was calm and thin, but I could hear it trickle over some rocks as it moved. The world around me seemed so much more alive than it had before.

"I'm going to head back to the car," Jules said. "Pax will bring you back to me when you two are done here."

"Are you sure?" I asked. My worry was more for Pax than for myself. I didn't want to be responsible for eating Jules's man-friend.

"Everything will be fine, Tera. Pax knows what he's doing. Mostly," Jules said with a smile.

Pax shot her a look. "Hilarious, Jules. We'll be fine."

"But what if I eat you?" I said.

Jules snorted as she burst into a laugh. I'd never seen her so smiley. It was nice to see her happy like that.

"Trust me, if I even think you're going to wolf out, I'll be running before you realize it," Pax said.

"If you say so." Jules came and gave me a hug goodbye. She waved to Pax before disappearing into the surrounding woods.

"So."

"All right, Tera," Pax said as he sat on the ground with crossed legs. "Controlling your transformation probably won't be something you can do in a day. This isn't going to be an easy journey, either. You're going to have to face the darkness in yourself."

"Why does that sound so cryptic? What does that mean?" I asked.

Pax laughed. "Sorry, I was trying the Jedi mentor thing, but it's way harder than Jules makes it look."

"You should probably just leave that to her, then."

"We are going to be doing some shadow work," he said.

"And that is?"

"Shadow work is one of the first things a witch should learn how to do. The shadow is the dark part of ourselves that we must address to grow. It is the parts of us we hide from the world. The ugly things we tell ourselves that no one knows. Your darkest fears, your biggest regrets. All of those things in culmination make our shadow self."

"Okay, but what does that have to do with my curse?"

"Your curse is rooted in your shadow; it feeds off your inability to understand your emotions and subconscious thoughts. Once you address your shadow, you can control your transformation. You will be able to control your actions while in your werewolf form. You will also even be able to make the change painless."

"That's amazing."

"There's one more thing you need to know about, though. The more you understand your shadow, the closer you will be to it. You won't ever be able to control the change on the full moon, and your shadow will be in the driver's seat, but you will be conscious for the entire time," Pax said.

"So, anything my shadow does during a full moon, I will remember?"

"Not only will you remember it, but you will experience it."

I thought about how broken I felt when I heard I had killed Mr. Fera. I couldn't imagine what it would've been like to remember every detail of what I did to that man. I thought about the beach and how many people were in danger there: Maggie, Tati, Ashlyn, Ben, and countless strangers. I couldn't risk putting anyone in danger like that again. I decided two things: I had to learn to control my transformation, and I could never transform on the full moon.

"Fine."

"Okay, close your eyes and focus on my voice," Pax said. "You are going to need to relax yourself until you are in a near trance state. Take a deep breath through your nose for a count of six. Now, hold that breath for a count of six. Exhale through your mouth with a sigh for another count of six. Continue to do this as you let your body relax, let the world around you fade away."

Meditating was a lot harder than I ever realized. Every sound drew my attention. The wind, the squirrels pitter-pattering across branches, deer breathing, and even Pax's heartbeat kept distracting me. Focusing on nothing seemed impossible when my senses wanted me to focus on everything. I tried to drain everything out by focusing on Pax's voice, but the more I focused on him, the more I could hear his breathing and tongue moving. I must've been stiff as a board because Pax could tell I was not relaxed.

"Tera, focus on yourself, your thoughts, your breath, your heartbeat. Just let my voice be background noise to those things," he said.

I did just that. I focused my attention on my breath, and soon, with each one I took, the tension left my shoulders as they slipped lower and lower into a relaxed place. My thoughts stopped racing as I let them resolve themselves with each breath. I pictured something in my mind that became clearer as I became more relaxed.

I could see the grove, but Pax was gone. I was sitting on top of the boulder. It was quiet. I looked around. I didn't see anyone, but I knew I wasn't alone. I stood on the boulder to get a better view of my surroundings. The trees that lined the grove were as far as I could see. Past them was a blackness that shifted like a thick smoke concealing whatever was outside the light. A low growl was coming from inside the darkness. The hairs on the back of my neck and arms stood up. My muscles were stiff as I stared into the blackness, waiting for something to step into the light. Sweat was sliding down the side of my face. I opened my mouth to speak but couldn't make any sound. I took a deep breath and tried to swallow the lump in my throat.

"Who's there?" I finally got out.

"You don't recognize me?" a voice said as someone stepped out of the darkness. I was staring down at myself—a version of myself I didn't know.

8

Selene

I closed the door as slowly as I could, trying to avoid making any sound. My goal was to get upstairs, shower, and change without drawing any attention to myself. I didn't have an explanation for Uncle Dan as to why Tera and I had been MIA. I didn't want to lie. I hated all the lying that came with being a witch.

As the door clicked shut behind me, his voice came from the kitchen. "Tera? Selene? Is that you?"

I exhaled and cursed under my breath. "Yeah, Uncle Dan, it's me."

"Come in here," he said.

I walked into the kitchen, where he was sitting in his work uniform, a cup of coffee on the table before him. He smiled at me. Behind his reading glasses, his crow's feet became more defined. His blond hair was littered with gray strands. He looked older than when I'd seen him last, before Mr. Fera's funeral. I expected him to be upset we hadn't been around, but he seemed more pleased to see me than anything else.

"What are your plans for tonight?" he asked.

"I'm going to get changed and head over to Tati's to help her with something." Aunt Jules said it was best to be vague. Being vague still felt like a lie.

"Are you and your sister busy on Saturday?"

"I don't think I am, but Tera left for an overnight school trip today. I don't know when she's coming back."

"I didn't know she had a trip coming up," he said before taking a sip of his coffee.

"Yeah, Aunt Jules signed the permission slip." I was throwing Aunt Jules under the bus, but I doubted Uncle Dan would ever ask her about it. "Aunt Jules is a chaperon of the trip, so I'm sure everything will be fine."

"I'm not worried."

"You're not?"

"No. You girls are adults and mature enough to handle yourselves," he said. "And I trust that if you need me, you will come to me."

"Thanks, Uncle Dan." The guilt I felt for lying to him grew more pungent after hearing that.

"Anyway," he said. "I am going to be going on vacation for a little while."

"You are? Where are you going?"

He stood and put his mug in the sink. I watched him in his silence. It was so odd to see him like this, relaxed and unquestioning. Then, he approached me and gave me a kiss on the head. "I am going on a trip across Europe with Liam. I'm not sure how long we'll be gone, but I'll call you both every week. We're leaving on Saturday, so I guess you'll need to tell Tera I said goodbye."

"Okay, I'll tell her," I said softly. Relief washed over me. Before I could think of another topic to raise, he walked out the front door without another word.

I headed upstairs and into the bathroom. I grabbed a towel from the closet and draped it on the shower's door handle.

I looked at myself in the bathroom mirror. I looked beyond tired.

The bags under my eyes were so dark I resembled a raccoon, and my skin was a few shades paler than normal.

I opened the shower door and turned on the water. There were candles on the bathtub's four corners. I picked up the one closest to me and took a whiff. Lavender. I sighed as the soothing scent entered my nostrils. Tera had left them after her last bubble bath.

Which wasn't the worst idea in the world, honestly. I decided I needed a bath instead of a shower. I flicked the drain switch so the tub would fill. Then, I grabbed a bath bomb and face mask from under the sink and placed them on the ledge beside one of the candles. I took my backpack off and pulled mine and Tera's phones out. I put them on the table beside the tub. Then, I took off my clothes and stepped into the tub.

The water was warm and soothing as I sat down. I took a deep breath and looked at the four candles around the tub. With a snap of my fingers, the candles sparked to life. A sense of accomplishment stirred inside me.

My relaxation was cut short just after I closed my eyes; a gunshot echoed through the bathroom. I sat up, startled. The candle's flames shot six inches higher before going out, leaving only twisting smoke.

Then, there was a ding and a vibration from one of the phones on the table beside me. I grabbed my phone, my hand still dripping with water. No notifications. I lifted Tera's, and I found the culprit: a text message from Ben.

My dad keeps asking about you. I told him things were over, but he keeps insisting I invite you over for dinner with him and my brother tonight.

I thought back to when I'd run into Ben's dad at the funeral. I'd heard a gunshot then too. Something was up with him.

I swiped open the text message. *What time is dinner?*

He responded in under ten seconds. *Wait. Are you serious?*

I shook my head and typed back. *Yes.*

He responded. *In an hour?*

See you then.

I stood and grabbed my towel. I wrapped it around myself, grabbed the phones and my backpack, and headed into Tera's room. I closed the door behind me and flicked the light on. *Tera's gonna kill me if she finds out about this*, I thought. *I'm going to impersonate her and trick her ex to investigate some kind of premonition I keep having about his father. All-Mother, who am I becoming?* I shook my head as I opened her closet and walked in.

I froze in the doorway. Her closet was like someone had shrunk a department store into one room. It was organized by season and color, which was absurd to me. Tera never organized anything but her closet, apparently.

I'm gonna have to ask her to look at mine when she's back, I thought as I ran my fingers over the clothes. Some of them still had tags on. What would Tera wear to meet Ben's dad?

I grabbed my phone and clicked Ashlyn's contact. *How am I going to explain this to her?* I bit my lip before clicking the call button. She answered on the second ring.

"Look who it is," she said. "I thought you'd forgotten about me."

"I need your help with something."

"What's up?" she asked.

I explained to her I needed to be Tera to go to dinner with Ben's family. Of course, I left out the important parts and replaced them with a horrible lie along the lines of "helping her rekindle her relationship with Ben." I was lucky that, aside from Tera and Ben, no one was more invested in their relationship than Ashlyn.

"I'll be there in two minutes," she said before hanging up.

I sat down at Tera's makeup table and plugged in her straightener. She spent a lot of time on her appearance. Well, she used to. I hadn't seen much of her over the last week. I had been so busy preparing for The Ascension while Tera learned to live with what had happened, which meant teaching herself control. Part of me feared that if she figured out how to control her curse, she might not want to break it.

Would that be bad? If she had control, did the curse need to be broken? I doubted Aunt Jules would give her a choice if it came to that. I wouldn't either. Tera needed to be cured.

The bedroom door swung open as Ashlyn burst in. She looked at me with a smile like the devil's. She walked into the closet and came out with several outfits on hangers. She dropped them onto the bed.

"Let's get this transformation started," she said as she approached the makeup table and began going through Tera's things. "Let me see these text messages."

I unlocked Tera's phone and handed it to her. She swiped through the short conversation and chuckled. "His brother is going to be there. Tera and I met him. He was an ass. Tera wouldn't go to this dinner without looking snatched. I know exactly what look to do."

Ashlyn went to work with the makeup. The way she worked with the brushes made me feel like a canvas. She even stuck her tongue out as she focused. Her sharp brown eyes scanned every inch of my face. She covered any imperfection she might have seen. After what felt like an hour, she stepped back.

"And we're done," she said with a proud look.

I turned to the mirror. I looked closer, trying to find myself under the mask Ashlyn had created. My bags were gone, my cheekbones were glowing, and my eyes looked intense.

"Wow." I couldn't see myself beyond the look Ashlyn had created. I looked more like Tera than myself.

"You know, Selene, you can look like this any time, right?" Ashlyn said. "Tera doesn't have a monopoly on using makeup."

"I guess I just never felt the need to wear makeup. I'm not trying to impress anyone."

"I don't wear makeup to impress people. I wear it for me. It makes me feel powerful. Like I'm painting my face for the battle of life every day," she said as she straightened my hair.

"I never thought of it like that."

"Yeah, my mother didn't teach me much growing up. However, she taught me that there is nothing more that the powers fear than the feminine," she said.

"That's probably why more women were burned during the witch trials than men. Even though there were just as many male witches."

"Men fear a powerful woman," she said.

"Only the weak ones," I said, wiggling my eyebrows. She laughed.

Ashlyn finished with the straightener and curled the ends of my hair. She sprayed a generous amount of hairspray over my head. I coughed as I stood and walked to the bed to look at the clothes she picked out—a black strapless dress with a leg slit, a red dress, high wasted jeans with a crop top, and a romper. I picked up the black dress and held it up.

"That's a good choice," she said. "It screams 'head bitch in charge,' but I don't know if Tera would wear that to meet Ben's dad."

"Hmm, maybe you're right, but would she wear it if she were single and looking to stir feelings in her ex?" I asked.

"Oh, you're evil," she said with a smirk. "Go put it on."

I went into the closet and slipped into the dress. It was a perfect fit; I zipped the back as far as I could on my own.

"What time is it?" I asked as I returned to the room.

"Six thirty," Ashlyn said. "You're supposed to be there already."

"Tera has never been on time for anything in our lives. Zip me up, please."

Ashlyn zipped the dress up, and I turned to face her. She was wearing the red dress that was on the bed.

"What are you doing?" I asked.

"Oh, you thought I was going to let you have all the fun?" she asked.

"I'm going with you."

"I don't know if that's a good idea." *What if something happens, and Ashlyn gets caught in the middle of it?* I thought. She wouldn't even understand what was happening.

"I should probably go alone."

"Ben would expect that I would be there. Tera wouldn't show up without some sort of backup," she said. "And since you can't be yourself and Tera, the logical choice is me."

I hated that she was right. I would not be able to convince her to stay. I decided I would just have to protect her if anything happened. "Fine. I'm driving, though."

"Perfect. That will give me time to fix my makeup in the car," she said.

After a short ride across town, we were outside Ben's house. I grabbed the pocketbook I brought from the backseat and checked to ensure the family grimoire was still there. It was. I hated the idea of carrying it around with me because I feared someone would grab it and end up bitten by the book's guardian. However, keeping it with me was the only way to build my connection with it. I grabbed Tera's phone from the pocketbook and texted Ben: *Here.*

Ashlyn and I exited the car and made our way up the long driveway toward Ben's massive house. It was an old white colonial with three above-ground stories and a balcony supported by six marble columns that framed the front porch with the front door in the center of the middle two. I had always thought it was so big that you could probably get lost for a week while searching for the bathroom. Ashlyn knocked on the door and looked back at me with a raised eyebrow.

"What do you think his parents do?" Ashlyn asked.

"Honestly, I don't know," I said, looking around at the property surrounding their home. They had to have had about twenty acres of land, most of which was wooded. Their nearest neighbor was miles away and beyond the woods. "I don't think Tera even knows," I whispered.

"Really?" Ashlyn asked.

"I don't think he ever really talks about his family."

"That's sus," Ashlyn said.

"I know."

Ben opened the door and looked at me with a beaming smile. He was wearing a baby blue polo and khaki pants. His hair was combed back, and his brown eyes were fixated on me. The crisp air I felt tickling my skin earlier was gone as a sudden wave of heat hit me. I was blushing, and if Ashlyn hadn't layered makeup on me, I'd probably be bright red like a freshly cracked glow stick.

"You look gorgeous," Ben said. I had no idea how to respond to him. I wasn't used to those kinds of interactions. Thank the All-Mother, Ashlyn swooped in and saved me from embarrassing myself.

"Thanks," she said as she pushed past him into the house's foyer.

"Oh, hey, Ashlyn," Ben said. He sounded disappointed that she was there.

I followed in behind her and past Ben. He put his hand on my shoulder. I looked back at him. His expression had changed, his eyes were glassy, and his smile had faded. He looked like he was in pain. Seeing Tera like this must have made it feel like his heart was breaking again.

"Can we talk alone?" he asked.

"Later. I don't want to start the night like this." I pushed away any feelings I had toward the situation and tried to be cold. He nodded and looked away from me.

"Okay. Later," Ben said.

It had dawned on me how terrible of an idea it really was. Not only did me being there cause Ben more pain, but it would also hurt Tera when she heard about it. I had to avoid being alone with Ben at any cost.

Ben led us into the kitchen, where they had a bartop counter. He pulled a chair out for me and offered to take my bag. I sat down and hung my bag on the back of the chair, telling him I'd rather keep it. Ashlyn sat beside me.

"I'll go let them know you're here," Ben said before leaving the kitchen.

Ashlyn smacked me on the arm and said, "Jeez, ice queen, maybe you want to be a little nicer to him."

"I don't even know what to say to him," I said. "And there is no way that I'm going to go off and have a private conversation with him."

"Try to flirt or something," she said. "We want to make him think Tera wants to get back together."

"Uh, yeah," I said with a sheepish grin. Ashlyn narrowed her eyes.

"That is why we are here, right?" she asked.

"Not exactly." I couldn't keep lying anymore.

"What! Then, what are we doing here?" she asked.

"I can't really explain that right now, but it's important. I promise."

"If it's important, then why can't you tell me?"

"I just can't right now. I will tell you everything later." I could hear Ben's footsteps nearing the kitchen. "I need you to trust me."

"Fine, but you better tell me when we leave," she snapped.

Ben came back into the kitchen alone. He said, "My brother will be down in a minute, and my dad ran out to get dinner. I hope you guys like Peruvian food."

"I love Peruvian food," Ashlyn said. "I once dated a Peruvian guy, and h—"

"I don't remember you saying she would be here," a man said as he entered the kitchen. That must've been Ben's brother, Will. Ashlyn said he was an ass, but she didn't tell me he was hot. He was wearing a black dress shirt and slacks. He looked at me and smirked. It sent a chill down my spine, and all the hair on my neck stood up. My instincts told me I needed to be on guard, like a predator had just entered the room.

"And there goes the night," Ashlyn said. "You should teach your brother some manners, Ben."

"Funny that you think little Benny could teach me anything," he said as he leaned against the counter behind Ben.

"Little Benny," I said with a chuckle. Ben's cheeks turned red. Ashlyn snorted, which de-escalated the situation even further. The four of us were left laughing for a few minutes before the awkwardness returned to the air.

"Something seems different about you," he said to me.

"What do you mean?" I asked. I could see Ashlyn shifting in her seat beside me.

"You don't seem as tense as when I first met you," he said. "Maybe it's because you haven't yet knocked the wind out of me today." He stood and moved to the other side of the bar beside Ben. He was looking at me like he was trying to read into me. "It was like you were inhumanly strong."

I kept my poker face tight; he knew something. I needed to cover for Tera. I raised my eyebrows and said, "Maybe you are just inhumanly weak."

Ben's phone chimed before anything more could be said. "Dad will be back in five. We should set the table, Will."

"I'll help," Ashlyn said.

"I have to use the restroom."

"It's just through the living room and to the right," Will said.

"You know she's been here before," Ben said.

"Thanks anyway." I grabbed my bag from the chair and took it to the restroom. I did not get lost on the way.

I put the seat on the toilet and sat on top of it. I pulled the grimoire out of my bag and put it on my lap.

"All right, I need to know the truth about Ben's father and brother." I put my hands on the book and closed my eyes. I tried to focus on what I wanted: the truth. The book shook as if to tell me to lift my hands. After I did, the book flung open, and the pages flipped. When it stopped, it opened a page that read, "Tea of truth." It was a recipe for a tea and a spell that would make those who drank it speak only the truth for a day.

"I can't use this. I don't have time to make tea and bring it back for them to drink." The book slammed closed with a low hiss. "Hey! Don't you hiss at me. This is important."

The book flung open to the page again. This time, sitting between the pages was a vial of brown liquid. I grabbed the vial and inspected it closely. I *don't even want to know how that got in there.* After my initial confusion wore off, excitement flooded me.

"This is perfect." I kissed the book. "You beautiful little grimoire, you're never leaving my side."

I read over the spell a couple of times before I slipped the book back into my bag. I put the vial in my bra and stopped to look at myself in the mirror. I fluffed my hair and checked my teeth. "Ben was right. You are gorgeous."

I left the bathroom and headed back into the kitchen, where Ben was taking a pitcher of water and a pitcher of sweet tea out of the fridge. *The All-Mother is smiling down on me today,* I thought as I walked to Ben. I grabbed the sweet tea from him.

"I'll get this. You just take care of that." I rubbed my hand on his back. He looked at me and smiled.

"Thanks," he said. I waited for him to leave the kitchen before I closed the fridge and put the tea on the counter. I pulled the vial out and opened it. I poured the liquid into the tea.

"Dark hearts and silvered tongues, let your lies be undone. With one sip of this tea, the truth will be revealed to me," I chanted lowly. I stirred the pitcher in a clockwise motion as I spoke.

I took the pitcher into the dining room, where everyone was seated. I put it on the table near Will. Ben's dad stood to give me a handshake.

"It's so nice to finally meet you," he said. I smiled at him before taking my seat next to Ashlyn and across from Ben. I hung my bag on the chair behind me, slipped my phone out, and texted Ashlyn: *Don't drink the tea.* She checked her phone and then looked at me worriedly. We watched as Ben's father and Will poured themselves glasses of tea. I grabbed the pitcher of water and my glass.

"Everything looks delicious," I said as I filled my glass. I poured some for Ashlyn and Ben as well. I raised my glass. "I'd like to make a small toast. Thank you for being so kind as to invite me over for dinner and also for raising such a sweet man as Ben."

"I'll cheer to that," Ben's father said as he raised his glass. He nudged for Will to follow. He did. Ben looked at me like I had said something offensive, and Ashlyn smiled nervously. Our glasses clinked together.

I took a smug sip of my water as I watched Ben's father and Will take drinks of their tea.

9

Tera-Sue

She looked at me with an evil smile. Her eyes were two different colors, one red and one blue. Her hair was unkempt, and her clothes were caked in dry blood. There was something sinister about her that made me uneasy. *Is this the darkness that lives in me?* I thought. *Is this my shadow?*

"I'm the real you," she said. "The you that stopped fighting her nature. The you who embraced being the killer we are. I let my anger take the driver's seat, and so will you."

"No. You're wrong. I'll never be a killer again! I won't let my anger out."

She let out a cackle that rang through the grove. "You can't fight against it. Once a killer, always a killer." Her voice was inside my head, like a whisper from the back of my mind. "You know you liked the taste of his blood."

"No!" I screamed as I fell to my knees and covered my ears. I could feel her approaching me. "You're not me! I won't become you!"

"You already have," she said. I swatted at her; her flesh tore under my nails.

"Tera! Wake up," Pax shouted.

I was jolted out of my unconscious state and back into reality. Pax was standing in front of me, clutching his right forearm. I could see blood dripping down his hand. There was a pit in my stomach. I looked down at my hands, and there was blood on the fingers of my left hand. I looked at Pax, tears filling in my eyes. I could feel myself still shaking with anger and fear.

"Tera, it's fine," he said. "Just a little scratch. I'll live."

I wiped my eyes with my clean hand. "I'm so sorry."

"You don't need to apologize. I expected this kind of thing when I agreed to help you."

"I can't control myself. Something worse could have happened."

"But something worse didn't happen. You can't give up over one hiccup. Keep going."

"What if I can't do this? What if I lose control and—" I took a deep breath before continuing. "And kill someone again?"

"You need to have faith in yourself for this to work. Doubt will poison any progress that we make," he said. "You need to trust yourself, Tera."

"How can I trust myself when a monster lives inside me?" she said.

"Your shadow self is not a monster, Tera. It's the parts of yourself that you don't understand, the parts of you that you refuse to accept." He sat down on a rock beside me. "Can I tell you a story?"

I looked at him for a moment, wondering why he even asked. He would tell me the story regardless of what I said. "Okay."

"When my daughter, Maya, was bitten, I drove myself crazy trying to cure her. I—"

I cut him off.

"Bitten?" I asked.

"Yeah, she wasn't cursed by a witch like you were. She was camping with a friend's family when they were attacked. She was the only survivor, but she was bitten," he explained.

"That's horrible."

"It was. I tried everything to break her curse, but I didn't have the right resources, and few people were willing to offer me help. Jules was the first person to jump to my aid. She helped me create a necklace like the one she made you. It was also her idea to teach Maya how to control the change. It almost got us eaten then too," he laughed.

"Really?"

"Oh yeah. Maya struggled with trying to confront her shadow self. The first few sessions left Jules and I staring down a massive yellow-eyed beast. It was terrifying. I read somewhere that bitten werewolves are more vicious than their born or cursed counterparts. They're not strong or dangerous, but they will stop at nothing to tear apart whatever they are chasing."

"How did you and Jules stop her from eating you?"

"Jules had a spell that would cause her necklace to appear on her. It was like pressing the button on a shock collar remote," he said, standing up from the rock and stretching.

"What happened? Did you break her curse?"

"No, we didn't," he said. "We found a way, but we didn't get to it fast enough."

"So, you can cure my curse!" I shouted as I leaped up from the ground in excitement. I started thinking about how nice it would feel to be ordinary again—to hang out with my friends without worrying about killing them, to be with Ben again, and even to go back to school. The simple things were the things I missed the most.

"No," he said. With that, all my excitement deflated. It was like a punch to the gut. I collapsed back down to the floor in disappointment. "It wouldn't work for you."

"Why not?" I asked.

"Because the cure we found was to kill the werewolf that bit her, and even that wasn't guaranteed to work, but we never got the chance to find out," he said. His voice was somber, and he kept his back to me. The topic was hard for him to even think about, let alone talk about. I had to know everything, though.

"What happened to her?" I asked.

"She was killed by hunters," he said.

Hunters? I thought. I stared at him, waiting for him to say more, but he didn't. We stayed like that for a while before Pax finally looked back at me. His cheeks were a tender red, and his eyes were glass.

"The key to facing your shadow self is not fighting against it but trying to understand it and the emotions behind it. Don't fight against yourself. Let yourself feel. You need to let go of control."

"Keeping in control is the only thing that's keeping me from wolfing out."

"What if fighting to stay in control is the only thing that is causing you to wolf out?" he asked.

I thought about the times I'd almost changed. I had been fighting against the things I felt to stop myself from changing. My eyes widened as I looked at him. He smirked. "I'm ready to try again."

Pax guided me back into a meditative state, but this time, I didn't need his guidance. It was like I could close my eyes and appear back in the unconscious world I had created. This time, I looked up at the boulder where my shadow self was sitting. Her crooked grin spread across her face when she saw me.

"Back so soon?" she said as she jumped down from the boulder.

"Yup," I said as I walked toward her.

"Are you ready to be the killer we've always been?"

"We're not a killer," I said calmly as I stopped only a foot away from her. "What happened to Mr. Fera was tragic, but it was an accident."

For the first time, I believed that. I grabbed her and pulled her into a hug. I kept a tight grip on her as she squirmed to get away from me.

"What are you doing!" she shouted.

I could feel the anger seeping out of her as I touched her. My skin felt hot, and my blood was rushing through my veins. I tightened my grip on her.

"I've been so angry about what had happened to him. I've been blaming myself for it. He's dead because of me. I can never take that back. I've hated myself because of it. I blame myself more than anyone. I hold anger at myself for it. I am angry at myself because it can happen again at any moment. I'm too weak to stop it. I can feel it now." I cried, but I couldn't stop speaking. She had stopped fighting me. "You let the anger take over you. You've projected it onto everything around you because you can't take being angry at yourself anymore."

Then, the anger drained out of me. She sobbed. Sadness replaced anger. She didn't have to say anything for me to understand her feelings. I was all too used to them. "We've pushed everyone away, haven't we? Out of fear for them and to punish ourselves. I pushed Ben away when really all he wanted to do was be there for us. I fought against Jules's hope for the cure. I haven't seen Selene in days, not because there was no time, but because I'm afraid to face her. I broke my own heart. I broke Ben's heart. We can't go on like this."

We stood intertwined in each other's grasp for what felt like hours before she faded away. I let my hands drop to my side. I stood there and sobbed for a while longer before my own voice spoke from behind me.

"Pathetic," it said. "You feel a few emotions, and now you're a blubbering mess."

I turned to look at who was speaking. It was another version of myself. This me was beautiful. I was almost envious of how perfect she looked. She had an aura of confidence that seeped out of her like a poison that made me feel beneath her.

"Who are you?" I asked.

"I'm you," she said. "The better you, of course. I am your true shadow self, not just some manifestation of your trauma. I am the you that you desire to be."

"I don't desire to be you."

"Oh, but you do," she said. "You wish you were never targeted for the curse. You wish you were a witch. You wish your mother never abandoned you. And you certainly wish that you weren't the dirty mongrel you are now."

My cheeks were hot again, and I balled my fist at my side. What annoyed me the most about her was that she was right. I wanted all those things. I took a deep breath and unclenched my fist. "Yes. I want all of those things, but I can't have them."

"You wish it were Selene that was cursed and not you," she said, crossing her arms.

"That's where you're wrong. I envy Selene because she gets to be a witch and isn't cursed, but I do not wish she was. I wouldn't wish this burden on her. If I had to choose to take on this curse or pass it on to Selene, I would take it."

"You're lying," she said. "I am what you desire—"

I cut in before she—I could finish. "You were what I desired but couldn't have. I understand why I had those desires, but you are not what I desire now. I want to be me. I know more about myself now than I did when you were created. You're nothing more than a representation of the anger and sadness I felt."

"You can't just get rid of me lik—" She was cut off by a growl coming from inside the darkness beyond the tree line.

Pounding footsteps approached us from outside the grove. The massive creature came into the light, and its black coat glistened like a thousand little stars in the night sky. It roared at her. She was frozen with fear when it lunged at her. It cleared thirty feet to her in seconds. It grabbed her by the throat with its massive teeth. The creature thrashed its head after gripping her.

There was a sickening crack. All the struggle left her body. The beast tossed her motionless corpse past the tree line and into the darkness before turning its attention to me.

It growled at me and snapped its massive jaws. The more I looked at this creature, the less I feared it. I extended my hand toward it. It dropped to all fours, where it was still taller than me. Its growling had receded to just a low grumble. I walked toward it.

It was warier of me than I was of it. It lowered its head so we were staring into each other's eyes. My reflection stared back at me through the clear film covering its eyes. Its eyes weren't mindless or animalistic but rather full of thought and emotion. It was like looking into the eyes of another human, not the monster I had made it out to be. I ran my fingers through the fur on top of its head. It was like silk between my fingers. It closed its eyes and exhaled heavily out of its nostrils. Its breath blew my hair behind me. I followed its lead and closed my eyes. I kept running my hand through its warm fur as I did.

Calm. That was the only thing I felt as I opened my eyes again. I was back to reality. The grove had darkened, and Pax was nowhere to be found. I closed my eyes and tried to listen for him, but all I could hear were crickets and other creatures of the night scurrying around. I knelt beside the rock where Pax had been sitting. There was blood on it. I touched it; it was dry. He had been gone for some time. I stood back up and looked around.

"I have no clue how to get out of here," I said to myself.

A breeze blew through the grove, and I caught the scent of honey-suckle being carried by the wind. *That smells amazing.* My stomach growled. *Smell.*

I looked down at my left hand, which still had Pax's crusted blood on it. I raised my fingers to my face and inhaled through my nose. Iron was the prominent scent, but there was another scent I picked up. It was subtle and reminded me of running water. I dropped my hand to my side and closed my eyes as I took a big whiff of the air. I snapped my eyes open as I caught his scent.

I guess being an apex predator has its perks.

I followed Pax's scent out of the grove and into the woods. Every time the night breeze hit my skin, I became excited. I wanted to run and cheer. It was like I had dropped the burdens I was carrying when I had left the grove. I ran. Tears of joy slipped down my cheeks as I did. I leaped over roots that stuck out of the ground with each one. I laughed.

Pax's scent was becoming stronger as I approached a road at the edge of the woods. I jogged for a bit on the road until Aunt Jules's car came into view. I burst into a sprint to get there. I stopped dead in my tracks ten feet from the back of the car. There was panting from inside it.

"Ew," I shouted.

"Oh shit," Pax said from inside the car.

I plugged my ears as best I could and closed my eyes. *I should've walked,* I thought as I tried to erase this moment from my memory. Five minutes passed before the car door opened, and I could safely open my eyes.

Jules was fixing her hair as she walked over to me. She was beet red. Pax was behind her with his shirt on backward and an arm wrapped in a bandage.

"We weren't expecting you to be awake already," Jules said.

"Clearly."

"Did it work?" Pax asked.

"Yes. I think."

"Are you sure?" Jules asked.

"Well, I petted the werewolf in my mind, and it didn't kill me, so yes, I'm sure." Pax looked confused, trying to follow my logic. "Trust me, it worked."

"How did you find us?" Pax asked.

"I just tracked your scent." I raised my hand, which had his blood on it, and wiggled my fingers.

"Tera, that grove is like five miles away," Pax said.

"Five miles," I repeated in disbelief. "I ran here in like fifteen minutes." They both stared at me like I had a spider in my hair. I shrugged. "What's for dinner? I'm starving."

Jules smiled. That must've been the first time she really smiled like that at me since this whole thing happened. It made my chest feel full.

"We'll pick up something on the way home," she asked.

"Is he staying at the house?" I asked, gesturing to Pax.

"Probably," she said with a scrunched nose.

"Then you need to buy me new headphones. I can hear through the ones I have now."

Jules laughed.

I hopped into the passenger seat of the car. I could hear Jules tell Pax with a chuckle, "Looks like you're in the back." She patted him on the chest as she walked past him and opened the driver's door.

The only thing that came to my mind whenever I saw them interact was Ben. *What am I going to do? Will he be safe now, or is it still too risky to be around him?*

10

Selene

It had already been ten minutes into dinner. I didn't think the spell was working. I kept waiting for something to happen. Nothing did. All that happened was a conversation about Ben's grades and his upcoming soccer game—nothing of actual substance. I glanced at Ashlyn out of the corner of my eye. She was chowing down on the chicken and yuca happily. Ben was staring at his plate in silence and wouldn't even look up at me. Will, on the other hand, wouldn't stop staring at me. I was too uncomfortable to even look in his direction. I looked at Ben's father, who made eye contact with me. He wiped his mouth and cleared his throat.

"So, Tera, Ben tells us you two broke up recently," he started.

"Dad," Ben said, but his father raised a hand to silence him.

"Um, yes, we did," I said softly. Ashlyn squeezed my hand under the table.

"Why is that?" His father asked.

"I've been sick recently, and the doctors don't know what is happening to me, but they are saying it's serious." I was making this all up on the fly. "So, I decided it wouldn't be fair to Ben or myself to be in a relationship right now. He means a lot to me, but I really have to focus on my health." I looked at Ben, who still wouldn't take his eyes off his plate.

"I'm sorry to hear that," his father said. "Is that why you haven't even touched your food tonight? Does your illness affect your appetite?"

Before I could answer, Will cut in, "Oh, come on, that's absolute bullshit. We know why she hasn't touched her food."

And the fun begins.

"Will," Ben said. He was shocked by his brother's outburst.

"Don't act all surprised, Ben. You think Dad was actually interested in having dinner with some girl who dumped you?" Will asked.

"I'm sorry, Ben," his father said. I looked at Ashlyn, who looked as confused as I was.

"Do you want to speak English, maybe?" Ashlyn said.

"Oh, sorry, let me catch you up to speed," Will said. "Your friend Tera is a fucking werewolf. A vicious beast that ripped out Mr. Fera's heart and ate it."

I knew it. "I'm a what?" I asked, trying to sound offended.

"Stop pretending. We've already caught you," Will said. "There's no way you are as strong as you are. It's not possible. I could hear you fighting the change in the bathroom at the beach house. You're a werewolf, and that's why you haven't touched your food. Or the silver fork and knife."

He was confident that there was a werewolf sitting at the table with him, and he was confident that that werewolf was Tera. All I had to do to destroy his theory was pick up my utensils.

"Really? I had no idea I was a werewolf," I said as I picked up my fork and used it to poke a piece of yuca. I took a bite and spoke while chewing. "Tell me more."

Even though he was right about Tera, which was bad news, I got so much satisfaction watching him register what I had just done. Ben's father looked just as shocked as Will had. Ashlyn chuckled.

"So, if I had been a werewolf, what then? Was I supposed to eat you for learning my secret?" I asked.

"No. We would've killed you," he said.

"You kill werewolves?" Ashlyn asked, mocking him.

"And other monsters," their father said.

"Wait, are you guys serious?" Ashlyn asked.

"It's kind of what we do, sweetie," Will said.

"What does that even mean?" I asked.

"We're hunters. A monster pops up. We go and kill it," their father said.

"And a monster killed Mr. Fera?" Ashlyn asked.

"A werewolf, to be specific," Will said.

"And so, you thought you would just kill me because you thought I was a werewolf?" I asked.

"Well, we had to be sure before we acted. We wouldn't want to kill an innocent person by accident. It's already bad enough that a monster is running around in our hometown. It makes us look incapable," Will said.

"Ben." He looked up at me with guilty eyes. "You too?"

"It's a family commitment. We've been hunters for generations. Benny hasn't gotten his first kill yet, though. We hoped this werewolf would be it," Will said.

"We'll have to wait until the next full moon to go hunting," their father said.

"What happens if you find nothing, then?" I asked.

"Then, the werewolf has left town, and we'll have to wait for the next reported killing to hunt it down and kill it," Will said.

Nausea was the only thing on my mind at that moment. I could feel that bite of yuca coming back up. I stood from the table and grabbed my bag and Ashlyn by the arm. "I think we should get going," I said before rushing to the front door.

Ben jumped up from the table and followed us. He grabbed me by the arm when we got into the foyer.

"Tera, wait," he said.

"No, Ben. I don't want to talk. I don't even want to even look at you or your crazy family right now." I pulled away from him and opened the front door. Ashlyn tugged on my arm to stop me. She turned back toward Ben and slapped him across the face.

"You ought to be ashamed of yourself for letting them talk like that to us," Ashlyn said. "They didn't have to make up shit just to make us uncomfortable."

We stormed out of the house and down to the car, arms linked. I got into the driver's seat and drove until I couldn't anymore. I pulled the car over to the side of the road and put it in park. I pressed my forehead against the steering wheel.

"Hey, it's okay," Ashlyn said. "Tera definitely dodged a bullet with those psychos."

I couldn't keep the charade up any longer. I was exhausted from all the lies. On one hand, everyone lied to everyone, and it made things so much more complicated. On the other, the lies protected us, like Tera's lie to Ben. I could control whom I told the truth to, so I did.

"Ashlyn, they were telling the truth."

"What?"

"Werewolves are real. Tera is one of them. And I'm a witch."

"Stop trying to mess with me, Selene. It's not funny."

I held my left hand out and focused my frustration on the center of my palm. A flame fluttered to life. Ashlyn's eyes widened as she watched the flame dance about in my hand. I closed my hand into a fist and extinguished it.

"How did you do that?" she asked.

"I told you. I'm a witch."

"My aunt is a witch, and she can't do that," she said.

"Different kind of witch."

"I can't believe you've kept this hidden for so long," she said. "Like I don't blame you, obviously secrecy is important. Salem proved that, but I mean, I would've never been able to keep a secret like this. I would've blurted it out when we were in first grade."

"I only just found out after my birthday."

"That explains why you and Tera have been acting so strange lately," she said.

"Yeah, Aunt Jules and I have been working on finding a cure for Tera."

"Wait. D-did Tera actually kill Mr. Fera?" she asked. I looked into her eyes, trying to find how she would react, but she had a serious look.

"Yes, it was her first full moon, and we didn't even know she'd been cursed. I think it was the waitress at The Grind. I haven't told anyone, but I think she was the witch who cursed Tera."

"Are you sure?" she asked.

"She's the only one who could've slipped something into Tera's drink," I said. I tightened my grip on the steering wheel. *I could've stopped all this if I hadn't been such an idiot and understood my visions from the beginning.*

"She's still in town," Ashlyn said.

"What? How do you know?"

"I've seen her. She's running a stand at the farmer's market. I've been there with my aunt a couple of times," she said. "We should kick her ass."

"I have to tell Aunt Jules. Maybe she can make that witch tell us how to break Tera's curse."

"Maybe we should tell Ben's family about her and let them kill her for Mr. Fera's death," she said.

I froze momentarily and thought about what would happen if Ben's family learned there were witches in town. They could hunt us all down and kill us just for not being human.

"No. Ben's family is not good news; I don't know much about hunters. In fact, I didn't know they existed before tonight. I have the feeling that if they learn there are witches in town, many good people will be in danger."

"Maybe you're right," she said. "They were ready to kill Tera without knowing if she was actually a werewolf, which she is, but still. They seem like the shoot first and ask questions never type."

"Let me make this phone call," I said as I exited the car and closed the door behind me.

Part of me regretted telling Ashlyn the truth. I didn't know if she could keep her mouth shut, and even if she could, I had dragged her into a world she didn't belong in. Part of me was glad to be honest with someone for once, but I didn't have much choice after that dinner. The suspicion would always be there. At least that way, she found out on my terms and not by snooping around and getting herself into trouble.

I called Aunt Jules and told her about everything that had happened. She was pissed that I put myself and Ashlyn in danger by snooping around hunters. She was even more pissed that I told Ashlyn the truth. I swore I could hear her turning red as she yelled into the phone. When I told her my theory about the witch who cursed Tera and that she was still in town, Jules got quiet. She told me she would pay her a visit on her own. I tried to argue with her. I wanted to go, but she shut me down and told me I had more training to do for The Ascension. She told me to go to bed and that Tati expected to see me in the morning. She hung up before I could say anything. I climbed back into the car and closed the door.

"She's upset?" Ashlyn asked.

"Oh yeah," I said as I started the car and drove us back to my house.

Ashlyn left after we returned to the house. She wanted time to process everything on her own. I couldn't argue with her about that. I often wished I had more time to process everything that was happening, but I was being thrown one obstacle after another. I hadn't realized how tired I was until I opened my bedroom door.

I flicked on the light when Tera said, "Are you wearing my clothes?"

My soul nearly leaped out of my body at how startled I was. I wasn't expecting her to be home, let alone sitting on my bed. I said, "Uh, yeah, they are. What are you doing home? Aunt Jules said you probably wouldn't be home for a few days."

"Yeah, Jules really needs to work on her time-estimating skills," she said with a shudder.

"Where is your necklace?" I asked.

"In my room. I'll only need it on the full moon from now on," she said.

"Really? That's amazing," I said as I sat down on the bed beside her. I could feel a tinge of worry in my stomach.

"So, why are you wearing my clothes?" she asked as she took a closer look at me. "Is that my makeup you're wearing too?"

I hoped I had more time to figure out how to tell Tera what had happened at Ben's house. I wouldn't lie to her or push it off for another day. I decided to rip the bandage off.

"Tera, I need to tell you something," I said as I pulled her phone out of my bag and handed it to her. She took it and looked at me with a raised eyebrow. "It's about Ben."

"What about him?" she asked.

"I've had this vision of a gunshot a couple of times, once when I bumped into his father at Mr. Fera's funeral and another time earlier tonight when Ben texted you and asked you to come over for dinner with his father and brother."

"Okay?"

"So, I—I, uh, impersonated you and went to their house for dinner to try and find out what was going on."

"You did what!" Tera shouted as she jumped up from the bed and started pacing around the room. "Why would you do that? Ben and I are broken up! I can't just show up for dinner at his house."

"Tera, that's not everything." I remained serious in an attempt to recapture her attention.

"What do you mean?"

"During dinner, I cast a truth spell on the tea that Ben's father and brother drank. They are hunters, and they were planning on killing you tonight after you failed their test at dinner."

"Their test at dinner?"

"Pure silver utensils you wouldn't have been able to touch. After I picked them up, they no longer suspect you are a werewolf, but Ben is one of them too."

"No," she said as she plopped back down on the bed beside me. "Ben would never be a hunter. He's too kind and gentle. He'd never do that."

"Ben was the one who was going to kill you," I said as I put my hand on her shoulder. She covered her mouth, and tears ran down her face. "I'm so sorry, Tera."

She buried her face in my chest and sobbed. We sat there for the rest of the night until we fell asleep.

11

Tera-Sue

I was jolted awake by Selene's phone ringing at eight o'clock in the morning. I lifted my head and wiped the sleep out of my eyes. Selene was already up and out of the bed. I patted down her bed, looking for the phone. It was in her bag on the floor next to the bed. I reached into her bag and dug around until I found her phone. I pulled it out and answered it.

"Hello," I said groggily.

"Selene, if you don't get your behind up and over here, your Aunt Jules will kick both of our asses," a familiar voice said.

"Sorry, this is Tera. I think Selene is already getting ready."

"Oh, hey, baby! How are you feeling? You gave me a real scare at the beach the other day." I realized it was Tati I was talking to.

"Sorry," I said as I sat up and looked around the room. I could hear a low hissing. I didn't know where it was coming from, but it was somewhere near me.

"You go get dressed too. I want you to come on by with Selene and spend some time with me," she said. "I could teach you a thing or two that Pax could only dream about." She chuckled.

"All right. See you soon," I said as I hung up. I was still seventy-five percent asleep and felt like I was hallucinating the hissing. I looked around the room. That was when I spotted a massive snake slithering into the bed with me. I jumped up and threw Selene's phone at it.

"Selene! Come quick, there's a snake," I screamed as I leaped out of bed and against the wall. My heart was thumping in my ears, and I distanced myself as much as possible from the snake.

Selene burst into the room. She looked at me and then spotted the snake on the bed.

"Did you go in my bag?" she asked.

"Yes, your phone was ringing."

"Hey," Selene said, snapping at the snake to get its attention. It turned and hissed at her. "Oh, don't you hiss at me! Get back in the book now."

The snake looked at me and then back at Selene. "Now," she said. The snake let out one last hiss at me before slithering off the bed and back into Selene's bag.

"You just keep a snake in your bag?" I asked.

"No, he's the guardian of our family's grimoire. If anyone who isn't bonded with it touches the book, the snake will come out and kill them," she said. Her tone made her statement sound like this was a normal occurrence. I could feel the shock on my face.

"Oh, and you just leave that unattended? What if someone goes in your bag to borrow something?" I asked.

"I usually don't let it leave my side. I keep a very close eye on it because of how dangerous it is," she said.

"Maybe you should keep it locked up or something. You know how Ashlyn is. What if she went in there for lipstick or something? She'd never see it coming."

"About that," she said. I didn't like her tone of voice.

"What?"

"I kind of told Ashlyn everything last night. So, she knows the truth about us now," she said.

"What were you thinking! You know Ashlyn can't keep secrets. You might as well have put it in the newspapers."

"I didn't really have a choice," she said. "She went to Ben's last night and heard everything they said. I didn't want to keep lying to her after that."

"I'm going to get dressed." I walked out of Selene's room and across the hallway into my own. I slammed the door behind me. I wasn't angry with Selene; I was angry at Ben—mostly. Okay, I was a little angry at her, but most of my anger was pointed at him. I couldn't believe that he was willing to kill me. He made me believe he loved me. The mere thought of him felt like a hand was squeezing down on my heart.

I checked my phone. I had five missed calls and a bunch of texts from Ben. I swiped them away. I had a couple of texts from Ashlyn as well. She wanted to hang out with Selene and me today. I invited her to Tati's house. If Selene wanted her to know the truth, then she wouldn't mind.

"You did what!" Selene shouted as she slammed on the brakes at a stop sign.

"I figured you wouldn't care since you seemed fine telling her everything."

"That's not the same thing, Tera. This could be dangerous," she said. "I nearly burnt down the house during my last training session."

"And I almost ate Jules's boyfriend. But I didn't, and the house is still standing, so I think we have plenty of control over ourselves. Plus, Tati will be there. She won't let anything bad happen."

Selene took a deep breath. "Fine, but I don't like this. If something happens, it's on us."

"Agreed." *We'll just have to make sure nothing happens.*

"Aunt Jules has a boyfriend?" she asked as she started driving again.

I explained everything about my little training session with Pax and how I caught him and Jules messing around. She laughed. Selene then told me about Jules's Ascension journal and how Pax's name had hearts next to it. She told me about all the things she would have to do for The Ascension. The car ride to Tati's was the most normal I had felt since all this started. We were joking and laughing like nothing had changed, and for a few fleeting moments, it felt that way.

When we pulled up to Tati's house, she was sitting on the front steps of her wrap-around porch talking to Ashlyn. Tati's house stood alone on the street; the nearest neighbor was miles away. She smiled at us; her teeth were so white that the sun reflected off them like snow. Tati met us on the walkway to the porch and pulled us into a hug.

"Ashlyn told me about your little adventure into the hunter's den last night," Tati said as she released us from her warm embrace.

Selene looked at me out of the side of her eye as she spoke. "It wasn't what I was expecting."

"Well, it's a good thing you went. Now you've thrown them off Tera's trail," Tati said.

"Should we still be worried about them?" Ashlyn asked as she walked closer to our little huddle.

"Hunters are always dangerous. Now that we've discovered them, we'll have to do something about them," Tati said.

"What do you mean?" I asked.

"We have to strike them first before they can do any damage."

"How are we going to do that?" Selene asked.

"With some magic, of course," Tati said. "Selene and I are going to do some training for The Ascension while Tera and Ashlyn go to the farmer's market and pick me up some things. I'll text you the list. When you get back, the three of us are going to deal with those hunters."

She pointed to Selene and Ashlyn. Ashlyn said, "Wait, I'm not a witch."

"Honey, you don't have to be a witch to do a little magic. I'll explain more when you get back," Tati said.

Selene and Tati waved us off from the porch as Ashlyn pulled away.

The first twenty minutes of the ride were silent. Ashlyn never let it stay quiet for too long. I knew something had to be on her mind.

"What's wrong?" I asked her.

"I'm just thinking about how messed up everything is," she said.

"What do you mean?"

"We're almost halfway through our senior year, and nothing is going like I thought it would," she said.

In the last few months, I had only been in school for a total of two weeks. It was the same story for Selene: she had been getting a crash course on eighteen years of witchcraft and history she'd missed out on. I had almost completely forgotten that it was our senior year. I hadn't even looked at any colleges.

"We're supposed to be having the time of our teenage years right now. We should be partying every night, going on college tours, and flirting with boys," Ashlyn said.

I laughed.

"We should be laughing, and you should be getting prom-posed to by that tall, hot soccer boy, but the world is so messed up," she continued.

I stopped laughing at her mention of Ben. As much as the thought of him confused me with anger and sorrow, I also felt happiness. I knew Ashlyn was right. We'd become so intertwined by my curse that we'd stopped living our lives.

"You're right. I want to go to college and prom. I want to party and flirt with boys." I wiggled my eyebrows at her on that last part. "So, let's do it."

"What?" she asked.

"Everything is crazy in my world right now. We should do normal senior-year stuff. I've got control over my curse now, so there's no reason we can't. I just want to feel ordinary again."

"Well, I think there are some things we need to add to our new definition of ordinary," she said.

"Like what?"

"Like cursing hunters and howling at the moon," she said with a smirk.

Ashlyn turned on the radio, and we sang at the top of our lungs and danced in our seats for the rest of the ride.

We pulled into the gravel parking lot of the farmer's market. It was a massive collection of white tents that housed hundreds of vendors selling things from home-grown fruits to handmade jewelry. It would take Ashlyn and me forever to navigate through the maze of people to find everything on Tati's list. After an hour and a half of searching, we were left with one item on the list: blackthorn thorns.

"Do people actually sell this?" I asked Ashlyn as I showed her the item on the list.

"Actually, when I came here with my aunt, there was a lady selling blackthorn berries. Maybe she has some," Ashlyn said.

"Do you remember where her tent was?" I asked.

"I think it was over here," she said as she walked off to her right.

I would've sworn we were walking in circles until I saw a large paper sign, "Blackthorn Berries," hanging over a tent. I patted Ashlyn on the arm and pointed toward the tent. I walked up to the folding table that acted like a counter. The woman behind the table had her back to us as she was packing some plastic bags with stuff.

"I'll be with you in a moment," she said without looking back.

I looked around the tent. There were herbs and fruits set up on tables around all four sides. Inside the tent were coolers with wicker baskets stacked on top. I spotted a small basket labeled "Blackthorn." It was filled with a couple of branches that had blueberries, with thorns protruding out from the little bustles and leaves.

Why would they sell the berries still attached to the branch like that? I looked around the tent at some of the herbs for sale: bay leaves, cinnamon, pepper, and rosemary. I kept looking. Wolfsbane, belladonna, and nightshade. *This must be a witch's tent.*

I looked over to Ashlyn to see if she noticed something off with the tent, but she just waited patiently, burning a hole in the woman's back with her eyes. Then, her face dropped in shock. I snapped my neck forward to find the woman standing in front of us with a wide smile. Her bad dye job and discolored forehead were burned into my memory—the waitress from The Grind on our birthday.

"What can I help you girls with?" she asked. Her voice was so peppy that it made me want to jump over the table and rip her face off. I clenched my jaw and fist.

"We'd like that basket of blackthorn berries," Ashlyn said.

While the woman turned around to grab the basket, Ashlyn grabbed my hand and squeezed it. I could feel my anger boiling up inside of me. I could hear the wolf's growl in the back of my mind. She wanted to come out, and I almost wanted to let her out. I would've let the wolf out to tear her to shreds if I didn't feel something bump into my leg. I looked down as a little girl walked by.

"Sorry," her mother said as she pulled her along. I looked down at the little girl and around at all the people shopping. I took a deep breath. *I can't let go. Not with all of these innocent people around*, I thought.

The woman turned back around and extended the basket toward me. I handed her the cash and grabbed the basket. She reached out, grabbed me by the wrist, and pulled me toward her. Then, she whispered something in my ear, something in another language—a language that felt as though it was weaving into my very bones.

I pulled away from her and felt my skin burn. I could feel my body fighting against me. I shoved the basket into Ashlyn's hands, along with all our other bags, and sprinted away. I pushed through people as

I rushed toward the gravel parking lot. I could feel my ribs cracking with each breath I took. I ran through the pain until I finally collapsed beside Ashlyn's car. My hands had already cracked as talons pushed off my fingernails.

I pulled at the car door. It was locked. I pulled again, even though I knew nothing would change. I could see my backpack on the floor by my seat. I felt my spine snap as my body collapsed. I held myself up with the door handle. I closed my fist and smashed through the window. I pulled myself halfway through the window and reached into my bag. I grasped my necklace that was loose in there. It burned in the palm of my hand, and I closed my hand around it.

I closed my eyes and focused on the burning. I focused on my breathing and my mind. I could feel my body cooperating with me again. I rubbed my thumb over my fingers, and they returned to normal. I could feel my legs again. I pushed myself up and out of the car.

I looked down at my shirt. It was covered in blood and cut up where I had been lying against the glass. I lifted my shirt and looked at my stomach.

There wasn't a scratch. The necklace had stopped burning. I slipped it into my back pocket.

Ashlyn came jogging into the parking lot. She was out of breath.

"Are you okay?" she said between breaths.

"Yeah, I'm fine," I said. "She must've used some spell to trigger my curse."

"Did you have to break my window?" she asked with a whimper.

"Sorry. It was locked, and I needed to get in. Unless you wanted to be dinner," I chuckled.

"I have a sweater in the back you can change into," she said as she put the bags in the backseat.

I grabbed it and pulled it over my tattered shirt. It was a plain black sweater that was stained with the scent of Axe. "This thing smells like a boy's locker room."

"It was that douchebag's. He's never getting it back," she said as she got in the driver's seat.

I called Tati on speaker. She picked up on the first ring. "We got everything. And we had a run-in with the witch who cursed me."

"Did anything happen?" Selene's voice came through the phone, filled with worry.

"She tried to trigger my curse, but I was able to control it."

"Good," Tati said. "Now there's one more thing we're gonna need."

"What?" I asked.

"We're gonna need the hunters' hair," she said.

"How are we gonna get that?" Ashlyn asked.

"Selene and I have tracked them down already. I'm going to get the father's hair. The three of you are gonna get the two boys' hair together," Tati said.

"We're going to go after Will first," Selene said. "He's at some bar. I'll send you the location and meet you there."

"Okay. See you there," I said as I hung up. I looked at Ashlyn, whose phone dinged with the location.

She pressed go on the GPS. I dreaded seeing Ben again.

12

Selene

I told Tera to stay in the car. I knew she wouldn't like what I had planned. Ashlyn and I walked across the parking lot and into the bar. There were a couple of motorcycles out front. Inside, my boots stuck to the floor with each step I took. A couple was dancing offbeat to classic rock playing over the speaker. The bartender was wiping down one of the tables with a stained rag. He shot us a glare but said nothing. Will was sitting at the bar with his back to us, nursing a beer. I reached into my coat pocket and pulled out a tube of lip gloss Tati had given me.

"Since when do you wear lip gloss with sparkles?" Ashlyn whispered.

"Tati and I did a lot more than just prepare for The Ascension," I said as I coated my lips in the gel. "You have the scissors?"

"Yeah," Ashlyn said.

"Good. Cut some of his hair when he hits the floor."

"What?" Ashlyn asked.

I didn't take the time to answer her. I marched right up to the bar while I still had the nerve to go through with the plan. I tapped Will on the shoulder. When he turned to face me, I slapped him across the face. The clap it made was loud. Ashlyn gasped.

"How dare you talk to me that way?"

"Tera, what—"

I cut him off. "You just threaten to kill every girl you meet? I thought you were more mature than your brother." I cringed as the words left my mouth. This was a bad plan. "I thought you were more of a man."

"I am," he said as he stood and pressed his chest against mine. He was built like bricks, hard and cold. His eyes were full of rage.

"Prove it." I tried to keep my glare intense as my insides gagged.

He leaned down and pulled me into his grasp. He kissed me. It was like I had been kissed by a frog that would never turn into a prince. It made my skin crawl. I pushed away from him.

"Are you drunk?" I shouted. Everyone in the bar was looking now. "Don't ever touch me again."

"I-I thought…" His voice trailed off as he rubbed his eyes. He reached out to grab my hand. I stepped to the side, and he collapsed onto the floor, unconscious.

I knelt beside him and whispered in his ear, "You were right. Tera is a werewolf. You made a mistake, though; you shouldn't have assumed she was alone."

Ashlyn came over and cut a small chunk of hair from the back of his head. She struggled to get a good amount because of how short it was. I held out a plastic bag for her to put it in. I stood and looked at the bartender.

"You should really call this pervert a cab. He's unconscious."

He rolled his eyes and grunted as we walked out of the bar.

"So magical knockout lip gloss?" Ashlyn asked.

"It's a powder Tati taught me how to make. I thought of mixing it in lip gloss because it would be less conspicuous that way."

"It doesn't work on you?" Ashlyn asked.

"The powder I made won't work on me. If someone else makes it, then yes, it would."

As we entered the car, Tera was eager to hear how it went. I filled her in on everything, including that I'd impersonated her again.

"Okay, you have to stop doing that," she said. "How come they keep falling for that? Am I that easy to impersonate?"

"I think Selene just pulls off a really convincing Tera," Ashlyn said.

"If it makes you feel any better when he wakes up, he won't even remember we were there."

"That makes me feel a little better," she said. "So, how was the kiss?"

"Disgusting. I think I might have to bleach my lips tonight."

Ashlyn and Tera laughed. I pulled the mirror Aunt Jules had given me out of my bag and placed it on the center console.

"Time to find out where Ben is." The joy left Tera's face at the sound of his name. Ashlyn looked at me with concern. "Are you sure you want to do this?"

"I have to," Tera said. Her expression was hard to read. I could only imagine how she felt.

I traced my finger clockwise around the mirror's edge.

"Mirror dark, mirror light, mirror wrong, mirror right, show me what my sister's heart fights," I chanted.

Ben's image flickered in the mirror. He was sitting with his feet in a pool. It was dark around him. The only light was the one from the pool.

"Where is he?" I asked.

"He's at school," Tera said.

"How do you know that?" Ashlyn said.

"He used to sneak into the school on the weekends and sit at the pool for months after his mom died," she said.

"Let's go." Ben's image faded from the mirror, and I slipped it back into my bag.

The school was empty and dark. When we pulled into the parking lot, the only car in front of the school was Ben's truck.

"I'm going in alone," Tera insisted. Her voice was low and gritty. Ashlyn nodded along in agreement. I disagreed, but I understood. I handed her a pair of scissors and a bag of knockout powder.

"Don't breathe it in."

"Okay," she said and exited the car.

Ashlyn and I observed as Tera walked toward the school and disappeared around the back. The only door that would be open was the one Ben used to get in. It was on the other side of the building and out of sight.

"You should drive around to the faculty parking lot so we can see her come out."

We pulled around the building and into the faculty parking lot. I spotted a car at the back of the lot. I knew that something was wrong. I looked at the door that Tera was supposed to enter through. It wasn't propped open the way it was supposed to be.

"Ashlyn, we have to go in there."

"What, why?" she said.

"Something is very wrong. I don't think Tera and Ben are alone in there."

"Let's go kick some ass," Ashlyn said as she eagerly jumped out of the car.

I threw my backpack over my shoulder as I exited the car. We walked up to the back door of the school, and Ashlyn tugged on the handles. The door was locked.

"Well, now what?" Ashlyn asked.

"We break in."

"How do you want to do that exactly?"

I looked at the lock on the door and focused on the keyhole. I snapped my fingers. A fire filled the keyhole on the door. I closed my eyes and focused on feeding the fire more energy, increasing its temperature. I traced my left index finger over my necklace in a circle to help me focus. The fire started to crackle and pop. It spit flecks of metal onto the ground as it continued to melt the lock. I extinguished the fire with a clench of my fist.

"Well, I guess that works," Ashlyn said. As she pulled the door open, molten metal sloped onto the floor from where the deadbolt used to be.

We jogged our way through the empty hallways and toward the gym. The school was an eerie place when no one else was around. It felt like a horror movie cliche. The gym door was propped open. I opened the door and looked around. I spotted someone standing at the doors to the pool with a rifle in their hand. They were too far away to make out any more about them.

"Ashlyn, there's someone with a gun on the other side of the gym," I whispered.

"Fuck."

"Go around into the girl's locker room from the hallway and into the pool that way," I said as I handed her a bag of the knockout powder.

"What about you?" she asked.

"I'm going to go take care of our guest in the gym."

"Are you crazy?" she whisper-yelled at me.

"Definitely."

Once Ashlyn was out of sight, I flung the gym's double doors open. The sound of the doors banging around caught the attention of the person at the gym's other end. I walked toward them. They pointed the rifle at me.

"Don't come any closer," she called.

I froze at the sound of the voice. There was something familiar about it. I took the risk and approached. She jiggled her gun at me.

"I said stop, Selene."

"Who are you?" I called back.

The person took a few steps toward me. My eyes had adjusted enough to see her face. Maggie Fera stood at the other end of the basketball court. She was pointing a rifle at me.

"Maggie? What are you doing?" I asked.

"Ben's dad called me," she said.

"Ben's dad?"

Then, I remembered. When I ran into Ben's dad at Mr. Fera's funeral, he said they were coworkers. Mr. Fera was a hunter. Maggie was a hunter.

"Tera killed my dad," she said.

"Maggie, you don't understand," I said. I took a step forward.

"Oh, I understand. She's a monster."

"No, she's not. She's a victim."

"She's a victim? Was she a victim when she pulled my dad's heart out with her teeth?"

"Someone did this to her. A witch. She's here in town still."

"Oh, don't worry. We know about the witches," she said. Her grip grew tighter on the rifle.

"You do?"

"Yeah, Ben's dad has one hostage. He'll rip her teeth out until she gives up the rest of them," Maggie said with a deranged smile.

Fuck. They have Tati.

"Maggie, these are people," I tried to plead with her.

"No, they're not. They're abominations. Monsters. Don't try to stop me from killing Tera. I will shoot you," she said.

She turned around and started walking back toward the doors to the pool. I snapped my fingers, and a line of fire erupted between Maggie and me. She looked back in shock. It took her only a couple of seconds to process what had happened. She lifted her rifle and pointed it at me. I braced myself. *At least if Tera hears the gun, she'll know something is happening.*

Just then, Ashlyn came crashing through the pool doors. Maggie turned her head in time to catch Ashlyn's fist to the nose. The punch knocked Maggie off balance and the rifle out of her hand. Ashlyn kicked the gun into the fire and threw a handful of knockout dust into Maggie's face. Maggie toppled over, unconscious like a bag of rocks. I extinguished the fire and rushed over to Ashlyn.

"That was so badass," I said as we interlocked fingers after a double high-five.

"I know," she said with a chuckle.

"We should get some of her hair." Ashlyn nodded. "Is Tera okay?"

"Physically, she's fine," Ashlyn said.

Ashlyn cut a lock of Maggie's hair as I made my way into the pool room. Tera knelt beside the pool with an unconscious Ben on her lap. She was running her fingers through his hair. She looked at me as I knelt across from her. We sat there for a few moments, just looking at each other. I broke the silence.

"We have to go. Tati's in trouble." Tera nodded. She gave Ben a kiss on the forehead and laid his head against the floor.

As we left through the gym, she looked at Maggie's unconscious body. Tears formed in her eyes. Ashlyn and I wrapped our arms around her and kept her close as we walked out of the school and returned to the car.

I took my phone out and called Aunt Jules.

"Hello," she answered. She sounded like she was struggling with something. I could hear someone else's voice muffled in the background.

"Aunt Jules, we need your help." I explained Tati's plan to curse the hunters, what happened in the school, and that Tati was in danger.

Aunt Jules sighed heavily. "I'll meet you at Tati's house in ten minutes. We need to come up with a plan."

Aunt Jules was already there when we pulled up to Tati's house. She was waiting in her car when we parked. She got out and grabbed a red cooler from her back seat. She was pissed. She handed the cooler to Ashlyn.

"Take this inside and put it in the fridge, please," she said. She kept her eye trained on Tera and me. I knew once Ashlyn was inside, we were going to hear it.

Ashlyn took the cooler and patted me on the shoulder. "Good luck."

Aunt Jules didn't wait for Ashlyn to get into the house before she started, "What were you two thinking?"

"We were just doing what Tati said," Tera said.

"Yeah, she said that we needed to get the hunters before they got us."

"And look where that leaves us now. They've got her." Aunt Jules shook her head. "You can't be wasting your time with things like this, Selene. You need to be focused on The Ascension."

"I have been focused. I'm trying to learn everything I can in a fraction of the time that all the other witches at The Ascension have had."

"Then, why did you let Tati put you all on this path? Do you know how dangerous hunters are? There isn't just one family of hunters; there are hundreds, and they won't just come to town to hunt Tera. They will hunt us all. You exposed yourself and put Ashlyn at risk," Aunt Jules shouted.

"We were just doing what we thought would protect everyone," Tera said.

"I would have handled it," she snapped.

"What are we supposed to do, Aunt Jules? Sit quietly in the corner and wait for your instructions? We have to be able to protect ourselves. What's the point of knowing I'm a witch if I have to wait for you to come rescue me?" I yelled. Tera looked at me with a shocked face. Even Aunt Jules was taken aback by my outburst.

"I need you both to be safe," she said quietly. "You're all I have."

"You can't shield us from the world. I won't be strong enough to help cure Tera if I have to rely on you to fight all of our battles alone."

Aunt Jules wiped tears out of her eyes. "We'll talk more about this after we save Tati."

"Wait. You want us to help?" Tera asked.

"I'll need you to help. The hunter has probably already called for backup."

13

Tera-Sue

"Aunt Jules is right. There are at least ten people there," I said as I returned to where our rag-tag group had gathered. They had numbers, but so did we. Jules had called Pax, who brought his son and Tati's sister. There were eight of us now. Ashlyn was in charge of driving the getaway car, which was a white van with no seats in the back and a unicorn painted on the side. The rest of us were huddled in the woods outside Ben's house, formulating an infiltration plan.

"How many of them are outside?" Jules asked.

"There are two on the front porch and one at the back door." Jules had me running recon because I was the fastest, the strongest, and had super senses.

"Aden, Selene, and Tera take the back door. They probably won't have silver bullets, seeing how they think you're dead. Try not to take any chances, though," Jules said. She had gone back to the school while we were waiting for the cavalry, tied up Ben and Maggie and sent a text to Ben's father saying that she'd killed me.

"That means we're taking the front door together," Paxton said as he nudged at Tati's sister. She rolled her eyes at him and started walking toward the front side of the house.

"Will you stop instigating her?" Jules said as she shoved him toward the house.

"She makes it so easy, though," he said with a chuckle.

Jules looked over her shoulder back at us. "See you inside."

We nodded as we started making our way toward the back end of the house.

"What's the plan?" Aden said.

"We get his gun, knock him out, and then go inside," Selene said. She had taken the lead of our small group as we walked. Something about her had changed. She would've never taken a stand against Jules, even when she was right, and she never wanted to be in charge of anything. *This curse is causing her to change just as much as it's causing me to.*

"You make that sound so easy, but how do we do that?" he asked.

"What's your divine gift?" Selene asked.

"Telekinesis, but I can barely move a stuffed animal across a bed," he said.

"Didn't you train for The Ascension?" she asked.

"My dad has been focusing more on the second trial with me. He said it's always been the hardest for our family," he said.

"I just need you to get the gun away from him. Tera and I can handle it from there," she said.

"I think I can do that," he said.

I had no clue what Selene was planning, but I had faith that when the time came, I would be able to wing my part. I wasn't a witch who could fling magic and knock people out with some pocket sand. I was a girl who was cursed to turn into a glorified dog. *What more value could I have than recon?* We reached the edge of the woods closest to Ben's back deck. The man guarding it stood at the stairs connecting the backyard to the deck. He had a rifle in his hands and his eyes glued to his phone.

Selene stood between Aden and me. She nodded as she stepped out into the backyard. We were only a step behind her as we walked toward the deck. The man glanced up from his phone at us, back down, and then back up. Startled, he dropped the phone and fumbled with his rifle. Aden made a violent wave with his hand. The rifle moved, but so did the man holding it. He tumbled down the stairs and onto the lawn. I doubted that was what Aden intended to do, but the gun slid a couple of feet away from him. The man pushed himself forward to grab it, but Aden waved his hand again. This time, the rifle flew to the other side of the yard. The man stood and turned to run back to the stairs, but as he did, fire erupted between him and them. The flames stood taller than the man. The man turned back toward us and pulled a knife out. Selene looked at me and nodded.

Part of me became excited as I realized this was my part of the plan. I got to beat up some thirty-year-old dude who was decked out in camo from head to toe. I walked until there were only about ten feet between us. The man charged at me. It was like I was watching a movie at half-speed. He moved so slowly when compared to me. I slipped past his knife with ease and ejected a small punch to his ribs. A loud crack rang through the air as my fist connected with his chest. The man gasped for air as he hit the ground. I stepped on his hand, which held the knife. It was like I was crushing a bug. The man screamed. I pulled the knife out from under my shoe and threw it onto the lawn.

Selene sprinkled dust on the man's face. The hunter fell fast asleep. His breathing was labored. I'd broken a few of his ribs with even a soft punch. I needed to work on controlling my strength.

"He won't remember the last two days," Selene said.

"Remind me never to get on the bad side of either of you," Aden said as he looked at the man.

Selene made a fist at the fire, and it vanished, leaving the grass crispy. We walked up onto the deck and made our way into the house. I cleared the kitchen and dining room as we entered. I listened for heartbeats around me. I could hear four more below us, and I could smell blood.

"There's blood. A lot."

"Where?" Selene said.

"Downstairs." I waved for them to follow me as I led them through Ben's house. I ignored the fond memories that flashed before me as I entered each room.

In the living room, Jules was sitting on the couch with her feet perched on an unconscious hunter on the coffee table. She made a shushing motion and pointed to the stairs. After a few moments, Pax came down the stairs.

"Clear," he said.

"Pax and Aden round up all the hunters. Make sure they get dusted and out of the house," she said. The boys nodded and went out the back door, probably to bring that guy around front.

"How many are downstairs?" she asked.

"I hear four heartbeats. Probably two hunters, Ben's father, and Tati."

"Tera, I love you, but you are the only one of us who will survive being shot. You need to go down there first. We need you to draw any fire that we might get," Jules said.

"Aunt Jules!" Selene said.

"I'm sorry, did bulletproof skin come with your new attitude?" Jules snapped back.

"We don't know enough about the curse to say she will survive," Selene continued to protest.

"She will," Tati's sister said. "I've seen one of her kind survive being shot with an explosive. Then, it tore the men who attacked it to shreds."

"Well, I guess it's settled then," I said as I leaped over the coffee table and opened the door to the basement. *I may as well be useful. Maybe it won't hurt that bad.* I descended the stairs.

At the bottom of the stairs was a hallway leading to the wine cellar.

Ben brought me down there once, right after his mom had died. He wanted to drink some of her favorite wine while we ate dinner. He made store-brand spaghetti and sauce, but he didn't care. He wanted the wine. The concrete walls clashed with the carpeted floors. The area near the wine cellar was an open, empty room. Ben told me it was for storage.

As I approached the end of the hallway, I could hear the heartbeats more clearly. Two were in the space just around the corner, just outside the wine cellar door. The other two were inside the wine cellar, and one was beating fast. The smell of blood was the only scent I could catch. I could only imagine what we would see when we opened that cellar door. I stepped out of the hallway and into the view of the two hunters guarding the door.

I never realized how much getting shot would hurt, but it was not nearly as painful as when my body pushed the bullets out. They shot me six times before they realized it wasn't doing anything. *I hope Pax was right and this will be painless,* I thought as I closed my eyes. I thought about the wolf I had seen when I was meditating. I focused on her. My bones cracked like I had just woken up from a long sleep. It wasn't painful; it felt good. Tension left my body with each pop and crack. One of the men whimpered.

I opened my eyes.

I was staring down at the men, who smelt like piss. I looked down at my hands to see a massive set of talons. I smiled at the men, or at least that was what I thought I did.

What they saw must've been terrifying because one of them started crying. I slammed one of them against the wall with a backhand. His body fell limp on the floor. I turned to the other one and growled. I grabbed him with my left hand by the head and shoulders and tossed him into the wall behind me. I turned to the first man I had smacked and ripped off his coat.

I held onto it and closed my eyes. I could see the wolf sitting beside me. I nodded to her, and she ran off into the distance.

The next time I opened my eyes, I was back to my human self. I wrapped the hunter's jacket around myself. I went to the bottom of the stairs. Jules and Selene were eagerly standing at the top of the stairs. I gave them a thumbs-up, and they came down.

Selene tugged on the door to the cellar, but it wouldn't budge. She kicked it in frustration.

"It's locked," she shouted.

"Step back," Jules said. She jutted her hand out toward the door, and it cracked under the influence. The door was launched into the cellar. Selene and I kept close to Jules as she walked toward the doorway.

Once in the doorway, we saw Tati tied to a chair, a gag in her mouth. There was blood all over her, and she was unconscious. Behind her was Ben's dad, a gun pressed to the back of Tati's head. He kept his eye locked on us. He didn't even seem nervous. His eyes were a fierce blue, nothing like Ben's. They were full of hate.

"What's your plan here?" Jules asked coolly.

"I could kill her and take as many of you as I can with me," he said.

"I doubt you'd get very far. I'd kill you the second you pulled the trigger."

"I'm sure you would," he said. Sweat was dripping down his forehead and into his right eye.

"You'd leave your kids fatherless? You'd leave them orphans?" Jules asked. None of her threats were empty.

"What are my options?"

"Put the gun down. We wipe your memory, and you get to live," Jules said.

"Then you monsters continue to kill people?" he asked.

"No one will die," Jules said. I was stunned by her compassion, even now.

"You're gonna keep your dog locked up?" he said. His glare shifted to me. I fought the urge to jump across the room and punch him. I looked at Tati, whose breathing was heavy. She had lost a lot of blood.

"She won't be like this for much longer. We're going to cure her," Jules said.

He let out a sickening laugh. It wasn't a hearty laugh but a focused one. He never moved the gun from Tati's head or his finger from the trigger. "There is no cure. She's a monster, and there's no changing that now. You're delusional."

"Enough. Drop your gun and surrender," Jules snapped.

"Sorry, but I can't. You're too dangerous to keep alive," he said as he pointed his gun at Jules. I could see his hand tensing as he neared pulling the trigger.

"Stop," a soft voice called over my shoulder.

It was hypnotic. It made me want to stop breathing. I looked back to see Tati's sister, her eyes trained on Ben's father. He had frozen in place. His face looked strained.

"Drop the gun," she said. Ben's father followed her orders and dropped the gun to the floor. He looked shocked. "Now, kick over toward the door."

"What are you doing to me, witch?" he asked. Still, his body followed her instructions.

"Amateur hunters," Jules said. She rolled her eyes. "You don't even comprehend the extent of our gifts, yet you want to hunt us."

"You're abominations, freaks of nature," he spat back at her.

"Freaks who bested you," Jules said with a smile.

"Not yet," he said. He pulled a knife out of his pocket and raised it into the air.

He moved so quickly that I knew I couldn't get to him before he stabbed Tati. Even Tati's sister was caught off guard by his last-ditch effort, but Jules wasn't. As soon as he wound up, she acted. With a flick of her wrist, his head twisted until we heard a snap. His body collapsed onto the ground, and the knife clattered beside it. I released the breath that had lodged itself in my throat.

Jules moved to Tati's chair, ungagged her, and pulled off her bindings. She was still unconscious.

"Reyna, help me," Jules called. Tati's sister ran to her side and helped Jules carry Tati out of the cellar.

I looked at Ben's father, and I felt sad. Ben had lost both of his parents; he was left with only Will. I knew the man deserved what he got, but part of me wished it had happened another way. He was too full of hate to hear what we had to say.

On my way out of the house, I went upstairs to Ben's room and stole a pair of pajama pants. I pulled the hunter's jacket onto my body and buttoned it up. It was in good condition, minus the tears toward the bottom from when I'd yanked it off the hunter.

Outside the house, all the hunters were piled on top of each other, unconscious. Jules propped Tati up in the van's passenger seat and closed the door. I stood next to Selene and watched as the others climbed into the van. Selene reached down and grabbed my hand. I squeezed. I knew what scared her the most about that day. It had been sitting at the back of my head. *What if he was telling the truth?*

Jules approached us. She looked exhausted. I wondered if the same thing worried her. If it did, she didn't show it. She fought to keep her grasp on hope.

"We have to burn down the house," she said.

"What? No, we can't do that," I protested.

"We don't have a choice. If they find his body, they will know something is wrong and wiping their memories will have been pointless," Jules said.

"What about Ben? He won't have anywhere to go. This is his home."

"Tera, I know you care about him, but we can't risk it. It will be safer for us and him this way."

"He'll be okay," Selene said. She had doubts in her eyes, but I knew I couldn't argue with them. I nodded and walked to the van. I watched through the open door as the house erupted into flames.

The weeks after that felt slow. We waited for Tati to recover, and the process was long and grueling. The witches completed their curse on the last three local hunters left: Will, Maggie, and Ben. Ashlyn and I had watched as they did an intricate ritual with poppets and blackthorns. They pinned each hunter with something specific. Maggie was given paranoia—which stuck well because she stopped showing up at school. People said she wouldn't even leave her house.

Selene cursed Will with sloth so he would lose all desire to hunt. Jules cursed Ben with impotence so that he wouldn't be able to hunt. It was the worst of the three. It affected more than just his hunting; he lost his ability to play soccer. He even quit the team, thus giving up his chance at a scholarship. It broke my heart to see him in so much pain, but my family was safe, so I had to deal with it.

Selene and I started going back to school again during the day. Ashlyn forced us to join the prom planning committee, which took up any free periods we had. During the evenings, we were at Tati's house, where Selene was training for The Ascension and helping to heal Tati.

14

Selene

Aunt Jules had turned Tati's house into Hogwarts. Pax and Aden had moved in to help care for Tati, but also so Aunt Jules could help train Aden for The Ascension. Somehow, he was behind me in preparation. Aunt Jules had turned her focus toward him and left me to my own devices. I had turned my focus away from the Trials of the Moon and Sun and to the Trial of Creation.

I was honing my skills in potion and spellcraft. I had finally finished the encyclopedia of North American herbs and moved on to studying their metaphysical properties from our family's grimoire. Thankfully, Tati had a greenhouse on her property stocked with nearly anything a witch could need. I had taken on tending to it during Tati's recovery.

I was preparing to make a salve to help heal Tati's wounds and speed up her recovery. As I moved around the kitchen, I watched Tera, who was sitting at the table.

"Are you writing in a diary?" I asked as I pulled bay leaves from the cabinet.

"I'm trying, but I don't really know what to say."

"Aren't you just supposed to write whatever you want?"

"Yeah, but I can't exactly just write everything in here. What if someone picks it up and reads about how I'm unhappy because I dumped my boyfriend after I turned into a werewolf? Oh, and he's a hunter whose dad my aunt killed with her magical powers," Tera said. She closed the book and sighed.

"I mean, most people would probably think you're writing a fiction story." I chuckled.

"Oh, and my sister, the witch, has conjured herself a sense of humor."

"What if I enchant it so that not just anyone can read it?" I asked.

"Can you do that?"

"I can try. I mean, how hard could it be? I read about how the grimoire was enchanted, and I may be able to recreate it on a smaller scale."

"As long as a murderous snake doesn't start slithering out of my journal, fine," she said.

I pulled a bay leaf out of the jar and dipped it into the elder tree water I was using to make the salve. I took the journal from Tera and traced a counterclockwise circle onto it. I placed the leaf in the circle's center.

"From prying eyes, I must hide the secrets that are placed inside. Banish them from those who seek, but Tera does not admit peeking," I chanted. I lifted the leaf and willed it to ignite with a flame. I traced it around the book so that the smoke touched every inch. Finally, I let some of the ashes sprinkle onto the book and placed the leaf into the sink to burn the rest of the way.

"Did it work?" Tear asked.

"Let's see." When I opened the book, it was blank. "Have you written in it yet?"

"Yeah, I have," she said.

I closed the book. "Okay, give me permission to read it."

"Selene, won't you please look at my journal?" she said.

I opened the journal, and this time, there was writing on the first page.

Dear Diary,

Fuck—

I laughed and handed the book back to her. "It works."

"Now, I can write about how annoying you are, and you'll never be able to read it," she said as she exhaled an exaggerated evil laugh.

"Oh, shut up and help me make this salve for Tati." She laughed and stood from the table.

"What can I do, chef?" she asked.

"I need you to get me the turmeric root out of the fridge."

She went over to the fridge and opened it. Then, she opened the freezer. I looked back to see what she was doing. She was standing at the fridge with the turmeric in one hand and the other opening Aunt Jules's cooler. She gagged.

"What is it?" I asked.

She slammed the freezer shut and handed me the bag. Her face was mortified.

"It's a hand," she said.

"A hand?" I asked. "Like a human hand?"

"Yup," Tera said. She tried to shake the image out of her head.

"Why on earth?" I asked.

"I have no clue, but that is disgusting," she said. "Oh my god, you don't think Jules is like the witch version of Jeffrey Dahmer, do you?"

"Uh, no, I don't think that she eats people."

"Then, how do you explain that?"

"I have no clue. Let's ask her."

I finished the salve. Tera and I brought it to Tati's room and put it on her wounds. Then, we went to find Aunt Jules, who was training with Aden in the backyard. Aden was improving with his telekinesis, but it was still dangerous to stand too close while he practiced. Aunt Jules had him trying to push a dresser. It wasn't moving, and whenever he waved his hand, a drawer shot out.

Aunt Jules sat on the porch with a stack of books and a legal pad. She was reading one of them and taking notes when Tera and I sat on the wicker couch across from her. She didn't look at us. She hadn't talked to me since we had saved Tati.

"Aunt Jules," Tera said as she cleared her throat.

Aunt Jules sighed heavily. She closed her book and looked at us. "What?"

"Well, we were doing some work in the kitchen, and I may have let curiosity get the best of me. We were just wondering why you have a human hand in the fridge?" Tera asked.

"It belonged to the witch that cursed you," she said.

"What? How did you get it?" Tera asked.

"I went to the farmer's market, took her from her stand, tortured her, and cut it off," she said.

"Why?"

"We might be able to use it to break the curse," Aunt Jules said.

"Did you kill her?" Tera asked.

"No, I couldn't. She's from one of the Original Covens."

"Which one?"

"The Dyer coven. Her name was Lucile Dyer," she said.

"Why did she do this to me?" Tera asked.

"Your grandmother promised your mother to Lucile's son. Your mother didn't fulfill that promise, so Lucile wants to make us pay for it."

"So, this happened because our mother didn't want to be in an arranged marriage?" Tera asked. Aunt Jules didn't answer her.

"When were you going to tell us you went after her?" I asked.

"When I figured out how to break the curse," she said. She wouldn't look at me.

"We're supposed to be working on breaking this curse together."

"We were. You were supposed to be preparing for The Ascension, but you got caught up in that foolish scheme to take down the hunters," she snapped.

I balled up my fists in my lap. Aunt Jules was blaming me for everything that had happened.

"I was just following along with what Tati thought we should do. You were the one who told me to train with her."

"You're smarter than that, Selene. You never do something you don't want to; you should have stopped it. You're not even ready for The Ascension," she said.

"Oh, I'm not ready? Is that why you're spending all your time teaching Aden? Because you don't think I'm ready?"

"You won't be strong enough in time, and I can't waste my time teaching you when you don't want to learn. I need to be able to focus on finding a cure for Tera."

Her words were a cold knife that stabbed into my gut. Tera sat silently beside me. There was nothing she could say. This was a battle between Aunt Jules and me.

"I don't need you to teach me. I'm strong enough on my own for The Ascension and to cure Tera. You've been holding me back," I snapped at her. I stood from my seat and walked away from Aunt Jules and Tera. I wanted my words to hurt her. I wanted her to realize how much she'd hurt me.

I glanced off the deck at Aden, who had stopped practicing to watch the scene unfold. My eyes darted to the dresser. My skin was hot with anger, and my mind was racing. I let my anger spill out.

The dresser erupted into flames. Aden flinched as it did. I stepped off the porch and walked past him toward the greenhouse.

Inside the greenhouse, the plants were flourishing. Since I'd started taking care of them, they had all become more vibrant. Some of them had even bloomed out of season. Being near them calmed me. I grabbed the watering can and filled it in the sink. I walked around the rows, feeling the leaves and soil. Most of the plants weren't toxic and were safe to touch.

I had my mission. I would not be attentive to any more than one plant today. I neared the elder tree in a massive pot on the ground. It was growing too large to keep in the greenhouse and would have to be moved outside. I felt its soil dry, even though I had just watered it the day before.

"You sure are thirsty, huh?" I said as I poured some water into its pot. I rub my fingers over its bark. I looked at the poppets that hung from its branches. It was what Aunt Jules had used to bind the curse on the hunters.

"Aunt Jules doesn't know this, but I think that you're the key to breaking Tera's curse." I read in our family's grimoire that Elderwater could be used to break some of the most powerful curses. I knew I wouldn't be able to use just any old Elderwater to break Tera's curse, though. I needed to wait for a powerful celestial event to charge the water. Aunt Jules had been working on her own to search for a cure, but so had I. That was why I'd taken up the task of caring for the greenhouse.

I moved on to watering the other plants. I hummed a lullaby as I did. I knew the plants liked it. Though if they didn't, it wasn't like they could tell me. A few other plants, like the elder tree, needed water even though I had watered them recently. Once I had finished my rounds, I made my way around to prune any dead leaves from them. There were none. As I walked around in search of the nonexistent dead leaves, soft footsteps entered the greenhouse. I looked toward the door to see Tati's sister looking around at the plants. She wore a tight red headwrap and golden earrings that sent a reflective sparkle across her cheeks. Her cheekbones were sharp, and her eyes were sharper.

"Do you need help to find something?" I asked.

"I was looking for you. Have you been caring for these plants?" she asked.

"Uh, yes, I have."

She reached out and touched the leaves of the plant beside her.

"Amazing," she said. She was so focused on rubbing the leaf between her fingers that I wondered if she had forgotten the real reason she was here.

"Why were you looking for me?" I asked.

She released the plant and turned her attention back to me.

"I heard the fight you had with your aunt," she said.

"The dead probably heard the fight I had with my aunt."

"I assure you, they did. I don't think that you are to blame," she said.

"You don't?" I asked. I was shocked.

"My sister has always had a stubborn streak. Once she has an idea, there's no changing her mind. If you had chosen not to help her, she would probably be dead from doing it on her own," she said.

"Oh." I didn't know what else to say.

"I wanted to say thank you for your part in saving her and caring for her," she said. "I realize I have not gotten the chance to thank anyone yet or even introduce myself. I'm Reyna. Thank you for what you have done and what you will do."

"What do you mean, what I will do?" I asked.

"I don't think your aunt realizes just how powerful you are," she said.

"What?" I asked.

"Look at these plants. I have never seen this greenhouse so alive, and I know it's not my sister's doing. I've seen her kill succulents."

"I've always had a green thumb, I guess, but it's just making sure they're cared for."

"This is not some simple green thumb," she said. "This is a sign that you possess one of the All-Mother's most powerful divine gifts."

"What are you talking about?"

"The breath of life. The ability to convert your raw power into life. I have met one other witch with this power. It is incredible. They can heal any ailment, cause the surrounding nature to thrive, and even bring the dead back to life. You are able to manipulate the life force of the world around you, strengthening them." Reyna pointed to a bush covered in flowers. "How else can you explain this bush blooming in the fall?"

"But I've already manifested two of the All-Mother's gifts."

She stepped closer to me and grabbed my hands.

"I have the feeling that you will manifest even more. There is still so much untapped power inside of you," she said. "Come with me. You need to see your own power to believe it."

Reyna led me out of the greenhouse. We walked past Aden and his crispy dresser. Aunt Jules had her eyes locked on us the moment we were in her view. Her expression was unreadable, but I wanted her to eat her words. I didn't meet her gaze.

We entered the house and passed through the kitchen. Tera was writing in her journal, and Pax was scarfing down a sandwich. Tera, with piqued curiosity now, closed her book and followed us. Pax followed behind her. Reyna led me up to Tati's room, where she was lying unconscious in the bed.

She hadn't woken up since we rescued her from the hunters. Aunt Jules thought she would wake after we patched her wounds, but that was two weeks ago. Her forehead glistened in sweat, but she still hadn't moved an inch. Reyna sat me down on the bed beside her.

"Take a deep breath in. Then, exhale and call out to her," she said.

Tera stood behind her, looking at me with confusion. Pax stood with his arms crossed. When he witnessed this, he would tell Aunt Jules, and she would regret the things she had said to me. I was driven by my desire to prove my power to her.

I followed Reyna's instructions and took a deep breath in. I leaned toward Tati's ear. I wanted this to work. I wanted Tati to pull through.

I let the breath go as I whispered to her,

"Tati, I know you can hear me. Wake up. Come back to us." A few moments passed, and nothing happened. I grabbed her hand in both of mine and brought it to my face. I closed my eyes and tried to focus on Tati. I thought about the plants in the greenhouse and how I had talked to and touched them. I focused on Tati and whispered to her again.

"Come on, you need to wake up now." I hummed the tune that I did for the plants. I could feel the eyes watching me from behind. They were hoping this worked as much as I did. This was the last-ditch effort that they were all banking on.

I doubted myself. I didn't believe I had the power to do this. Aunt Jules's doubts crept their way back into my head. *"I can't waste my time teaching you." What if she was right? What if I'm not strong enough?* I thought. My doubts were taking hold of my mind when Tati squeezed my hand.

I snapped my eyes open to look at her. She smiled, her eyes still closed.

"You're just full of surprises, aren't you, honey?" Tati said. I yelped joyfully, and I shifted to hug her. Tera met my excitement as she climbed over the bed to hug her from the other side.

"I told you that you had the power," Reyna said.

I looked back at her and saw Aunt Jules standing in the doorway, looking at us. I felt triumphant. I smirked and then turned back to finish my embrace with Tati.

The rest of the night, we filled Tati in on everything that had happened and how we had rescued her. Reyna gave Tati a tough time for being so reckless. Aunt Jules didn't even talk to her. Tati knew she was upset and told us she would take the time to talk to her in the morning. I was glad we would be at school for that conversation because I knew Aunt Jules would do a lot of yelling, and if I were there, she'd probably turn her sights on me.

15

Tera-Sue

The car ride to school was silent. Selene was clutching the steering wheel so tightly that I feared she would leave an imprint. Aden was in the backseat with his eyes locked on a book Jules had assigned him. I was forced to sit in the tension they left in the air. Selene was still pissed with Jules after their fight, and she took some of that out on Aden. I felt bad for him. Jules had thrown him in the middle of her and Selene's battle. I wondered if she had done that to make Selene jealous, to motivate her. Whatever the real reason was, it motivated Selene. She was able to wake Tati up from her comatose state and heal all her wounds. Tati was up cooking breakfast when we left for school. Jules kept up her furious demeanor and silent treatment. Only Pax and Aden heard anything from her.

I was used to Jules lecturing me, and she was used to me doing whatever I wanted anyway, but when Selene did the risky thing instead of the responsible thing, it shook her to her core. I had never seen Selene get like that. She had something to prove. I just didn't know who she had to prove it to. Once we arrived at school, Selene was ready to ditch Aden and start her day. I let her go and volunteered to walk Aden to the main office.

"You know you don't have to read that while you're here. You can take a break and just do normal things."

"I don't really have time for normal things," he said.

"Then, why are you here?"

"My dad wants me to be here," he said. He still hadn't looked up from the book. I grabbed the book from his hands and closed it. "What the hell?"

"Your dad wants you to be here, so be here, not in this book."

"I can't waste my time. I'm not ready for The Ascension yet," he said as he tried to get the book from me.

I held the book out to the opposite side of me and pushed on his chest with two fingers. Aden slid back as I pushed.

"I don't think burying your nose in this book will help you get ready, either."

"There's not much else I can do. I am barely going to pass the first trial, and the other two are even harder," he said.

"If only we knew a witch who was ready for all three trials and could help you."

"No. She won't even look in my direction. There's no way she'll help me. Your aunt would also probably stop training me if I asked her for help."

"I think she would help you, and you'd just have to hide it from Aunt Jules." *Selene would love it if she could teach Aden something Aunt Jules couldn't.*

"Sneaking around doesn't sound like a smart plan," he said.

"Probably not, but then again, what other witch do you know that can bring someone out of a coma with just a few whispered words?" I asked. We turned into the main office.

"I'll think about it," he mumbled as we got in line to talk to the secretary.

There were a few other people in the main office: the students waiting to make the morning announcements, the students waiting to talk to the principal, and the students waiting for their turn with the secretary. They were all familiar faces except the one in front of us in line. He was new; he had to be. I would've remembered that chiseled jawline and sharp cheekbones. That was all I could get from his side profile, but I was eager to see him turn around. He reached the counter and handed the secretary some paperwork. She looked through it over her glasses, licking her thumb as she turned each page.

"Well, sweetie, this looks all good. Let me just input you into the system and print out your schedule," she said as she booted up the computer. The ancient desktop sounded like it was about to take off from the desk and fly away. The clicking of the mechanical keyboard rang through my head. "All right, sweetie, first and last name."

"Dean Almonte," he said. His voice was deep and raspy. The secretary started typing again.

"You're next, so I'm gonna go. Don't want to be late. I'll see you later," I said to Aden. I left the main office and could still hear the keyboard clicking halfway down the hallway.

When I reached my locker, Selene was talking with Ashlyn, who was holding a thick binder. I opened the locker, dropped my backpack inside, and hung up my modified hunter chic coat. I cut it shorter to get rid of tatters and ironed on some patches. I closed the locker and slid into the conversation.

"I don't think this is a good time to organize a school dance," Selene said.

"This is the perfect time to organize one. We got a win, and we need to celebrate it," Ashlyn said.

"What are you talking about?" I asked.

"Ashlyn thinks we should be throwing a dance," Selene said.

"No, I don't think anything. We are having a school dance. I already got it approved by the principal, and as the prom committee, it comes down to us to plan all the dances."

"I told her I don't think it's a good idea. I have little more than a month to finish preparing for The Ascension," Selene said.

"I think it's a great idea."

"What?" Selene said.

"Yeah, we deserve this. We beat the hunters." It felt wrong to celebrate destroying Ben's life, but I told Ashlyn we'd do normal senior things.

"Exactly," Ashlyn agreed.

"You'll still train for The Ascension. We'll plan the dance during our free periods."

"Wait. What?" Ashlyn said.

"Fine, only during our free periods," Selene said.

"Perfect. You get to train, and we get to have some semblance of a normal senior year."

"Now that is settled, I'll see you bitches later. Can't wait to decide on a theme," Ashlyn said.

School days went much faster after all the things that had happened recently. Some classes mattered less. I didn't see the point of worrying about logs and exponents. Math and science couldn't explain what happened to me.

Gym became my favorite class. It was the only time I could spend my pent-up energy, even if it was only a fraction of it. That day, we were told we'd be going outside to play some sports or walk the track. Ashlyn demanded we walk the track. In the past, I would've fought her on that, but I couldn't risk playing sports with other students; they were just too fragile. As we walked, Ashlyn rattled off all her ideas for the dance. I focused on listening and watching the people play on the field.

There were three groups: one playing flag football, one playing soccer, and the last playing volleyball. I spotted Aden in the football group. He looked like he was having fun. He was shorter than the other guys playing and even some girls, but that made it easy for him to slip in between the other players. The new guy, Dean, was also playing with that group. He was one of the quarterbacks, and he was fast. When he was running the ball, none of the others could even touch him. His dark hair was wet with sweat, and he had a streak of white hair. Ashlyn must have realized I wasn't listening to her because she had turned her attention to their game as well.

"Well, would you look at that," she said.

"What?" I asked.

"You do notice boys other than puppy-eyed hunters who want to kill you," she said.

"That's not funny. Ben wouldn't have killed me," I said, but I doubted myself. After I saw how much hate was in his father, I questioned what kind of person Ben really was.

"It doesn't matter now. He couldn't kill you if you ran into his knife," Ashlyn said as she pointed to the soccer group.

Ben was lying on the floor in the middle of their playing field. Some people playing on his team were shouting at him for being so bad. One of the teachers went over and checked on him. He was fine, just stewing in his crushed pride. He stood from the field and walked the track. I could hear his team celebrating his departure. My heart hurt.

"I hate seeing him like this," I said, keeping my eyes on him as he walked on the other side of the track.

"He literally led you into a trap where he was going to kill you," Ashlyn said.

"That doesn't make it hurt less." *He's lost everything. His mom, his dad, his home, and now he can't even play soccer.*

"Tera, don't get any dumb ideas. The curse is the only thing keeping them from hunting you," Ashlyn said.

"What if there was another way?" I asked.

"There's not. His dad was a psycho, his brother was a psycho, and he's a psycho. Forget about him. Look at the hottie playing football," she said. Ashlyn sucked at consoling people, but she wasn't wrong. Ben was dangerous, but I loved him.

After gym, I sat through a few more periods of pointless classes. I scrolled through colleges in the library while I waited for Selene and Ashlyn. None of the schools caught my eye, but I knew I'd have to look at them in greater detail again soon.

I shut the computer down, opened my journal, and started writing. I poured every feeling I had about Ben into the pages. I wrote about when I'd met him, our first kiss, the first time he'd told me he loved me. I wrote about our first fight, how he was there for me when my first dog died, and how I was there for him when his mom died. I wrote about when I found out the truth about him and the time he'd tried to kill me. I wrote about how I was still madly in love with him and how I hated to see him. The way he confused me. I had written so much that my hand cramped up, and so did my heart. Writing it down didn't make me want to let go of him; it made me want to pull him closer.

"What are you writing? An essay?" Selene said as she sat down at the table beside me.

"An essay would be less painful. I'm writing about Ben."

"Tera, I know it hurts to see him around school and to think about him. Maybe you should talk to him," Selene said.

I looked at her in awe.

"What?" I asked.

"Talk to him, try to get some closure. He couldn't hurt you if he tried. Maybe talking to him will let you figure out how to let go of him."

"Are you feeling okay?" I asked as I put the back of my hand on her forehead. "Who body snatched you?"

"I'm fine," she said as she swatted away my hand. "I'm just saying that it might be better for you. You won't be in danger or anything, so why not?"

"Yeah, maybe you're right. I'm going to go do that. Tell Ashlyn that I'm fine with whatever theme you guys decide for the dance." I stood and grabbed my journal. I left the library and made my way into the hallway.

I charted my path to the cafeteria so that I avoided any hall monitors that might have been around. The cafeteria was packed with students, but Ben wasn't there. I went to the gym and sneaked into the pool room. He wasn't there either. I looked at the pool's clear water and thought about the last time Ben and I talked.

I had sneaked into the pool room through the gym, holding the door so it didn't make a sound behind me. Ben was sitting with his feet in the pool and his back to the door. He was just staring at the water. I wondered what he was thinking about. It reminded me of all the times I would find him there, just sitting with tears in his eyes as he thought about his mom.

"Ben," I said softly. He didn't jump or flinch like I expected him to. He just glanced over his shoulder at me.

"What are you doing here?" he asked.

"I wanted to talk to you."

"You haven't answered any of my calls or texts," he said. He stopped looking at me.

"Ben, what was I supposed to say? It's okay that your father and brother told me they were planning to kill me?" I asked. I felt bad for lying to him and pretending they were wrong about what I was, but it was too dangerous to tell him the truth now.

"You could have at least heard what I had to say," he said. "I don't know why they were talking like that. I don't even know why you agreed to come to dinner."

I wouldn't have if it were actually me. I took a few steps closer to him before freezing in place. *What if he tries to attack me? I shouldn't get closer.* It hurt to think that Ben would have been able to hurt me.

"I'm sorry. I shouldn't have gone. And I shouldn't even be here now. I just can't help myself. Ben, I lo—"

"You're the one who broke up with me." He got up and turned to face me. He took a few steps toward me. I had never seen him so angry. "You ripped my heart out. Every time I look at you, I feel it happening again. I look at you, and all I hear is you saying, 'I just don't love you. I never will.'"

He spat my own words back at me. I would have rather he plunged a knife into my heart. I didn't want to say more, not when I knew he would end up forgetting it all. I told myself that we'd have this conversation again and that it'd go differently next time.

"I'm so sorry, Ben." I reached into my pocket, grasped a handful of the knockout dust, and threw it into his face as he opened his mouth to respond. He looked betrayed as he collapsed. I caught him on his way down and rested his head in my lap. I snipped a small lock of his perfect blond hair.

I walked back into the gym from the pool area. I didn't know where else Ben would go, where else he felt safe.

Then, it came to me. I went to the door that led to the field and saw it was propped open. There was no gym at that period, so I knew it wasn't open for a class. I walked outside and saw Ben standing on the field, trying to kick soccer balls into a net.

He missed every shot he took. He grunted each time a ball bounced off the goalpost or flew over the net. I walked to the field and stopped about twenty feet from where Ben was.

He stopped kicking at the balls as soon as he spotted me. He didn't smile at me or even give me a longing stare. Ben looked at me with angry eyes. I knew I deserved them. We stared at each other, silent for a few moments, before he started walking off the field. He walked right past me without even a glance.

"Ben," I called after him. He stopped walking, but he didn't look back at me. He didn't respond. "Just talk to me, please."

"I don't have anything to say," he said. Ben started walking again. I jogged after him.

"Then just listen to me." I ran around him and put myself between him and the door. His eyes were glassy and wouldn't meet mine. "I'm sorry. I've been so stupid; I broke up with you because I was scared of the changes that were happening in my life. I didn't want to put you through the pain of what was happening. I wanted to protect you, but when I did, I hurt you more than I could've realized. Ben, I loved you, and everything we had was real."

He was still silent, but his shoulders weren't as tense as before. I could feel my own heart tensing as I prepared myself to continue.

"I know so much has changed in your life since then, and I'm sorry for it. A lot has changed in my life too. I don't think we should get back together. I'm not ready for that. I don't even really know who I've become yet. I just wanted you to know you're not alone. I'm still here for you. I'll always be here for you."

Ben grabbed me and pulled me into a hug. He put his head on my shoulder and started sobbing. I rested my hands on his back and tried to fight my own tears.

16

Selene

Ashlyn had pretty much planned the entire dance by herself. All I had to do was listen to it. She wanted red and black balloons to match the school colors and an archway outside the gym doors so pictures on the actual red carpet she was ordering would look presentable. The theme she had picked was something about masquerading in Hollywood. She even planned on providing masks to all students to ensure they followed the dress code, though she assured me we could pick our own if we wanted.

I was glad she had done all the creative thinking on her own. I didn't want to waste more energy than I had to on this dance. I was in charge of getting volunteers to sign up for setting up the gym the day before the dance.

The bell saved me from having to deal with any more of Ashlyn's dance mania. It was the last period of the day and the easiest: English. When I sat down in class, a boy was sitting in Tera's usual seat. He was new to the class. He had soft green eyes and dark brown hair with a white streak running through it. He wore jeans and a black T-shirt. In the center of his chest, I noticed a necklace charm. It was a tree inside a circle with tiny purple crystals as the leaves. He didn't look like he wanted to be there, although not many people did in high school.

"Excuse me. I'm sorry, but that's my sister's seat," I said in my kindest tone.

"I don't see her here," he said with a stone face.

"It's still her seat," I snapped.

"Then, when she shows up, I'll move."

Deep breath, Selene. Don't light his books on fire. He's just a punk kid who is being an ass to get to you. Just smile and nod. I did just that. I also prayed that Tera would show up on time for class once in her life.

The bell rang to indicate the start of class. The teacher waited a few minutes before they started their lecture. No one came into the class late. The teacher stood in the center of the class. Our desks were arranged so the two halves of the class were facing each other.

"We are going to start a new unit in class this week. We are going to talk a bit about our expectations from the novel *Frankenstein* by Mary Shelley. What do we know?" they asked.

"Frankenstein is the monster with the green skin and bolts in his neck, the one that walks around with his arms stretched out in front of him," one boy said.

The teacher nodded as they listened.

"Actually, Frankenstein is the doctor, not the monster," one girl said.

"That's very relative, don't you think?" the rude boy beside me said.

"Ah, we have a new student. I forgot," the teacher said. "What is your name?"

"Dean," he said.

"All right, Dean. Why is Frankenstein being the monster relative?" the teacher asked.

"I think Dr. Frankenstein himself is the monster. He's not what most people would consider a monster to look like, but he is the monster in the story. He created this creature and abandoned it to its own devices, where its only goal becomes to torment its maker after people treat it like an abomination," Dean said.

"Dr. Frankenstein might be a monster in his own right, but that doesn't excuse his creation's actions." I had read Frankenstein in ninth grade when Aunt Jules gave it to me as a Christmas present. "We are not what those who create us are. We become defined by our own actions and choices. If you choose to act like a monster, regardless of your motives or intentions, you are a monster."

Dean looked over at me with an unreadable face. He could hide behind any poker face he wanted, but I knew I had gotten under his skin. The teacher chuckled.

"Well, this is the kind of discussion I like to see. I can already tell that this book is going to have you all thinking intensely. Once you get your books, I want you to spend the rest of the period reading it," they said.

The teacher passed our books out, and I started flipping through the pages. I didn't mind rereading books for class, but there was something about rereading Frankenstein that felt more drawn out.

By the time the last bell rang, I had only reached the third chapter. I closed my book and got up from my chair when I noticed Dean was standing beside his desk, waiting for me.

"Can I help you with something?" I asked.

"Looks like your sister was a no-show," he said.

I hadn't even noticed Tera had never shown up to class. It wasn't like her to skip a class. Sleep through them, yes, but skip one? No. I worried that her conversation with Ben had taken a turn for the worse. I regretted telling her to talk with him.

"Looks like it."

"If you didn't want me to sit next to you, you could've just said that," he said.

"That wasn't what it was about. I actually have a sister who sits there." I rolled my eyes at him and walked out of the room and into the crowded hallway. Dean followed me.

"Sorry, I didn't mean to insinuate that you made up your sister. It has just been a long day. I was a dick. It's hard being the new kid as a senior," he said. His apology felt strange, like it didn't belong in his voice.

"Well, usually, things are easier when you're not such an asshole," I said as I stopped at my locker.

"Let me start over. Maybe I could give you a ride home?" He was desperate.

I couldn't tell why, though. *Is he that desperate for a friend?* I thought.

"That's nice of you to offer, but I have my own car." Hope drained from his face as I said that. I'd taken his olive branch, thrown it on the floor, and lit it on fire. I felt a little bad. "But yes, we can start over."

"Okay, cool. I'm Dean," he said as he held out his hand for me to shake. I took it. His skin was soft, and his shake was firm.

"I'm Selene." I took my hand back and finished packing to leave. I pulled my keys off the hook Tera had set up in the locker and felt my heart skip a beat when I saw the car key was missing. *Did Tera take the car? Where the hell did she go? Did she just leave me stranded here?* A hundred other thoughts flew through my head, some of them angry, others worried. I closed the locker and smiled at Dean.

"It looks like my sister took the car and left me here."

"First, your sister is MIA. Now, your car is MIA. I think I'm questioning your sanity," he said.

"Me too," I said with a sigh. To top it all off, like this moment couldn't get any worse, Aden appeared at the locker.

"Are we ready to go?" he asked.

I didn't have a problem with Aden. I had a problem with Aunt Jules using him to make me jealous. It didn't help that his face was so punchable. It was like all the things testing my patience were coming to a culmination at this very moment.

"Friend of yours?" Dean asked. He eyed Aden up and down.

"You know this guy, Selene?" Aden asked, matching Dean's energy.

"Aden, this is Dean from my English class. Dean, this is Aden, my aunt's boyfriend's son. Now, enough of your pissing contest. I have to figure out where the hell my sister is. Thank you."

I called Tera's phone six times, and she sent all of them to voicemail. I called Ashlyn next. She hadn't seen Tera since their gym class, but she offered to come and pick Aden and me up. I told her I would let her know if I needed her.

"Can you drive Aden home for me?" I asked Dean.

"What?" they asked in unison.

"You offered to take me home, but I need to talk to someone else before I can leave. If you really want to be my friend, do me this favor. I'll owe you big time."

"Fine," he said. "But I'm keeping my seat in English."

"Deal." *Tera won't need it after I kill her.*

I walked with Dean and Aden to the parking lot, where they got into a rusty old Mustang and left. I spotted Ben's truck, where I would ambush him and interrogate him as to the whereabouts of my love-struck sister.

I waited hours outside Ben's truck for him, playing Solitaire on my phone on top of the hood.

"Selene?" he called.

I sat up and shot daggers at him with my eyes. I could see the fear on his face as I leaped to the ground beside him.

"Where's Tera?" I demanded as I poked him in his hard chest.

"I don't know. I haven't seen her in a few hours."

"What did you say to her? I can't find her anywhere; she just took the car and vanished."

"What? Why are you here and not talking to the police or your aunt?" he asked.

"I'm not exactly on speaking terms with my aunt right now."

"What? Tera is missing!"

"Yeah, and it probably has something to do with what you said to her when you two talked earlier. You and your stupid brown puppy eyes! What did you tell her?" I asked and slapped his shoulder.

"Ow, nothing. We talked about my life, and I talked to her about my dad and my house and my brother and how now I can't even kick a soccer ball properly," he said.

"What did she say to you?"

"She said that if she could fix it, she would, but she was just being nice. It's not like she can magically fix my problems."

No. She wouldn't try to break the curse, would she? She can't do that.

"Ben, I need you to take me to Tati's house right now. I know where Tera is."

Ben didn't ask any questions as we drove to Tati's house. When we pulled up to Tati's house, our car wasn't in the driveway or the street. Tera wouldn't have parked in the open where someone would see her. She wanted to execute her plan in secret.

"I'm not staying here. I'm coming with you," he argued.

"Ben, I need you to stay here. If Tera shows up while I'm inside talking to everyone, you will be the first to catch her," I lied.

"All right, fine, but in fifteen minutes, I'm coming in," he said.

"Just wait here," I said as I exited the truck and closed the door behind me.

I cut through the house to sell my lie to Ben. I avoided running into anyone as I did because I didn't have time to stop and talk. I exited the house through the back door. I walked down the back porch steps and toward the greenhouse. I could feel Aunt Jules's eyes on me as I walked. She was sitting on the porch reading. I didn't have time to worry about her, though. I needed to stop Tera. Inside the greenhouse was a long trail of dirt that led out of the other door and into the woods. I jogged as I followed the trail. I came to a spot in the woods where Tera was standing next to the elder tree, still in its pot. The smell of gasoline filled the air.

"Tera, stop!" I shouted. She whirled around to face me. Tears were streaming down her face. I approached her.

"Please don't try to stop me, Selene. I can't let him live his life like this. Why should he suffer because I am a monster?" she asked.

"Tera, you're not a monster. You are a good person. Ben will be fine."

"He's not like them. I know he's not. He is gentle and kind. He wouldn't hurt us like them," she said.

"We don't know that, Tera. Please don't try to break this curse. It's the one thing that's letting you live a semi-normal life."

"I can give up normal for him," she said. I could see the resolve in her eyes. She lit a match and tossed the match into the elder tree's pot. She was too quick for me to stop her.

"Tera, no!" I screamed as the plant burst into flames.

The smell of gasoline and fire filled the air. I rushed toward the flames, but Tera grabbed me and turned me so they were no longer in my view. I tried to squirm out of her grip, but she was too strong. I couldn't use my power to manipulate them because I couldn't see them. I wasn't strong enough. I couldn't save the tree, the poppets tied to its branches, or the hope I had for it to help cure Tera. I wanted to cry out for help. I wanted Aunt Jules to come and fix it, to clean up our mistakes again. I couldn't find my voice to call out for help. I was powerless as Tera held me in place until the fire had died down. Then, she released me.

I ran to the tree's ashes and waved out the last of the fire. There was nothing left of it except ashes. I ran my fingers through them as I searched for the little sliver of hope. There was none. Tera came toward me to comfort me.

"Selene, it's okay. We'll be safe still. They're not going to hurt us."

"No! We're not okay! That tree was the best chance of a cure we had. It's gone."

I sobbed. Tera froze, truly taking in my words. She stared at me for a few moments before she walked away. I tried to use my power to save the tree. I whispered to it and buried my hands in its ashes, but nothing was working. I kept trying for what felt like hours. I became so ingrained in trying to bring ashes back to life that I didn't realize I wasn't alone until Aunt Jules put her hands on my back.

"Selene," she said softly.

"No, I'm not done yet. It's still not alive," I said and clenched onto the ashes.

"It's gone. There's nothing we can do now," she said. She guided me up from the ground.

We returned to the house, where she sat with me on the porch. Aunt Jules just looked at me, not saying a word. She pulled me in for a hug and patted my back as I sobbed into her chest.

17

Tera-Sue

Sometimes, I did dumb things. That time, I did a really dumb thing.

I didn't regret breaking the curse we had put on the hunters. I was happy it had helped Ben get a small piece of his world back. It was worth the scolding I received from Jules and the silent treatment from the other witches. Even Tati wouldn't talk to me. I understood why they were angry, but I did what I thought was right. I regretted destroying the sliver of hope Selene had found for breaking my curse. It was like I was back to square one.

If there was no way to break the curse, it just felt like there was a matter of time before I killed another innocent person. I also feared that I had broken something inside of Selene. I had never seen her so distraught. Selene was always in control of herself. She rarely ever cried. After that, she wouldn't even look at me. I couldn't undo my mistake, and the more I thought about it, the more I doubted I would do anything differently. I was willing to suffer for an eternity so that Ben could feel happy for a moment.

Our rides to schools in the days that followed were silent. I stared out the window at passing cars. I navigated my days only talking to

Ashlyn, and even she gave me a hard time at first. Selene didn't come to any of the dance planning sessions we had. Ben and I hadn't spoken since the day it all happened. We'd returned to reserved and longing stares from across hallways and fields. In English, Selene let my seat get taken by the new guy, Dean. I was forced to sit on the other side of the classroom and listen to them whisper back and forth about nerdy book stuff. That was how my days went until the Friday before the dance, fourteen days before The Ascension.

Jules had summoned us to Tati's kitchen, where I would be the most hated person in the room. I stood in the doorway and listened intently to her speaking.

"As you all know, The Ascension is just a couple of weeks away now. That means that our town is going to be filled with more witches than ever. All the Original Covens will be here, and we will be graced by a visit from one of the All-Mother's children," she said.

"Only one of her children?" Selene asked.

"Yes, at least one of them always attends The Ascension. There could be more than one, but that's unlikely, and that's not what we need to be worried about. The entire Dyer coven will be here. That means Lucile will have backup with her, and we are going to be targets, especially you, Tera," she said. Everyone in the room cast harsh glances at me except for Selene. She had worry in her eyes.

"I've concocted these protection pouches for each of us," Jules continued. She passed out little black pouches to each of us. "They should protect us from the effects of any witchcraft. I want you all to keep them on you until The Ascension is over, and I don't want anyone going around town unnecessarily. That means after school, you will come straight home and won't be going anywhere this weekend."

"We can't do that," Selene said. "Saturday is our school dance, and I already bought my dress."

"Selene, it's too risky to be going out to a silly dance, especially alone.

I don't care how powerful you're becoming. I won't let you put yourself in any more danger," Jules said.

"I won't be alone. Tera will be there," Selene said without looking at me. "So will Aden."

"I wi—" Aden went to speak, but Selene cut him off with an elbow to the ribs.

"If you're worried about us, you can sign up to be a chaperon. All of you can," Selene said, pulling a sheet on a clipboard from her backpack. Tati reached over the table, plucked the clipboard from Selene's hand, and filled it out.

"You kids are not missing that dance. Despite everything that has happened to you this year, you're going," Tati said, pushing the clipboard into Reyna's hands.

"Even if you make some questionable choices, I will not argue against the fact that you all deserve to feel ordinary for one night," Reyna said and signed the sheet. She shot me a look as she handed the clipboard to Pax. He looked at Jules with a tilted head.

"I think it might be fun for us too," he said. He signed his name and handed the clipboard back to Selene. She looked at Jules, enjoying her victory, and then held the clipboard out to her.

"Come on, Aunt Jules! It's just a school dance," she said. Jules rolled her eyes as she took the clipboard and filled out the sheet.

"Fine, we will all go to this dance," she said, handing Selene her clipboard back. "Now get to school. When you get home, we're doing extra training."

"Thanks, Aunt Jules," Selene said, hugging her. Aden sighed in protest, giving his dad a fist bump on the way out. I followed behind them. I was glad things were back to normal with Selene and Jules. It only took me fucking up worse to fix it.

"Tera," Jules called as I went to follow Aden out of the house. I stopped and looked. "Be careful, please," she said. Her eyes told me more than that, though. They told me she forgave me and loved me. I nodded before leaving the house.

The car ride wasn't as silent as I had become accustomed to. Instead, Aden and Selene talked about The Ascension's trials and the other witches being in town. I could easily tune them out because I didn't understand half of what they were talking about. When I exited the car at the school, I spotted Ben standing at his truck talking to some girl. A tinge of jealousy swelled inside me. I had sacrificed so much for him, and he would never realize it, which hurt me more. A hand gripped my shoulder.

"Are you coming?" Selene asked. We hadn't walked together into the school since that day, but there she was, waiting with Aden for me.

"Yeah." I walked beside them, still silent, listening to their conversation.

"So, this dance… Are you going with anyone?" Aden asked her.

"Yeah, I guess I am. Dean asked me to go. As a friend, of course," she said.

"Oh," he said somberly.

"You can come with us," she said. "I figured we were all just going as a big group." She shot me a look, pleading for help.

"Yeah, of course we are. Ashlyn will be with us too," I chimed in.

"All right then. I'll go with you guys," he said.

"Could you also help us set up today during lunch?" she asked.

"Yeah, I can do that."

Once we entered the school, Aden went his separate way from us. Selene and I walked in silence to our locker. Ashlyn was pacing in front of our locker when we got to it. She looked stressed. *This dance must be driving her crazy.*

"You guys aren't fighting anymore. Good," she said.

"Not exactly." Selene looked at me. "What's wrong?"

"Well, I saw something terrible this morning. You two are going to have not to be fighting to figure out how to deal with it," she said as she rambled on.

"What is it?" I asked.

"Maggie Fera came back to school this morning," she said.

"Well, that's just fantastic," Selene said as she pinched the bridge of her nose.

"Do you think she remembers anything?" I asked.

"I don't think so. She came up to me and hugged me like nothing happened," Ashlyn said.

"That's good! Then, we just have to pretend like everything is normal. We can't afford to do something that might trigger her memory," Selene said with a cold side-eye at me. "Or the memories of the others."

"All right then. We just pretend like we're all still friends with crazy hunter bitch," Ashlyn said with a nod. "Let's get on with this day. We have a dance to decorate for."

Ashlyn had swindled the principal into excusing us from our classes for the day so we could supervise the dance setup. All the gym classes had been recruited to help set up as well. Ashlyn spent the first few hours of the day ensuring that the gym was spotless. I was afraid that the finish would come off the ground because of how many times she ordered it to be scrubbed.

Selene managed to get every sports team to dedicate their lunch periods to helping. She could be persuasive when she wanted to be. I was tasked with arranging tables for the buffet. It would've been no challenge for me to carry them out two at a time on my own, but people would've stared. So, instead, I had volunteers do all the carrying while I directed them to follow Ashlyn's floor plan. After the tables had been all set up and decorated with red and black tablecloths and centerpieces, the second wave of volunteers came in.

I stood with the gym door to the field propped open as the DJ backed his truck up to the door.

"Need some help?" Ben asked from behind me. I didn't look back at him.

"Uh, actually, that would be great. Could you grab a few other people to help the DJ carry his equipment in?" I asked, without looking back at him. He sighed and walked over to a group of students.

When Ben returned with three other people, the DJ was ready to unload. I held the door open for them as they worked together on carrying things into the gym. Ashlyn waited to guide them to the DJ's designated spot.

I kept my distance and went to the other side of the gym to help Selene construct the archways over each gym door. Getting the archways together wasn't the hard part; the hard part was getting the plastic vines to wrap around the archways without breaking. I must've broken fifteen vines before Ashlyn pulled me off the archways to help her get the boxes of masks from her car.

The masks Ashlyn had ordered were handed out to anyone who didn't come with their own. They were black plastic half-masks held on by an elastic string. I grabbed two boxes from her backseat when I spotted three fancier masks. One was red with gold accents and ruby gemstones, one was a black lace mask, and the last one was teal with silver beads. Each only covered the eye portion of the face.

"Those are so cute." I put the boxes on the roof of her car and closed the door.

"I'm glad you like them. The red one is yours," she said.

"Ashlyn, I didn't even buy a dress for this dance. I was just going to wear the black one I have."

"Oh, sweetie, you can't wear that one. Selene wore that to dinner with Ben's family, and she's wearing black," Ashlyn said.

"I'll just have to go in my pajamas then," I said with a sigh.

"Oh no, you won't. We're going dress shopping when we're done here."

"I'm supposed to go straight home after school."

"We'll be done before school is over, and I'll make sure you're home before Jules even notices you're gone," she said. "Now come on, we've got to get these masks into the gym and start selling some tickets."

Ashlyn's sales tactic was to wait until the day before to sell all the tickets so everyone would rush to buy them simultaneously. She wanted it to seem like many people were interested in going, so even those who didn't want to go had FOMO and bought a ticket. I couldn't say she was a marketing genius, but crowds came rushing to buy tickets when the announcement was made. Nearly every student bought a ticket or two. Ashlyn had gotten the principal to approve that students could bring non-student dates, which piqued the attention of even more students. When the crowd had finally cleared and Ashlyn and I could breathe again, we were left with five tickets. Our dance had nearly sold out.

"Are there any tickets left?" Maggie Fera asked softly as she approached the table. It was hard for me to picture her as dangerous; she was so timid and sweet.

"Yeah, there are some left." I could feel Ashlyn tensing up beside me, but I kept my cool. *She doesn't remember the truth; she would've come after me already.*

"Can I get two, please?" she asked. I took her money and ripped her off two tickets.

"You're bringing a date?" I asked as I handed her the tickets.

"Just a family friend."

"All right, we'll see you tomorrow night."

With a wave, I closed the money box and locked it.

"Family friend," I whispered to Ashlyn.

"You think she's bringing another hunter?" she asked.

"Let's hope not," I said as I got up.

Ashlyn and I left Selene to finish setting up the gym while we went dress shopping. The only job left was blowing up the balloons. I kind of wished I had gotten to stay and help. Selene looked like she was having fun watching Dean and Aden struggle to blow up balloons. However, if there weren't exactly one hundred fifty balloons, Ashlyn would notice.

The dress shopping trip was the most stressful thing that year for me. Whenever I put on a new dress, I could see all my flaws poking out. Those mirrors were designed to make me feel worse about myself. Ashlyn wouldn't let me stop trying on dresses until I found one I fell in love with.

She made me wear a mermaid dress, big puffy sweet sixteen dresses, and even some bride's maid dresses. I wondered if she was trying to help me shop for this dance or taking notes for her wedding.

Finally, she showed the employee the mask I had. After a few minutes of frantic searching, they came out with one I loved. It was a sleek, deep red princess dress—not a ball gown, but still elegant.

"This is the one."

18

Selene

I laughed as a balloon squeaked across the gym out of Dean's hands. He and Aden had been fighting with the balloons for almost an hour. I had fifty blown up on my own and was enjoying the entertainment from watching them struggle to blow up their respective fifty. Pretty much everything else seemed to be done, and the other volunteers were heading back to class.

"I'm going to make one last round and make sure everything is ready. I can trust that the two of you will finish this up, right?"

Dean looked at me with red cheeks and no breath left in his lungs. He gave me a thumbs-up. I could see Aden nodding as he blew up another balloon.

I grabbed my backpack from in front of the closed bleachers and slung it over my shoulder. I went to the back door that led out to the field and pulled on it to ensure it was shut. I looked around to make sure that Dean and Aden were the only other people in the gym. They were. I took a pouch out of my backpack and sprinkled black dust over the door's threshold. I moved to the next door that led out of the school and repeated the process.

Jules was confident that Lucile Dyer would try something now that there were more witches in town. Part of me hoped she would. I would use the dance as a trap. I created a spell that would act as a barrier, but it wasn't designed to keep uninvited guests out; it would stop them from using magic unless I wanted them to. The spell wasn't guaranteed to work, but I had packed that dust with many potent ingredients, including some of the ashes from the elder tree. I had faith it would.

I had dusted the threshold of every entrance to the school and had gone completely unnoticed. That was until I dusted the entrance to the student parking lot.

"Selene?" Dean questioned as he approached me.

"Dean," I said, startled by his sudden appearance. He raised an eyebrow at me.

"What are you doing?" he asked. *Fuck.*

"You'd just think it's silly," I said as I hid the dust pouch behind my back.

"Try me," he said.

"It's a, uh, superstition my aunt has," I lied. "She says that you should sprinkle this at the door every time you host a party so that everyone who attends will be safe."

"So, you're doing it here?" he asked.

"Well, at all the doors. Technically, Tera, Ashlyn, and I are hosting this party, right? I just thought. You know what, never mind, it is silly."

"No, I don't think it's silly at all. Can I see it?" he asked as he held out his hand. I handed him the pouch. He took a bit out of the pouch and sprinkled it along the threshold, leaving behind a thick black line. "Like this?"

"No," I laughed. I pinched some from the bag and lightly sprinkled it over the threshold so that it wasn't a visible line. "You're putting too much. It only takes a little, so no one would notice if they walked over it."

Dean followed my motions and sprinkled some himself. That time, he did it perfectly. I watched his face. His thick eyebrows twitched as he concentrated. *Why is he doing this?* Guilt tickled my chest.

"I guess you can call me superstitious now too," he said as he handed me the pouch back.

"I guess I can." I put the pouch back into my backpack.

"I am going to borrow my uncle's van for tomorrow night so I can pick everyone up," he said.

"Sounds good."

"I'll see you at seven o'clock sharp," he said. He gave me a grin before walking out the door.

I watched him as he walked away from the school. There was something about Dean that felt different. It was like he understood what was happening to us, like he understood me better than anyone else.

"Dean," I called as I pushed the door open.

"Yeah?" he called back. He turned to look at me with a tilted head and raised eyebrow.

"How 'bout that ride home you offered me?" I asked. He took a moment to think about it before nodding with a smile. I texted Aden as I followed Dean to his car to tell him to drive himself home and where to find the keys.

Dean drove a matte black Jeep Wrangler. It was covered in mud and dust. I carefully approached the beast from the passenger side and tugged on the door handle. Nothing. I tugged again. Still nothing. I looked through the car to the driver's side, where Dean was patting himself down. I glanced down at the car. The keys sat on the driver's seat.

I laughed, and as I did, Dean pressed his nose against the driver's window to look into the car. His cheeks turned bright red as he saw the keys.

"Well, so much for that." I joined him on the driver's side of the car.

He still had his face pressed against the window.

"I guess I'll have to take another rain-check on driving you home," he said. "I'm going to call a locksmith."

"I'll wait with you."

He pulled his face away from the window to look at me.

"Really?" he asked. His voice was soft and a little suspicious.

"Yeah, I don't have anything important to do tonight," I lied. I had plenty of important things to do, but none seemed to matter much at that moment.

"Thanks. Just hold on one minute," he said. He took out his phone and called the locksmith. I had nothing to do but listen to him as he spoke. His voice was a low growl, but his tone was calm.

"This isn't the first time you've done this, is it?" I asked when he hung up.

"Not even close," he chuckled. "I can be a bit of an idiot. My mom used to tell me to be glad my head was attached. Otherwise, I would've lost it already."

"Do you agree with her?" I asked as I took a couple of steps toward him. He looked at me and scrunched up his nose, like my question hurt.

"Sometimes, it's hard not to," he said. Dean looked away from me, back toward the car. I put my hand on the side of his shoulder. He was hot—so hot I could feel it through his denim jacket.

"I don't." Dean was one of the top students in our class, and even if he was a little clumsy or forgetful, it didn't make him stupid. He looked back at me, and I could feel the suspicion in his gaze.

"Can I show you something?" he asked.

"After the locksmith gets here?"

"No. It's actually not that far from here, just in the woods past the football field."

I couldn't help but laugh at how sketchy that sounded. I could tell the nuance of it was lost on him. He didn't even realize how odd his request was.

"Sure. Although I should warn you. Wandering alone into the woods with me could be dangerous," I mocked.

"Shouldn't you be the one afraid of me?" he said with a chuckle as he led the way around the back of the school.

"Please, I deal with things scarier than you before breakfast every morning."

He laughed.

"Your confidence is really inspiring," he said as we stepped into the wooded area past the football field.

"Oh?" I asked as I stepped over protruding roots and mud puddles.

"You make it seem like you're invincible. Like nothing could ever touch you," he said. He reached back and offered his hand to support me as we climbed up a steep pile of rocks. I took it. His grip was firm and warm as he hoisted me up the pile without an effort.

"A lot of things have changed recently." Tera always used to be the confident one, but she'd become more high-strung since she was cursed. Perhaps that made me seem more confident. "I wasn't always like this."

"Maybe, or maybe you just never realized you were," he said as he pointed me to the right of the forked path we were on.

Maybe. I mindlessly walked forward, lost in thought. I walked until Dean grabbed my waist and pulled me to a halt just before I walked off a small cliff.

"Whoa," he shouted as he pulled me back and into his arms.

"Thanks," I said with a heavy exhale.

"Are you okay?" he asked.

"Yeah, I'm fine," I said as I took a step away from him and out of his grip. "How much farther?"

"Not much," he said. He took the lead again, taking a left away from the cliff. We walked for another few minutes before we came to another cliff. This time, though, mist filled the air around us. It was like the water droplets were fairies dancing around us as we entered this opening in the woods.

"What is this?" I asked.

"Come look," he said and waved me over to the path's edge. Down below us, a waterfall splashed into a river.

"That is gorgeous," I said as I watched more water droplets fly up toward us. "How did you find this place?"

"I found it one night while I was on a walk," he said as he took a seat on a tree stump.

"Late night walks in the woods? That's pretty risky around here," I said and took a seat on the stump next to him.

"I guess you're not the only brave one," he said. "I come here almost every day now. It's the perfect place to escape from everything."

"Everything?" I looked at him. He turned his head to look into my eyes. His soft green eyes were refreshing. My heart beat faster as he leaned a little closer to me.

"Well, not everything," he said.

I leaned a little closer to him until we were only inches away from one another. I could feel my breath colliding with his when a loud ring jolted us away from each other. He sighed loudly before pulling his phone out. He glanced at it and then back up at me.

"The locksmith will be there in twenty minutes. We should start heading back."

I nodded and followed him out of the woods and back to his car. Once we were inside the car, our ride was silent. When the car stopped outside Tati's house, I turned to look at him. His cheeks were red.

"Hey," I said, putting my hand on top of his. "I had a really great time. Thanks for driving me home."

"You're welcome," he said with a nervous smile. "I'll see you tomorrow night."

I hopped out of Dean's jeep and closed the door. I had one more thing to take care of before I could get excited about the dance. I had to tell Aunt Jules what my plan was. She would be furious with me for even thinking it was smart, but I was ready to fight her on this one. I would not let Lucile Dyer or anyone else get the drop on us. We were going to be prepared.

"It's a genius plan," Aunt Jules said.

"I know it's dangerous, but we have t— Wait, what?" I was caught off guard by her agreement.

"I think it is a great plan, and these spells are almost bulletproof. You've really come such a long way from lighting my lawn on fire," Aunt Jules said. She looked through the pages of notes I had on the spells and workings I had been doing.

"Oh, uh, thank you." My heart warmed.

"There's only two things I have to suggest," she said.

"What?" I was eager to hear her feedback.

"We should make a hex bag to amplify the power of your spell. We would need to get it onto her person, though. In her purse, maybe," Aunt Jules said. "The second thing is a gift I will give to you tomorrow. You'll need to get her blood to make this plan work. Can you do that?"

"I can make both of those things happen."

"Good, then let's make a hex bag," Aunt Jules said with a smirk.

Aunt Jules and I spent the rest of the night together. We made the hex bag and dinner together in the kitchen. I was careful not to mistake the bone powder for Parmesan cheese. We all ate together as one big family, and that was the first night that everyone had forgiven Tera for breaking the hunters' curse. We all knew why she had done it, and none of us could say we wouldn't have if we were in her position.

I had already started looking for other ways to cure Tera, but none looked as promising without the Elderwater. However, I had hope.

After dinner, Aunt Jules and I watched as Tera turned and went for a run in the woods. Dinner almost came back up when she changed, though. It wasn't as disturbing as the first time I had seen her change, but it was like her skin was too small of a fabric that split and ripped, falling to the ground in chunks. As the sun set and the night came, Aunt Jules and I sat on Tati's porch and watched the stars while we waited for Tera to return. My mind kept going to how Dean had acted at the school, how he seemed like he wanted to be a part of our world.

"If Tati or Pax weren't witches and just humans whom you still loved, would you tell them the truth?" I asked.

"The last time we had a conversation like this, you went and told Ashlyn everything," Aunt Jules said. "Who is it now?"

"This guy, Dean. He's becoming our friend, but I think he realized we have a secret." I also told her about how he had helped me prep the barrier spell at the school without him knowing. However, I conveniently left out everything that happened after that.

"Do you like him?" Aunt Jules asked, shock in her voice.

"No, Aunt Jules. He's just a friend," I said. My cheeks warmed.

"I think you should tell him. I've learned recently that keeping secrets doesn't really protect anyone," she said. "Just be absolutely sure that you can trust him. That's all I ask. There are so many hunters crawling around this town that I couldn't even tell you who's dangerous anymore."

"Yeah," I agreed. I thought about Ben and Maggie. We hadn't expected either of them to be dangerous to us. Even if Tera thought Ben was harmless, I couldn't trust him. I had seen the cold look in his family's eyes while they discussed killing Tera. They were monsters. We sat outside for a little while longer until Tera crunched up the backyard's cold grass naked. Aunt Jules wrapped her in a blanket.

"I heard something else out there," Tera said.

"Like a coyote?" I asked.

"No, a lot bigger, but I couldn't find it. I was chasing it for a while, but it kept avoiding me," she said.

"Maybe it was just a person who was hiding from the massive creature prancing through the woods," Aunt Jules said.

"Maybe," Tera said. She didn't sound convinced.

Inside the house, we all cuddled and watched a tragic romance about a girl who got into an accident from texting while driving. After the movie ended, I cleaned up the popcorn and did some of the dishes. Pax followed me into the kitchen.

"Hey, what's up?" I asked as I dried my hands and hung the towel on the oven door.

"There's something I want to tell you," he said. His voice was odd and low. Pax and I hadn't spoken much since he and Aden had joined our little group. I had heard about him from Tera when she talked about her time in the woods.

"Okay." I nodded, waiting for him to continue.

"It's about something that might help you cure Tera. Something I haven't even talked to Jules about," he said. "There is a grimoire considered to be the most powerful spell book in existence. It is said to have every spell ever cast and how to break every one of them."

"Why are you telling me this now?" I asked.

"Because this book is only a myth, and I know Jules won't chase after it. At The Ascension, you could get a lead on it from the All-Mother's child if you win," he said.

I could feel my heart racing.

"What's it called?" I asked.

"*The Book of the Damned*," he said.

The name echoed in my head as I went to bed. I lay awake with excitement about the dance and excitement about the new possibility of a cure. I counted the wall panels before I finally drifted to sleep.

I was jolted out of my sleep by Tera banging on the door. I checked my phone. It was eleven in the morning.

I jumped out of bed and opened the door. Tera was standing there, an enormous, excited smile on her face.

"Ashlyn is already here. We have to start getting ready," she said.

"We have, like, eight hours before the dance."

"I know, but Ashlyn is going to take at least that long on our hair and makeup," she said.

"Makeup? We're wearing masks."

"That doesn't mean anything," Tera said. She grabbed my wrist and dragged me down the stairs into the kitchen.

Ashlyn had transformed Tati's kitchen into a salon. There were mirrors and makeup covering the table. I felt like I had just walked into a Sephora. Ashlyn was already fast at work on Tati's makeup, and Reyna was pulling Tati's hair into box braids. Aunt Jules waved me over to a plate of food.

"Good morning, sunshine," Tati said.

"Good morning. How early did you all start getting ready?"

"Started braiding at nine," Reyna said.

"I started her makeup about an hour ago, but I'm almost done," she said. "Then, I can start on Tera's hair and makeup."

"When am I up?" I asked.

"I should be done with Tera in about two to three hours, and Reyna should be done with Tati around then too," Ashlyn said as she shifted to Tera. "You and Jules will be at around two o'clock."

"Until then, though, we will be helping Aden train for The Ascension," Aunt Jules said.

"Okay," I said with a sigh before eating the rest of my breakfast. I knew that helping Aden train was just a cover for Aunt Jules to test me. *She's still doubting me.*

When we headed out back, Aden was already out there, sliding the dresser around on the lawn with a wave of his hand. I was impressed that he was finally able to move it. Pax was still standing fifty feet away from it. He had little faith that Aden wouldn't hit him if he were any closer.

"All right, Aden, it's time to see how you're doing with the Trial of the Moon preparation," Aunt Jules said. Aden nodded.

The dresser erupted into flames. Aden leaned in toward the flames and stared intently. I could see their reflection in his eyes. It was like he could see something in those flames that we couldn't see. He nodded.

"I see an athame with a sapphire in its handle," he said.

"Very good," she said. The flames extinguished.

"On the night of The Ascension, an item will be placed into a box. If you choose the divination ritual, you will be asked to identify the item," Aunt Jules.

"Oh, and here I was thinking predicting the future was enough."

"I doubt it will be much harder for you to find out the item. You are able to scry with ease," she said.

"The thing Aden really needs help with is the Trial of Creation. He is just struggling to grasp what I tell him," she said.

"I want you to walk him through creating a spell," she said. "Maybe he will have more luck seeing your process."

"I'll take a crack at it, I guess. Aden, come with me to the greenhouse."

Inside the greenhouse, I sat Aden down at my workbench. I slid the family grimoire away from him so that he wouldn't try to touch it.

"Do you know why I brought you here?" I asked.

"Because the most important part of a spell is the herbs you use?" he answered.

"No. The most important part of a spell is your intention. While the herbs do matter, they bring your intention into reality. You must first determine your goal."

"Uh, okay. I want to cast a spell for protection," he said.

"That's a good one to start with. Now that you know what your intention is, you need to find herbs that will complement that. You need to understand their metaphysical properties. You shouldn't just use any herb for any spell. Now, go around the greenhouse and pick three herbs you think will help the spell."

Aden took his time inspecting the plants as he walked around the greenhouse. He pulled some bay leaves and basil; both were good for protection, but basil wouldn't have been one of my choices. He was hesitant to grab his final herb. He stopped in front of the aconite, wolfsbane. He stared at it momentarily before he reached out to pluck one of its leaves.

"Stop," I shouted. Aden looked at me, confused.

"You haven't even read a single book on herbs, have you?" I asked. He shook his head in shame. "That plant is very dangerous. You shouldn't handle it with your bare hands. It's toxic. If wolfsbane is used to ward off werewolves and vampires, imagine what it can do to humans."

"I didn't know."

"You need to know the herbs available around you before you can even start casting spells, let alone creating them." *All-Mother take me, I sound like Aunt Jules.* "The herb I would've chosen is angelica. It's very potent for protection."

Aden nodded at my scolding, plucked some of the angelica, and brought it over to the workbench. He filled the herbs into a mortar, saving one bay leaf. He ground the herbs. I guided his hand so that he was grinding the herbs clockwise.

"Every little thing you do matters. The motions you make have meaning. Clockwise circles bring energy toward you. Use that for spells of protection, love, and luck. Counter-clockwise circles banish or send energies away from you. Use them for spells of cleansing, banishing, and hexes."

"How did you learn all of this so quickly?" he asked.

"I read all the books that Aunt Jules told me to, and I spent a lot of time studying our family's grimoire. After Tera was first cursed, I couldn't be ripped away from the books. Even after, I insisted Aunt Jules teach me more about The Ascension. I still kept studying."

"Jules barely wanted me to focus on the books. She wanted me to jump right in and gain experience by doing," he said.

"That's probably because you started even later in the game than I did. How come Pax didn't teach more of this stuff before now?"

"My dad wanted me to live an ordinary life. He didn't really want me involved in this world after what happened to my sister," Aden said.

"What happened to her?" I asked.

"She had the same curse as Tera, but she was bitten by another werewolf, not cursed by a witch. She wasn't careful and turned into the woods one day, and hunters found her." Aden's voice trailed off. I didn't need him to finish his story. I knew how it ended.

"I'm sorry."

"I was only a little kid. I don't even remember her, but because of her, my dad kept me out of this world as long as he could," he said. "One day, I slammed my door without touching it while we were arguing. He had to come clean about everything."

"I knew nothing about this world either until I watched my sister rip off her own skin and turn into a massive beast," I said with a shudder. The images from that night would never leave my mind.

"I hate that they lied to us," he said.

"I do too." I thought about my conversation with Aunt Jules the night before. "I understand why they did it, though. They were looking to protect us."

"Don't you think we'd be more protected if we knew about the things that could hurt us?"

I hated to think about it, but he was right. Lying didn't protect anyone but the people who were lying—whether it was us lying to the world about our existence or to each other about the things we didn't want to share. Maybe if Tera and I had known the truth, I could have been able to stop her from ever being cursed. The maybes didn't matter, though. We couldn't change anything that happened.

I took a black candle from the workbench drawer and placed it in front of Aden. Once he finished grinding the herbs into mush, he took the candle and carved the word "protection" into it. He rubbed the herb mixture into the carving and lit the candle. He waved the bay leaf over the flame to whisk the smoke toward himself.

"I am protected," he repeated with each leaf movement. After he said it twelve times, he put the leaf down and stopped speaking.

We just sat there and watched as the candle continued to burn. The wax droplets slipped down the side of the candle and pooled at the bottom. When Ashlyn sent Tera out to summon me to the kitchen, the candle was half its original size but still burning strong. I patted Aden on the back before leaving him to watch as his spell finished.

Tera's hair was like a mane of dark fur that fell into loose curls at her shoulders. The sunlight reflected off her face with a sparkle. Ashlyn had gone all out.

"You look like a porcelain doll," I chuckled.

"I feel like I belong in a corset and powdered wig," she said.

"Tell me what it's like to be married to Edgar Linton," I asked mockingly.

"Bite your tongue. We both know I could never choose a boy like that when there is a man like Heathcliff around," she said with a hand over her heart.

"I didn't know you actually read *Wuthering Heights*," I said, shocked.

"I didn't. I watched the movies," she said. I gave her a playful elbow to the side.

When I entered the kitchen, Ashlyn yanked me into the chair and whipped me around to face the mirror. Aunt Jules sat in Reyna's chair beside me, her long red hair pulled back into a Dutch braid. She read a book with black binding I hadn't seen around the house before. I tried to catch a peek inside, but Ashlyn pulled me back in my chair by my hair.

"We are going to keep your look simple but sexy," Ashlyn said as she straightened my hair. "You're the only woman here with two boys fawning after her, so we are going to give you a look that says you're a bad bitch who doesn't need either of them."

I could feel Aunt Jules, Reyna, and Tati with eyes all on me. I glared at Ashlyn in the mirror. She stuck her tongue out.

"They aren't fawning after me. They're just friends."

Ashlyn shrugged and continued working on my hair. After an hour of straightening my hair, Ashlyn moved to my makeup. She decided she wanted to keep that simple too. She gave me a light dusting of foundation and moved to eyeliner and lipstick. She chose a bold red lip. When I was done, I stood and turned toward everyone in the room.

"You look stunning," Tati said.

"All right, go get dressed and help Tera get into her dress," Ashlyn said as she swatted me out of the kitchen. I followed Ashlyn's demands.

19

Tera-Sue

I wrestled with my dress as I pulled it out of the bag. It was way too big for me to put on alone. I fell onto the bed as I tried to kick the bag off the end of the dress. I cursed it under my breath. I looked toward the door as it squeaked to announce someone coming into the room. It was Selene, already in her dress. She looked amazing, like a model who had just come off the runway. Her black strapless dress fit perfectly with her hair and makeup; Ashlyn had outdone herself.

"Need some help?" She laughed at me.

"Yes, I do."

Selene pulled the bag off the bottom of the dress and helped me climb inside it. I slipped my arms in the holes and flattened out the ruffles in the front of the dress. I adjusted the skirt so it sat correctly on my hips.

"All right, zip me up, but be careful. This dress is only a rental. None of us can afford to buy it."

"You look like a princess. Of course, this dress costs a fortune," Selene said as she zipped it in one quick motion. I cringed at how swift she was. "Oh, relax, the dress is fine."

Selene sat on the bed, looked up at me, and gestured toward the mirror. I walked to it so I could look at myself. Selene was right. I looked like a princess, and I kind of felt like one. Butterflies were dancing in my stomach as I looked at myself. I stopped looking at myself and sat on the bed beside Selene.

"Are you worried that something might happen tonight?" I asked.

"No, I'm not. We are all going to be together, and this time, we're ready."

"I'm nervous."

I grabbed the protection charm Aunt Jules had given me off the nightstand and tucked it into my bra.

"Why?" Selene asked.

"I'm afraid to let myself have fun, to feel safe." *Things could go wrong at any moment, and I could hurt someone.*

"I won't let anything happen to you, and anyone who tries to hurt you will be sorry they did. Anyone," she said. That meant Ben.

"A year ago, we would've gone to this dance without a second thought, but now I'm wondering if I am putting other people in danger by living my life." I hadn't talked to anyone about this because I always knew what their response would be, but now that I had destroyed the best shot we had at a cure, it felt heavier on my shoulders.

"Tera, you have full control over yourself. You're not going to hurt anyone. This won't be your life forever. I'm going to break the curse," she said.

"This has to be the worst senior year in the history of senior years," I chuckled.

"Maybe the worst one so far."

"Well, I feel bad for the one worse than this. I haven't even applied to any schools yet, and it's almost December."

"Neither have I," Selene said. "I forgot all about applying to colleges."

"We need to do that," I sighed as I leaned against her shoulder.

"Yeah." She rested her head on mine.

We sat there for a while in silence, just staring off into the distance. I could hear everyone chatting in the kitchen, Pax chopping wood in the backyard, Aden sitting on the porch. I had become so accustomed to hearing everything around me that it felt normal. The days during the full moon, when I had to wear my necklace, were like wearing noise-canceling headphones. Everything was so dull around me. The world seemed dimmer and quieter.

The floorboards creaked and whined softly as someone came up the stairs. It was Jules, and she had some boxes in her hands.

"Look at the two of you. You both look so beautiful," she said. She brought the boxes over to us and put them on the ground. Two of them were shoe boxes; one was a smaller box, and the last one was a long, thin box. She reached down, picked up the small box, and handed it to me.

"What is this?" I asked.

"I know I should wait until your prom for this, but with everything that's happened so far this year, I didn't want to wait. This was your mother's. She left it with me for you," Jules said.

Selene and I had never met our mother, and no one ever really talked about her. We barely knew anything about her. When we were younger and would ask Aunt Jules about her, she would always say, "I'll tell you when you're older." It made sense now. She had been all tied up in this big secret world we'd only just discovered. I knew there was more to the story of what had happened to her, but I didn't want to ask. I didn't want to ruin the moment.

Jules handed Selene the long, thin box. She nodded for us to open the boxes. It was filled with tissue paper. I separated the paper and felt something cold. I let the small object sit in the center of my palm. It had some considerable weight for its size. It was a golden brooch with emeralds decorating it. It was in the shape of three spirals that connected. I looked over to Selene and saw her holding a decorated knife with a sapphire in its handle.

"A knife and a pin."

"It's an athame, and that's a triskelion brooch," Selene said as she rolled her eyes at me.

"They've both been in our family for generations," Jules said and fastened the brooch to my dress.

"Be careful with that thing! You just stabbed me," I joked. Jules didn't even seem phased.

"Come downstairs for some pictures before your ride gets here," she said.

I stared at Selene, who was ready to go with her, dagger in hand. She looked back at me, confused before she realized.

"Oh, let me put this away," she said.

I slipped my red heels on with Jules's help before going downstairs. The kitchen was empty, and Ashlyn's makeshift salon had been packed up. Outside, by the flowerbeds on the front lawn, Ashlyn posed for photos by herself. She had roped in Aden as her photographer. He stood there, awkward in his suit. She switched poses in every photo, wearing her puffy dark blue dress with frills. She looked like she had robbed Cinderella of her ballgown.

Tati handed me my mask and urged me to get into the pictures. I tied the lace ribbon of the mask behind my head tightly. I shook my head to make sure that it wouldn't come off. I was ready to steal the show. I walked in front of one of Ashlyn's shots and twirled in my dress so that I was looking at the camera over my shoulder. Aden turned to follow me and snapped some pictures. Tati whistled in approval of my poses.

"You look gorgeous," she cheered. Ashlyn pulled me toward her, and we took some shots together.

"I can't believe you just stole the spotlight from me," she joked.

"Oh shush, you look like a princess," I said with a smile.

"You look like the queen," she said.

"You both look like Disney vomited on you," Selene said as she descended the stairs. Her black lace mask made her lipstick pop. Her sleek dress and velvet clutch matched perfectly.

Her black heels clicked with each step. She was serving villain vibes; I was there for it, and so was Aden. He turned the camera toward her and started snapping photos. She didn't even glance toward him until she was between Ashlyn and me.

Soon, a limousine pulled up. We all looked at each other. The back door opened, and Dean stepped out. He was in a sharp tux with a white blazer and black lapels. His hair was gelled back, and he smelled of freshly cut wood. The mask he had on made him seem even more mysterious. *Ashlyn is a genius.* I tried to keep my jaw from dropping.

"Oh my," Tati said as she fanned herself. "That's a case waiting to happen."

"You're like double his age," Reyna laughed.

"I am not. I'm only twenty-five," Tati pouted.

"Twenty-five for the last ten years," Reyna whispered to her.

I held my chuckle back from listening to their bickering because no one else likely heard it. Ashlyn leaned into Selene and me.

"Did you know he was getting a limo?" she asked.

"No, he told me he was bringing a van," Selene whispered back as Dean walked up to us.

"Hey," he said, with his gaze focused on Selene. I could have sworn I saw panic in her eyes. Ashlyn must've seen the same thing.

"Hi, Dean," Ashlyn said. He looked disappointed. Ashlyn took charge and started guiding everyone into positions for large group photos. She handed the camera to Aunt Jules, who was a surprisingly good photographer.

After about thirty minutes of photographs, we all piled into the limo and headed to school. Selene sat next to Dean, practically on top of him. She whispered in his ear, and he nodded, though I couldn't hear what either of them was saying. The music was too loud. She slipped something into his pocket before she sat up and moved away from him.

I hadn't ever seen Selene flirt with anyone before, so I figured she must've liked him, and it was clear he liked her. Aden was seeping with jealousy beside me as he watched.

When we reached the school, the line to enter was so long that it wrapped around the other side of the building. Ashlyn led us into the building, cutting the line. Inside, the gym was empty, and the DJ had just started playing music. We claimed a table right by the dance floor area. The boys left their jackets at the table and went to get us all some refreshments. Selene slid her clutch under Dean's jacket. Ashlyn grabbed both of us and dragged us onto the dance floor.

As we danced and let ourselves have fun, more and more people filed into the gym and onto the dance floor. Soon, we were surrounded by people on all sides, nudging against each other as we danced. I looked around at our group. It was the first time in months that I felt happy.

I noticed Dean wasn't on the dance floor. I looked around but didn't see him. I did spot Maggie Fera, Ben, and Will all clustered together at a table. I nodded in their direction. Selene looked over at them but didn't stop dancing. She whistled and caught their attention. Will furrowed his brow at her. Ashlyn and Selene flipped them off simultaneously without missing a beat of their dance. *Nothing is going to ruin tonight.*

Dean joined us on the dance floor. Standing close behind Selene, he whispered something to her. She turned to face him and wrapped her hands around the back of his neck. She stood on her tippy toes and whispered something back to him. They danced like that for a few moments without whispering anything more before they separated and rejoined the group of us.

Everything was perfect until the DJ played the first slow song. Dean and Selene paired off. Ashlyn and Aden paired off, even though he looked scared. I was left alone, which I attempted to use as a time to get a break, but that was cut short when Ben cut me off before I could get to the table.

"Hey," he said.

"Uh, hey." I could feel the hairs on my neck standing up.

"Listen, I know things are still awkward between us, but do you want to dance?" he asked. He held his hand out to me. I should've said no. I should've walked away from him, but I could feel my heart fluttering with joy. I nodded and took his hand.

On the dance floor, I let him take the lead. Our bodies were inches from touching, and our eyes were locked on each other. Everyone else on the dance floor faded away. It was just the two of us. I could feel myself getting lost in his eyes, in the memories that came with touching hands with him. It was like I was feeling every time we had ever touched at once, every memory and breath returning to me in just a moment. I let our bodies finally touch, and I rested my head on his chest as we swayed. I could hear his heart beating, racing just as fast as mine. If time ever had to stand still, I prayed it would be at that moment. Every problem and worry vanished inside his arms.

After a few slow songs, the DJ picked up the pace. We ended up in the center of the dance floor. I stepped back from him. I opened my mouth to speak, but he spoke first.

"I have something for you," he said. His eyes were tense.

"You do?"

"Yeah, it was my mom's," he said as he reached into his back pocket. "It was one of the few things to survive the fire."

"Ben, I couldn't take something that special."

"I need you to have it," he said. He looked so hurt inside that I couldn't argue with him.

"Okay."

"Hold out your hand," he said.

I did as he said. I held out my hand. He took out a ring with a large diamond. *An engagement ring?* I thought. *Why would he give me that?* My confusion ended when he dropped the ring into my palm. A searing pain shot through my body as the ring made contact with my skin. I flinched, and the ring fell to the ground. I looked at my hand as I watched the burn the ring had caused begin to heal. I looked up at Ben. He looked terrified.

"Silver." I realized what he was doing. I looked off the dance floor to where Maggie and Will were standing, watching us. I stepped away from Ben as I felt a pit growing in my stomach.

"Tera," he said and went to grab my arm.

I slapped him across the face before he could touch me. The slap echoed so loud that it caught everyone else's attention on the dance floor. Selene and Ashlyn rushed to my side, and Dean put himself between Ben and me. I could see Jules coming toward us from the punch bowl.

"You got a problem, buddy?" Dean barked at him.

"Are you okay?" Selene whispered to me.

I nodded. "I need to just go to the bathroom."

"We'll go with you," Ashlyn said.

"No, I need to go alone."

They both nodded to me as I made my way off the dance floor. I didn't look back as I jogged past Jules, out of the gym, and down the hallway.

Once in a hallway by myself, I stopped jogging. I felt sick to my stomach. I leaned against one of the walls and took a couple of deep breaths.

Ben is just like his father and brother, a hunter who wants to kill me. It doesn't matter if I love him. He wants to kill me. I fucked up. I broke that curse to help him. I put us all in more danger.

I sat down against the wall. Helplessness swelled up inside me as I started crying. I pulled the protection charm Aunt Jules had made out of my bra and held it up to my head. I prayed it would fix this mess. Heeled footsteps clicked against the floor, racing toward me.

The charm was ripped from my hands and flung across the hallway. I turned my head in shock to see Lucile Dyer standing thirty feet from me in the hallway. She wore a purple sequin dress and had a purse slung over her shoulder. I looked down at her arm. It was covered with a huge bandage.

"I've been looking for you," she said.

20

Selene

I pulled Dean away from Ben and stepped in front of him. Ben looked at me with wide eyes. He opened his mouth to speak, but I cut him off.

"Leave. Now. This is the only chance you're going to get to make it out of here. Take the rest of the hunter scum with you," I said through gritted teeth.

Ben said nothing and left the dance floor. Then, he, Maggie, and Will left the gym. I whirled around and went to walk off the dance floor and chase after Tera when Dean grabbed me by the shoulder.

"What was that? What happened?"

"I'm not too sure," I lied. I had an idea of what had happened.

"You said you were going to tell me the truth."

"I will. We all will, but there's still something I need to do tonight."

I grabbed my clutch off the table and left the gym. I checked the bathroom closest to the gym, and Tera wasn't there. I took my phone out of the clutch and texted Aunt Jules.

I think it's time.

She sent me back a thumbs up. I started walking down another one of the hallways. I checked all the rooms looking for Tera. I was halfway down the hallway when a scream came from an adjacent hallway. I ran toward the scream.

I turned the corner to see Tera curled up on the ground. Lucile Dyer stood between us. She was trying to force Tera's change. She had her back to me, so she hadn't noticed I was there yet. I willed a wall of fire to form between Tera and her. She glanced back over her shoulder at me and giggled.

"Aw, that's so cute that you think that will stop me. You know your aunt should have told you about your power sooner, then may—" She was cut off when I clenched my fist. She choked and gasped for air. Tera stopped struggling on the ground.

"What were you saying?" I asked her as I tilted my head.

"H-how?" she forced out.

"I set a trap for you, of course. I was hoping you'd come here and try something. I cast a barrier on the school that gave me control over the use of magic inside the school. So, if I don't want you using it, you can't," I explained. I clenched my fist tighter, and she coughed in response. "You see, I've concocted the perfect punishment for you. As much as you deserve to die, I think that will be too kind for you. Instead, I'm going to take away your magic."

"What? No!"

"Yes. I'm going to bind you so that you can never cast another spell again. You will never curse anyone again." I could see the fear in her eyes as I walked toward her. I took my athame out of my clutch and dragged it across her right cheek until she bled on it. I pulled a poppet out of my clutch. I stabbed the athame into the poppet and pulled it out slowly so that the blood would be inside and on the poppet. I took a black string out of my clutch and wrapped the poppet away from myself and toward Lucile Dyer.

"I bind you, Lucile Dyer. Magic shall not serve you until the trees and the stones, the earth and the sky, the sun and the moon become one," I chanted as I wrapped the poppet.

After the last bit of string had been wrapped, I held the poppet. I willed it to ignite.

As the poppet burned, Lucile began to wretch in pain. Her skin was turning red from the heat. She fought for a few seconds before she fell unconscious. I waited until the poppet was nothing but ashes in my hand. I stabbed her directly in the shoulder and pulled the athame out. I sprinkled and rubbed the ashes into her wound. I put my hand on her forehead and whispered in her ear.

"When you wake up, maybe you'll be no more dangerous than a fly."

Her wound healed with ash inside.

I waved out the wall of fire that separated us from Tera and ran to her. She was unconscious on the floor from fighting the change. I sent Aunt Jules a help text message.

"I got her, Tera," I whispered. "I got that bitch."

Aunt Jules came into the hallway with Pax and Aden, who helped lift Tera and carry her to the car. We all stepped over Lucile and left her there to be found by one of the janitors or wake up on her own.

The dance had died down since Tera had run out. Only a couple of people were left on the dance floor, slow dancing. Ashlyn was already cleaning up with the help of Tati and Reyna. Dean sat at the table alone, just staring at the dance floor. I went to him.

"You know you can dance to a slow song by yourself, right?" I asked.

"Only if you want me to be the one everyone talks about the next day."

"I've probably already earned that title."

"No, your sister definitely beat you there."

"Definitely," I said with a sigh.

"Is she okay?"

"Yeah, they took her home already."

"Who was that jerk that she was dancing with?"

"That was Ben. Her ex."

"That was Ben? Ashlyn made him seem like Prince Charming or something, but he just seemed like a dumb jock."

"Usually, he is like Prince Charming. I don't know what happened tonight." I knew Ben was a hunter, but even then, he was still kind.

"Well, the dance was fun for the most part," he said.

"Yeah, it was."

"How did your thing go?" he asked.

"It went well."

"Guess you owe me some explanations now?"

"I guess I do." I had enlisted Dean's help to sneak the hex bag into Lucile's purse earlier in the night in exchange for the truth.

"Well, I have the limo for like another two hours, so we could go to dinner," he said.

"Let's go."

I told Aunt Jules we were going to dinner. Ashlyn had decided not to join us and had hitched a ride back to the house with Tati. Aden was the only one who wanted to join us. The limo ride to the restaurant was just as fun as the dance because we let the music blast and danced the whole time. Aden even poked out of the sunroof and cheered at passing cars. He needed a boost from Dean to reach.

At the restaurant, the waitress sat us in a booth. I wondered if she'd assumed we would be loud and obnoxious and had placed us far away from her other customers. I sat alone on one side of the booth, and Dean and Aden sat together on the other.

I kept my eyes glued to the menu. I could feel Dean's eyes on me. I wanted to tell him the truth, but I couldn't tell another person Tera's secret without her knowledge. She had been pissed when I told Ashlyn. I thought about just telling Dean about my secret, but then he would ask about Tera, and I would have to lie again. I finally put the menu down and decided that I would have to tell him a half-truth. Dean and

Aden were engaged in a conversation about the menu and about what looked good.

"The chicken parm looks really good," Dean said.

"It does, but I'm a vegetarian," Aden said. I didn't know that.

"Oh really? Well, they have eggplant parm too."

"Hmm. What are you getting?" Aden asked as he turned to me.

Fuck. All that time looking at the menu, and not a second of it had been spent looking for something to eat. It was time to go with a classic.

"I'm probably gonna just get chicken fingers and french fries."

Dean laughed at my answer. "We come to a fancy restaurant, and that's what you're gonna get? You were staring at the menu for like ten minutes."

"Well, nothing really caught my eye on the menu," I lied.

"What's wrong with you? How can you not like Italian food? Is it the garlic? Oh god, are you a vampire?" he asked with a chuckle.

"No, I'm not a vampire. I'm a witch." I figured it was best to just rip the band-aid right off, and since we were already close to the topic, I went for it. Aden looked at me in shock. Dean started laughing. "I'm not joking."

"I thought you were going to tell me the truth, not a fairy tale."

"Give me your hand." I held out my hand.

"What?"

"Selene," Aden tried to protest, but I silenced him with a glare.

"If it's only a fairy tale, nothing will happen."

Dean placed his hand inside of mine, palm up. I held it tightly and pulled my athame out of my clutch. Dean's hand tensed up, and he tried to pull it away. I laughed.

"Relax, I'm just joking with you."

I released his hand and placed the blade of the athame in the palm of my hand. I applied some pressure and pulled the blade. A hot, stinging pain filled me, but I kept a steel expression. I let the blood from my palm run down my fingers.

Dean watched with fear on his face. I closed my hand into a fist and closed my eyes. I had never healed myself before, and I wasn't even sure I could. The sting of my cut turned into a searing pain that felt like I was holding fire in my hand. The pain then vanished. I opened my hand and glanced down at it. The cut and blood were gone. I showed my hand to Dean.

His expression was shocked, but something felt off about it. I met his eyes. On the surface, they were bright with shock, but I knew they were trying to deceive me. Dean was hiding something behind those gorgeous green eyes, but I wasn't sure what.

"There."

"Th-that's amazing," he said as he looked at my hand closer. He grabbed it and traced his coarse fingers over my palm.

"Wow, you're getting great at that, Selene," Aden said as he peeked at my hand.

"You knew she could do that?" Dean asked and looked at Aden.

"Well, yeah, I've seen her do a lot more than that. To Selene, that was just a parlor trick. She can work some serious magic," Aden said, nodding. He had been my test dummy for working with my new power. I had cut him and stabbed him, with his consent, of course, and then healed him at least fifty times before the dance. Though, he told me it felt like cool water was washing over his wounds, soothing him. That was not the experience I had.

"Really?" Dean asked.

"I just practice a lot."

"I practice too, but I can't do half of what you can," Aden said. He seemed discouraged.

"You'll get there."

"Wait, you're a witch too? Or are you a warlock?" Dean asked.

"I'm a witch. Warlocks are not good news. They are oath breakers. I never want to be known as a warlock," Aden said.

"Oh. Can you do stuff like that?" Dean gestured to my hand. Aden waved his finger toward the salt, and it slid across the table to him. Dean looked at him in shock. "So, what about Ashlyn and Tera? Are they witches too?"

"Not exactly," Aden started.

"No, they aren't, but they know about us," I cut him off before he said anything about Tera. I didn't want to tell Dean everything just yet, especially not when I was suddenly getting the feeling that he was hiding something from us.

"That's really cool," he said.

We didn't talk about it after that. For the rest of our time in the restaurant, we laughed about the dance and ate.

The ride home in the limo was tamer than our ride to the restaurant. We were winding down after a long night. I felt an ache in my muscles, as though I had been drained of all my energy. I was finally feeling the consequences of expending the power I used to best Lucile Dyer. Thinking about that moment brought joy to my chest. I made her pay, not only for cursing Tera but for killing our father too. I smiled. That was a good night.

Dean walked us to the porch. Aden went inside and probably crashed into his bed. Dean stood awkwardly at the bottom of the steps. I waved him up to follow me around the porch to the back, where Aunt Jules usually sat. She was fast asleep by then. We sat down at the loveseat that overlooked the acres of land Tati had.

The sky with a thousand little white dots. The only light was from the moon. Dean was tense beside me. I looked at him and placed my hand on his knee.

"I want you to know that telling you about us wasn't something I did lightly. I know you are getting close to everyone, and I just think that you deserve to know the truth about us."

"Thank you," he said softly.

"There are people that want to hurt us because of what we are. I need to know that I can trust you."

"You can. I'd never do anything to hurt you. Any of you."

"You can trust me, Dean."

"I do," he said. *Then what are you hiding?* He moved his hand on top of mine. I felt a chill crawl up my spine. The hollow feeling filled my chest. *Am I about to get a vision?*

"Ben, the guy from the dance. He's a hunter. So are his brother and the girl they were with." I tightened my grip on his leg, trying to force the vision to come out.

"Hunters?"

"Yes. They hunt down supernatural beings and kill them."

"Well then, I won't let them get near any of you."

We sat there for a few moments in silence. His oath hung in the air between us. He checked his watch for the time.

"I gotta go. It's almost time to return the limo," he said. I grabbed his hand with the watch on it. I looked at the clock face hidden beneath the piece of glass. "What are you doing?"

"Come here," I said and pulled him off the loveseat and to the banister. I stuck his watch out in the moonlight. I caught a glimpse of myself in its face.

I traced a clockwise circle on its face and closed my eyes. I felt the hollow in my chest growing deeper. The hair on my arms and neck stood up. I opened my eyes and looked into the watch's face. I saw the full moon and images of a wolf howling. A metal pyre was ablaze with green fire, and I was standing over it. The last thing was a man with blood-red hair. He looked directly at me, and the watch's face cracked. I jumped back.

"What the hell?" Dean asked as he looked at the watch still on his wrist.

"I'm sorry." I was trying to decipher the vision in my head, but I couldn't figure it out on my own. I needed to wait until everyone was awake.

"What happened?" he asked.

"It was a vision."

"Not a good one, I'm guessing."

"I don't know. You should go." I practically pushed him to the front of the house and off the porch. He gave me a sad smile and wave as he walked back to the limo. I waved back at him.

Inside, I took off my shoes and sneaked around the house so as not to wake anyone. Upstairs, I opened Tera's door. She was unconscious and snoring louder than a stampede of elephants. Her hair was a tangled mess, and she was drooling. I closed her door and crept into my room.

Once inside, I grabbed some wipes off the dresser and rubbed off the makeup I still had on. I slipped into pajamas before climbing into bed. My head hit the pillow, and the next thing I remember was waking up.

I rounded everyone up for a meeting in the kitchen. I explained my vision and what I saw. Aunt Jules had her intense thinking face on. She was staring through me with cold eyes and tight lips. Her nostrils flared every few moments. Everyone else in the room was waiting for Aunt Jules to speak. At times like that, I realized how well Aunt Jules had led us. Everyone had faith in her to make the right decisions. Even though we weren't all technically from the same coven, she unified us. We relied on her, but more importantly, she always succeeded.

"The man at the end of your vision sounds like Sevran. The All-Mother's son," Aunt Jules said.

"Why did I see him?" I asked.

"It must have something to do with The Ascension. He must be the one coming to it," she said.

"So, what do we do?" Tera asked.

"It's time to finish getting ready for The Ascension," Aunt Jules said. "Since we are the ones that called for The Ascension this year, we have the burden of hosting it. That means every witch attending it will be invited to stay on this property for the days leading up to it."

"I'm not sharing a room with any random backwoods witch," Tera said.

"They won't stay in the house. They will have brought tents and will stay near where The Ascension will happen. It is to mimic the time when the covens first received their gifts from the All-Mother when they were nomadic," Aunt Jules explained.

"What do we need to do to prepare?" I asked.

"We need to set up a ritual space and bless the ground. We will need to pick a spot for it. It should be in the woods somewhere on the property," Aunt Jules said. We all looked at Tati, who was biting her nails.

"There is a clearing in the woods with a big pond we can use," she said.

"Draw us a map to the clearing. Selene and I will head there and start the blessing," Aunt Jules said. "Pax and Aden should get the ritual pyre and carry it to the clearing. Reyna, send a message to all the covens. Let them know an Ascension spot has been determined. Tati and Tera, harvest any herbs we might need for The Ascension from the greenhouse. If there is anything missing, just run to the store and get it. Take my card."

Everyone dispersed to their assignments. Aunt Jules carried two ornate golden flasks as we walked through the woods. She had me carrying a bag of salt. Once we were a decent distance from the house, Aunt Jules spoke.

"Selene, there is something you need to understand about this Ascension."

"What?" I asked.

"Sevran is the All-Mother's child represented by the Trial of Creation. He will keep a keen eye on everyone during that trial, but he will have decided who is the most promising long before that. The one deemed most promising during The Ascension gets to ask for one thing from him, and if it is within his power and knowledge, he must grant it," she said. I already knew what I would ask for—*The Book of the Damned*. However, I couldn't tell Aunt Jules that.

"So, I can ask him about a cure for Tera," I said with a nod.

"You can, but there is something else you need to know about him," Aunt Jules said. "When Lucile Dyer tried to curse you both the first time, Sevran was there and agreed to do a ritual that would erase the curse, but there was a price."

"What was the price?" I asked.

Aunt Jules was looking ahead of us, but I could see tears pooling in her eyes.

"The price was that your mother needed to sacrifice herself."

"What?" I froze in my tracks. A thousand questions were flooding through my mind. *Why would she do that? Why didn't Aunt Jules tell us this before?*

"I didn't tell you this because your mother never wanted you to know," she said. "It was her last wish."

"Why tell me now?" I asked. I felt a sadness bubbling up inside me.

"Sevran is a cold man, and he will try to use it to test you. I wanted you to hear it from me and not him," she said. I walked again with her.

"How many more secrets are you keeping from us?"

"That was the last one, but it wasn't really my secret to share," Aunt Jules said.

That phrase rang in my ears. I understood that. I wasn't frustrated or annoyed that Aunt Jules kept this from me. I was just sad to learn the truth.

"I won't tell Tera."

Aunt Jules just nodded.

At the clearing, we blessed the ground. Aunt Jules asked me to create a massive perimeter of salt in the shape of a half-circle, which touched the pond at two points.

The pond was more like a small lake. The sun and treetops were reflected on its surface. I tossed some salt in the lake and disturbed the image before I sprinkled salt inside the half-circle I had created. Aunt Jules sprinkled water from the flasks around the ground too.

Once we were both finished, we stood in the center of the perimeter and joined hands. I closed my eyes.

"All-Mother bless us and this ground so we may perform The Ascension to honor the gifts you have bestowed upon us," Aunt Jules chanted.

At first, nothing happened. However, as she continued to repeat herself, I could feel the air around us changing.

It was like energy was swarming around and filling into us. I could feel myself becoming stronger with each second. A thunderclap made me jump and open my eyes. Aunt Jules laughed at me.

"We're all done. Let's get back to the house. We've got training to do," Aunt Jules said.

We walked back toward the house and out of the clearing. As we stepped out of the perimeter where I had laid the salt, I felt the surge of power drain out of me. The blessed ground was giving us a power boost.

21

Tera-Sue

The woods around the clearing were filled with activity. There were birds in every tree and squirrels prancing around in every bush. I could hear the groups of witches talking and laughing in the distance. With The Ascension starting later that night, all the covens had at least one member present. Even Lucile Dyer was there, but she didn't dare look in our direction. After what Selene had done to her, I was surprised she showed up. Her son came over to our small campsite, apologized for her actions, and gave us her grimoire to use to break the curse. Jules dove into it headfirst and hadn't come up for air. Selene was impatient, waiting for her turn.

I strolled through the woods outside the clearing. Something felt wrong to me. I could feel the thing I was chasing the other day in the woods. It was watching us still. I could hear it shuffling around the tree lines, rustling in the bushes around the circle's perimeter. I followed it farther from the clearing when voices in the opposite direction caught my attention.

The creature was heading straight toward them. I was silent as I walked toward the voices. I froze when I recognized them.

"Do you see these tracks? Werewolf?" Will said.

"She's close," Maggie said.

"I'll call for some backup for tomorrow night," Will said.

They are looking for me, but they're waiting for the full moon to engage. They must want to make sure I can't turn back.

"We should keep tracking these and see where they lead us," Ben said.

My heart sank when I heard him. He was just as willing to hunt me as the others. I stalked my way back toward the clearing. I knew they wouldn't follow me because the only tracks I was leaving were human. I gave up on following that unknown beast through the woods.

The clearing's perimeter was lined with tents and people. In the clearing's center sat a large stone pyre with a lit fire. I looked around for any familiar witch. I spotted Reyna meditating outside her and Tati's tent. I speedwalked to her.

"Reyna," I said in a hushed voice. She opened one eye and looked at me.

"What?" she asked.

"I think we have a problem." I explained the hunters were in the woods not too far from the clearing. She shook her head at me.

"We need to set up an early warning system," she said.

"How do we do that?" I asked.

"I should be able to make something quick," she said. She stood up and went into her tent. I waited an hour for her to come back out. She handed me a drawstring backpack. "Carry this."

We headed into the woods and walked a mile from the clearing to set up the warning system. Reyna pulled a ribbon out of the bag and tied it to the tree closest to the pond.

"We will need to spread them out a few feet and create an arc around the clearing," she said.

"How will this alert us that someone is coming?" I asked as I tied a ribbon to the next tree.

"When someone crosses over this barrier, the fire in the pyre at the center of the clearing will change color," she said. "Tie them tight. If one falls off, the alters might not work properly and could warn us too late."

I triple-knotted every ribbon I tied. I kept my mind focused on the task at hand. If my thoughts wandered, I would be thinking about things and people I didn't even want to remember.

It took us hours to set up all the ribbons, and when we'd finished, we still had the mile trek back to the clearing. Reyna, I learned, was not a woman of many words. She only spoke to me after we began our walk back.

"It's not your fault," she said.

"What?" I asked.

"We do not blame you for what you did. You loved that boy. No one could've known that he would want to hurt you," she said. I didn't look at her. I just thought about how stupid I had been. I regretted breaking the hunters' curse, but there was nothing I could do about it.

"I just wish I wasn't so stupid."

"We are all a little stupid, and we all make mistakes. It's what makes up people," she said.

"I feel like I'm always making mistakes."

"Mistakes happen as we grow. You've just been growing a lot lately," Reyna said as she wrapped an arm around me. We walked the rest of the way back to the clearing like that.

When we got back into the clearing, the sun was setting. The witches were now all standing outside their tents and staring at the pyre. As we approached, I realized they weren't staring at the pyre but at a man behind it. He was tall and wore a sharp black suit. His face was lit up by the pyre's flames, stern and emotionless. He looked around at the witches with a smirk.

"Let The Ascension begin," his voice boomed. I felt a chill shoot down my spine. It was finally time for The Ascension. Worry washed over me as Selene, Aden, and four others stepped up the pyre.

"And so, it starts," Reyna said under her breath as we joined the rest of our group.

Jules was standing at the head of the group with her focus locked on the red-haired man. One witch walked to the pyre and cut her hand. She let her blood drip into the flames. It spat and hissed with approval.

"Boleyn," she said. The next witch approached the pyre and cut herself.

"Fryer," he said.

The trend continued. With each witch that added their blood, the flames grew taller.

"Novak."

"Black."

"Gloria."

"Crowley."

Next, Pax walked to the pyre and cut himself.

"Aradia," he said.

"Laveau," the man after him said in a thick accent.

"Dyer," Lucile's son said as he added his blood to the pyre.

"Valentine," Reyna said as she did the same.

Jules went to the pyre next. She nodded to Selene before fixating a fierce gaze on the red-haired man.

"Nikoalidis," she said as her blood dripped in. The flames shuddered with joy.

The last woman approached the pyre. The flames were now five feet tall and whipping back and forth. She dropped her blood in.

"Le Fay," she said. The fire shot higher into the sky, illuminating the entire clearing for a moment before slipping back down to its original size.

"The Trial of the Sun begins now," the man said. He pointed to one of the participants, and she nodded. "What is your gift?"

"I have the gift of the tempest," she said softly.

"Summon your storm, witch," he said.

The girl closed her eyes and held her hands above her head. The clouds in the sky swirled around, turning black and growing. Sky growled with thunder.

"Pass," the man shouted. The girl opened her eyes and nodded before rejoining her family. He picked the next participant.

"What happens if someone fails?" I whispered to Tati.

"I've never seen it happen, but I've heard that their coven will be punished by the All-Mother. They will be shunned by all other covens," she said.

"That sounds horrible."

She nodded.

The next participant displayed their shape-shifting abilities by turning into a bunny. It was the most adorable thing I'd seen. I wondered if Pax could change into other animals as well or if he could only do wolves. The man pointed out his next participant. It was Aden.

"What is your gift?" the man asked.

"Telekinesis," Aden said.

"Show your power. Push me, witch," the man said.

Aden had a determined glint in his eyes as he jutted his hand out toward the man. The man's suit jacket and hair ruffled as though a breeze had hit him. He slid back not even an inch.

There was silence before the man chuckled. "Pass."

Aden rushed back to our group. He was shaking with fear. I patted him on the back but kept my attention on the participants. The next two also used telekinesis. Neither moved the man farther than Aden had, but they both passed.

Selene was the last one standing before the man. He smirked at her.

"What is your gift of choice?" the man asked.

"Pyrokinesis," Selene answered in a cool tone. She had her arms crossed.

"Summon your flames then, witch," the man said.

Selene didn't move or gesture. She just kept her eyes locked on the man. He raised an eyebrow at her.

"Summon your flames."

As the last word left his mouth, flames erupted from the ground on both sides of Selene. Some of the observers gasped. The flames twisted and slid across the ground to join in front of her. They grew in height as they wrapped around one another and stood tall above the ground. The flames formed the shape of a snake, which then bared its fangs at the man.

He let out a loud chuckle of approval. "Pass."

The flame serpent flickered out, and Selene walked back toward us. Some of the other witches whispered to each other. Jules glared at Selene.

"Selene, don't waste your energy on flashiness. You'll need every ounce," Jules said.

"That was nothing. With the blessed ground feeding my power so much, it felt effortless," Selene said.

"What?" Jules asked. "The blessed ground?"

"You don't feel the power from being here?" Selene asked.

"No," Aunt Jules said. The others in the group didn't either.

"Selene is so gonna win."

"It's not a competition," Jules said with a shake of her head.

"I'm so gonna win. Sevran was entertained by it," Selene joked.

"All-Mother help me," Jules sighed.

Sevran clapped his hands, drawing everyone's attention back to the pyre. "It is time to begin the second trial."

A man rushed to his side with a black box. Sevran held it in his hands and turned toward the pond. We all inched closer to the pond and farther from the fire. The moon's reflection was large in the pond. I felt excitement swim through my body as I saw it. With the full moon the next day, I could feel my nerves on edge. It was like seeing the moon made me want to go running through the woods. Sevran put the box by the pond on the ground.

"There are six items in the box, one to represent each participant since each of you has chosen divination as your second trial. This will be simple. You must divine the object that represents you inside the box. Open the box and see if you are correct," Sevran explained.

He waved for the participants to join him. He shoved the first girl in front of the box, and she was given a small mirror. She gazed into the mirror for a few moments before she looked up.

"A rose thorn." She opened the box and pulled out the thorn. Sevran nodded.

The next participant used tarot cards to divine that there was a die inside the box for him. The following participant threw a pouch of bones to the ground and inspected them. They found a pen inside the box for them.

Aden was next.

He sat down in front of the box with the pond at his back, like all the other participants had. He was handed a tray with a fire lit on it. Aden stared into the flames for a few moments. He observed them as they swayed.

"It's a pin of a mouse," he said. He opened the box and pulled the pin out.

There were only two participants left, Selene and one other witch. Of course, Sevran left Selene to go last. The next participant used a mirror just like the first and discovered a poppet inside the box. Selene, without being told, took her seat between the pond and the box. Someone tried to hand her the mirror. She put her hand up.

"I don't need that," she said.

Sevran kept an unreadable face as he watched her.

Selene turned to the pond behind her. After staring into it for a moment, she tapped her hand against the pond's surface. Her touch sent ripples that danced across the pond's surface. An image came into view.

It was the black box being opened. A hand pulled Selene's dagger from inside it. Silence filled the air. Everyone watched Selene turn toward the box and pull out her dagger. It was as simple as that. She gave a smug look toward Sevran.

"Very good. You've all passed the first two trials. Now, it's time for you to prepare for tomorrow's trial. You will need to create a living creature," he said.

Everyone started to whisper and talk in shock. He held his hand up and silenced them all. "We will start tomorrow night after dark. You will go first."

She nodded and then returned to the group.

"It's one thing to create a spell or potion, but it is another thing to create life. This trial is completely unfair," Jules said.

"Can that even be done?" Aden asked.

"I don't know. It's never been done before at an Ascension," she said. "Sevran himself has created monsters, but he is not a human witch. He is the All-Mother's son, so his power is nothing like our own."

"There must be a trick to this," Selene said.

"Why would he give us a trial we would all fail?" Aden said.

Selene smirked.

"Maybe he didn't," Selene said.

"What are you getting at?" I asked.

"Aunt Jules, does it say anywhere that The Ascension is meant to be done alone? Wouldn't it make more sense that we all took on the last trial in unison, like the covens received their gifts in unison?" Selene asked.

"You may be onto something. A single witch may not be strong enough to create a new life, but many witches working together may be," she said.

"Come on, Aden. We have to go talk to the other participants," Selene said. He nodded and headed off with her.

"I'm going to talk to some of the witches about your curse. Do you want to come with me?" Aunt Jules asked.

"No. I think I'm going to go relax in the tent."

I lay in my sleeping bag, staring at the red ceiling of the tent. I could hear the fire crackling from the pyre and witches laughing. I could hear the stillness of the woods around us. I knew the creature was still out there, and I knew the hunters were out there with it. I wondered what would happen if they found that creature. If they had come toward the clearing, the witches would have to kill them. Kill Ben.

Whenever I thought of Ben, it hurt less to do so. I was slowly healing from the breaks in my heart. Having him actively trying to kill me helped a bit with that.

I closed my eyes and let his face disappear as I fell asleep.

The next day was spent waiting for the sun to set and the moon to stand high. I wore my necklace all the while, and it burned. As the sun disappeared behind the horizon and night came into view, the searing pain the necklace caused me only worsened. I could barely handle the sensation that walking gave me, let alone standing to watch the final trial of The Ascension.

Jules had set up a chair for me with the group. I appreciated the gesture, but that didn't stop me from wanting to tear my own flesh off of my body to stop the burning. I took a deep breath, trying to focus on watching Selene unfold her scheme.

"You may begin," Sevran said with a smirk toward Selene.

"Glad to," she said. She stepped up to the pyre and sprinkled something into it. She glanced over her shoulder and nodded to Aden. He stepped forward and added something to the pyre.

"What are you doing?" Sevran asked.

"We're standing together, just like your mother intended," Selene snapped back.

The next witch stepped forward and added something to the pyre. Sevran's smirk turned into a smile. Selene was right. Of course, she was.

The rustling of the tents behind us caught my attention. I turned to look, catching the tail end of someone crawling into our tent. I stood from my chair and struggled through the pain to get to the tent. Everyone was too distracted by the trial to notice I was slipping away.

I thought I was home free until I reached our tent. There was someone inside. I yanked up the flap, intending to catch the culprit.

"Who's in here?" I said sternly.

"Me," Lucile Dyer's head came out of the tent as she stood upward.

I tried to step away from her, but with the necklace restricting me, I wasn't fast enough. My eyes widened as I saw she was dangling one of the barrier ribbons in front of my face. Before I could react, she grabbed my necklace and ripped it off.

22

Selene

"We're standing together, just like your mother intended," I snapped at Sevran.

His vicious smirk turned into a smile as he nodded for us to continue. I waved for the last of the witches to put their ingredients into the pyre. I sprinkled the last of the elder tree ashes into the pyre. After the last witch dropped her ingredient in, I dropped the rest of the ashes in.

The fire shook as we continued to manipulate it. I offered a thumbs up. They joined hands and chanted. I closed my eyes and put my hands inside of the flames.

It was a sensation I knew I'd never get used to. It was like sticking my hands in warm water. I had to split my focus to keep the fire from burning me while also absorbing power from the blessed ground. I listened to their chanting, waiting for the perfect moment to finish the spell.

Once they chanted their last verse and hummed in unison, I leaned toward the fire and took a deep breath through my nose. I focused on the extra energy flowing through me. With steady and calm breath, I exhaled into the fire, willing life to come forth from inside. I replicated the feelings I'd had when I was healing Tati. Every ingredient that went into the pyre was once alive. All of them had fragments of life force I needed to awaken. I could reach out to this life force. I could touch it.

I reached the bottom of the pyre, scooped up the ashes in my hands, and held them out of the flames above my head. I waited, letting the energy flow through me and to the ashes. I could feel everyone's eyes on me. All the participants were relying on me; their covens were relying on me. That must've been what Aunt Jules always felt like—the weight of everyone's fate on her shoulders. *And you don't really know if you can do it.*

A chirp echoed, and then a second one followed. I felt the ashes moving in my hands. They ignited into flames. A phoenix took off from my hands and soared through the air. I laughed with joy. The witches behind me began to clap and whistle. Even Sevran clapped. I looked back at Aunt Jules, who had a wide smile.

I watched as the smile on her face melted.

I turned back to see that the pyre's flames were now green. A gunshot rang through the air, and the phoenix came crashing toward the ground. I looked around and could see men stepping into the clearing with rifles. I whipped my head around.

We were surrounded.

A blood-curdling scream rang through my ears. I turned back and looked past the crowd to see Tera had changed. She howled before mauling the woman standing in front of her. She paused at the sight of a man coming into the clearing beside her with a rifle. She slashed him with one of her massive claws, and he fell to the ground before she dashed into the woods.

"Aunt Jules," I shouted. She was engaged with some of the hunters and tossed them around like rag dolls.

"Go after her," she shouted. I ran toward our tent, where she had mauled the first person. Lucile Dyer was lying on the ground, bleeding out. She coughed up blood and looked at me.

"Help me," she said. I looked at her hand and saw Tera's necklace and one of the alert ribbons.

"You did this to yourself," I said. I pulled Tera's necklace out of her hand and stepped over her. I sprinted into the woods fire to a pair of hunters and ran out of the clearing.

I could hear the commotion in the clearing prominently throughout the woods. Gunshots and screams rang out with each step I took. I was following the fresh prints Tera had left, but I had doubts about catching her. She moved too fast for any human to be able to chase her down. My only hope was that she would stop. Even as an only hope, it was a bad thought because she would probably only stop to kill someone else.

As I continued to run through the woods, I could hear growling ahead of me. It was deep and violent. *Tera must've cornered something and is trying to kill it.* I came to a massive boulder; Tera was on the other side of it. I heard a familiar voice.

"I can't believe you've been lying to me all this time," Ben said.

I moved around the boulder and into Ben's sight. He jumped slightly but didn't stop pointing his gun at Tera, who was backed up against the boulder. She could've easily killed him before he pulled the trigger. For some reason, she hadn't.

"Selene, get out of here," Ben said.

"Put your gun down, Ben. I won't let you hurt her."

"She's a monster, Selene! She's covered in blood," he said.

"She's not a monster! That's my sister."

"That changes nothing," he said.

"Then why haven't you pulled the trigger? Why hasn't she killed you?" I asked. His eyes widened. *I'm getting through to him.* "Think about it, Ben. That's Tera, the same girl you confessed your love for on top of the Ferris wheel."

"Shut up," a voice said from behind me as I felt the barrel of a rifle press onto my back.

"Maggie."

"Ben, shoot her. We don't have time to waste," Maggie said.

"Ben, don't. You love Tera. You can't kill her."

"I said shut up," Maggie yelled as she smacked me with her gun. My ears started ringing, but I could hear Tera growl at Maggie. I fell to the ground and turned to face Maggie, who had her gun pointed at my face. "I should've shot you in the gym."

"You remember that?" I asked.

"I remember everything," she said as she readied her rifle.

A howl filled the air. I looked back at Tera, but her head was tilted to the side as she listened. A vicious growl rumbled from behind Maggie. A massive white werewolf with sharp green eyes stalked behind her.

Before any of us could react, the animal slammed Maggie into the boulder. The familiar crunch of bones rang out. She slid to the floor, lifeless, with open eyes.

I swallowed the lump in my throat as the beast approached me. A gunshot popped as a bullet hit the beast's shoulder. It collapsed onto its back and began whining in pain. I scrambled to my feet and turned to face Ben, who now had his gun back on Tera.

"Ben, stop it." I stepped between him and Tera. I felt my hair standing up. A gun was in my face, and an uncontrolled werewolf was at my back.

"Get out of the way, Selene," Ben said.

"I can't, you know that. Put your gun down, please."

"This is what my dad died for, Selene. I have to do this," he said.

"Even if it breaks your heart?" I asked. "Even if you'll just end up dead too?"

"Yes."

"I'm sorry it has to come to this, then." I was ready to turn Ben into a marshmallow when twigs snapped from beside us.

The white werewolf pushed itself back up and turned its attention to Ben. Ben spun his gun toward it. I willed Ben's pant leg on fire. He screamed and kicked to make it go out. The white werewolf dashed forward and bit Ben's shoulder.

Ben screamed and pulled the trigger again. The wolf jolted back, releasing him, and rolled off him. They were lying side-by-side.

I waved the flames on Ben's leg out and sucker-punched him in the jaw to knock him out. The white werewolf was breathing heavily beside him. It thrashed. It was reverting to its human form, probably from the amount of silver that had been pumped into it. I turned to Tera, who growled lowly.

"Don't you growl at me." I stepped closer to her. She snapped her massive jaws at me, but I didn't stop. I held her necklace in both hands. I leaped forward and tied it around her massive wrists. She released a howl of pain before she shrank in size.

I closed my eyes. I hated watching her change. It made my stomach turn after the first time I had seen it.

I felt her arms around me.

"Thank you," she whispered. I hugged her back.

"Don't ever make me do this again," I laughed.

"I'll try not to," she laughed. We heard a cough and turned toward Ben. Laying on the ground beside Ben, naked and covered in blood, was Dean.

"Oh my god!" I jumped to his side.

"Dean's a werewolf?" Tera asked.

"I guess so. I didn't know anything about it." His wounds were not healing. It didn't look like he was getting any better. "He's not healing."

"It's the silver bullets. You have to pull them out," Tera said.

"Oh, disgusting," I said as I stuck my fingers into his shoulder wound. He began to thrash and scream in pain. "I need you to hold him down."

Tera did just that while I squished around in his shoulder wound. I felt the bullet with my fingertip, and I forced my fingers in deeper.

When I pulled the bullet out, I dropped it onto the floor and turned my attention to the second wound in his stomach. *Abs are attractive until you have to pull something out of them.* It was like pushing my finger around inside of warm, rock-hard Jello. I pulled the bullet out and sighed with relief. We looked at his wound. It still wasn't healing.

"Um, Selene, I don't think he is breathing," Tera said. I put my finger on his neck and couldn't find a pulse.

"I can't catch a break." I put my hand on his forehead and my other over his heart. I closed my eyes and leaned down so my lips were next to his ear. I had woken Tati from a coma and healed plenty of flesh wounds, but I had never brought anyone back from the dead. I didn't have the power boost from the blessed ground outside the clearing. Still, I had to try. I had to do something.

"Dean, come back to us, please," I whispered. "It's not your time yet."

I tried to pull energy from around me as I attempted to breathe life back into Dean. I was becoming frustrated because it wasn't working. I kept trying.

"Selene," Tera said.

I ignored her and pounded on his chest with my fist. He grunted as I made contact. My eyes snapped open, and I inspected him. His wounds were healing, and he was alive. He wasn't conscious, though.

"I did it." I smiled at Tera.

"How do we get them back to the clearing now?" Tera asked.

"We definitely can't carry both of them."

"No way. Let's just leave them here and come back for them," Tera said as she pulled Ben's coat off and zipped it up. She didn't ask me to heal his wounds. She probably wanted him to suffer a little.

"I hope everything is okay in the clearing," Tera said. I listened to see if I could hear any gunshots or screams, but there were none.

"It's a lot quieter now."

We hiked our way back to the clearing. There were no signs of any other hunters. In the clearing, the witches piled up the dead hunters and tended to the injured witches. Aunt Jules stood alone, closest to the pyre, staring in our direction when we stepped into the clearing. Relief filled her face. She smiled as she walked to us.

On the other side of the clearing to our left, I spotted Will and another hunter stepping in. Will's gun was pointed directly at Aunt Jules. She must've seen my face shift because she turned to face him. As she turned, Will pulled the trigger and shot a bullet through her head.

Aunt Jules hit the ground.

The moment moved in slow motion. I couldn't find words. I couldn't find anything but a guttural, primal scream. The ground beneath me felt like it was shaking. All the energy and power from the blessed ground funneled into my body as my scream filled the landscape. My hair floated around me. I shot my hands out toward him.

Lightning flew out from my fingertips. The other hunter pushed Will out of the way and was hit directly by the lightning. His body convulsed rapidly as all the power I had just absorbed flowed out of me and into him. He burst like a water balloon. Will broke into a sprint back into the woods.

I ran to Aunt Jules and fell to my knees beside her. Tears blurred my vision. Tera came diving down on the other side of her. She was crying.

"Selene," she said.

"I know." I put my hand over her heart and the other over her forehead, covering the gaping hole there. I closed my eyes and tried to focus my mind. I leaned in next to her ear.

"Aunt Jules, please, we need you," I whispered. My voice cracked as I talked to her. "You need to wake up. Come back, please."

I could hear Tera cry. I tried to muster up energy from the blessed ground, but it was all gone. I had used it all on the hunter. I could hear more people beginning to gather around us. I kept my focus on trying to bring Aunt Jules back.

"Oh, baby," Tati said as she tried to comfort Tera.

Tera became hysterical. I tried to keep myself together, but I could feel the tears filling up underneath my eyelids.

"Aunt Jules, don't do this to us. We can't do this without you. I can't do this without you." I rested my head on her chest and sobbed. "No! No! You don't get to do this! You don't get to leave me!" I screamed as I pounded on her chest. I felt a hand on my shoulder. I didn't want to move. I didn't want to give up. The hand pulled me up and into a soft embrace.

"Come on, baby," Tati said. I let Tati guide me back to her tent as my tears soaked her shirt and my sorrowful screams were muffled.

23

Tera-Sue

The weeks after Aunt Jules's death were dark. It felt like the sun never came back up again after she was gone. Everything everywhere reminded me of her—reminded me she was gone. I just wanted to be numb. I wanted to sit alone in my room while the days passed by because I thought I knew pain before. I thought breaking every bone in my body during the change was pain, but I was wrong. There is no pain like losing a loved one. My heart broke a thousand times from the moment she died. The worst part was that things kept changing, moving on without her, and I couldn't do it. Not that soon.

Selene was the stronger twin. She put herself together and kept a strong face for the funeral and the days after. She didn't crack in front of anyone, not even in front of me. She organized the funeral and collected Aunt Jules's things from the school. Neither of us had been back to our house. Not even Selene was strong enough for that.

The funeral was bittersweet. We were all there, sharing memories and laughs about Aunt Jules, but she was gone. Everyone in town was there to pay their respects to her closed casket. The Original Covens stuck around to do the same. Ben came to pay his respects but also to apologize for his part in it. His perspective had shifted after Dean bit him and infected him with our curse. He didn't dare let Selene spot him, though. He feared what she would do to him. Most of the time, I was on my feet being confronted by strangers who wanted to tell me how sorry they were. I just nodded and smiled at them. The only time I was seated was when it was time for the eulogy, which Selene was giving.

She stepped up to the podium in her black dress with a hard expression. She didn't have a paper with her, and for a minute, she just stood there in silence. We all stayed silent with her. She looked at the casket and then back out at the audience.

"Aunt Jules was the person who fixed everything. Any mistake we ever made, she was there to clean it up. She pushed us to be better, smarter. She was the one person who held us all down in the hard times. I'm not really sure how to do this without her. This is one thing I was never prepared for. I hope to be even half of the woman and leader Aunt Jules was. Thank you all for coming," she said before she stepped down from the podium.

Selene was right. Aunt Jules fixed everything. She raised us. After the funeral, we couldn't go home. No one heard from Uncle Dan since he left for Europe. All of our calls to him went to voicemail. We stayed with Tati, while she and the others tried to find him. Tati comforted us at every turn and gave us anything we needed. Having people to share the pain with felt good. We all lost her, but we also all were able to appreciate the life she had lived. We were all navigating this new world where a piece of us was missing, and we were learning how to do it.

Ashlyn was the one who pushed me to live a normal life the most. She forced me to write my college essay and start applying to schools. I got into UNCC and submitted my deposit. Ashlyn also forced Selene to apply to schools. She was accepted into every school she applied to but chose UNCC as well. It was easier to stay closer to home, and that school was only an hour away. Ashlyn was going to NYU. She wanted to explore New York City and all its men. We didn't do prom; it just didn't feel right. Ashlyn didn't fight us on that. It was a full moon anyway, so we had other things to deal with.

Ben had undergone his first change since Dean had bit him, and he was adjusting to the werewolf life. Selene made them both necklaces like mine to suppress the change. Dean and I trained Ben on controlling his change, but he struggled so much with it that Pax needed to take over. Things were awkward between Ben and me.

Nothing monumental happened in our lives after The Ascension. Selene was still digging up information on a cure, but as far as we knew, the leads were thin. I picked up a job at The Grind to make some extra money, but that was nothing special. Graduation was the next big event.

I started the day with an entry in my journal, which had changed purposes since I had first started writing in it. I had made it where I still talked to Aunt Jules, where I pretended she was still there with us.

Aunt Jules,

Today, we are graduating. After the year we've had, I can't believe we made it. I know that this just means our lives are going to change even more than we get ready for college, but it feels satisfying to have made it to the end. Six months without you has been harder than I could've imagined. I wish you could've been here to watch us walk across the stage and get our diplomas. I know you would've been proud. I miss you so much. So does Selene. I think it has been the hardest on her. She thinks she needs to be the one to fill your shoes. Even if we both know those shoes are too big for anyone to fill alone. I know you'll be watching over us today.

Love you always,

Tera

I wiped away the tears that filled my eyes as I wrote to her. I closed my journal and left it on my nightstand. I checked my makeup in the mirror to ensure my mascara wasn't running. I flattened my skirt with my hands before I headed downstairs. Tati and Selene were already downstairs in the kitchen, waiting for me.

"You both look beautiful," Tati said. Selene and I had worn the same royal blue dress for graduation.

"Thanks."

"Let's go before we're late," Selene said as she rolled her eyes at me.

Tati drove us to the school, where we put on our black caps and gowns. We headed to the football field, where chairs and a stage had been set up. The bleachers were serving as seating for guests. Tati left us to go get a seat. As we walked onto the field, Ashlyn ran up behind us and jumped between us, wrapping her arms over our shoulders.

"We did it, bitches!" she shouted.

"Woo-hoo!" I cheered. Selene laughed.

"I have to say, I love the color choice. Royal blue looks amazing on me," Ashlyn said as she walked in front of us and flashed us her romper. "You guys look okay too."

"It was Selene's idea," I said, doing a twirl with my gown.

"Since when did you become so fashion savvy?" Ashlyn asked her.

"It meant to represent how we made it through this year together," Selene said.

"Kind of like we're a gang?" Dean asked as he and Aden walked onto the field behind Selene.

"Or a club? Maybe a coven?" Aden asked.

"No, like a family. I know Tera and I wouldn't have gotten through this year without all of you. I also know some of you would probably be dead without me." Selene gave Dean a playful elbow. "We finished one journey together, and we're going to start the next one together."

"Damn, if only we had some champagne," Ashlyn said before grabbing Selene into a hug. She waved for the rest of us to join in for a big group hug, and we did. Selene squirmed out of the circle's center and cut someone off who was walking past us.

"Ben," she said. He looked terrified to see her, but I noticed he was wearing a royal blue button-up like the rest of the boys.

"Selene," he said nervously.

"You don't get to get out of this," she said. His face was filled with worry, and she let him stew in it for a moment before she continued. "You're one of us now, whether or not you like it."

Ben's worry melted into a smile. Selene pulled him in for a hug, and Ashlyn happily dove in, leading a second group hug. We stayed like that for a few moments, just laughing and joking in the embrace. We separated as it was time for the ceremony to begin. After a couple of long and boring speeches from the principal and a couple of senators, the valedictorian and salutatorian talked, and their speeches were more entertaining. I could feel myself falling asleep in my chair as the people dragged on and on, speaking. I must've fallen asleep a little because I felt Selene poke me in the side.

"Tera, pay attention. We're next," she whispered.

Our row stood and walked to the stage, where the principal called our names, and a bunch of people shook our hands before someone handed us a diploma. We waddled our way up the stairs and onto the stage. Selene stood in front of me, waiting to hear her name.

"Selene Nikoalidis," the principal called. Selene glided across the stage, shaking hands and smiling in photos.

"Tera-Sue Nikoalidis," the principal called. I tried to follow Selene's lead, but I felt much less elegant than she looked. I didn't trip, though, so that was a big positive.

Once we were safely back in our seats, we hugged each other and squealed a bit. Maybe only I squealed. Still, it was an exciting moment. We waited for the tassel turning and the tossing of our caps. I chucked mine as high as I could. I didn't care if I never saw it again. Selene threw hers only a foot in the air so she could catch it. We grouped back up with everyone and took pictures together. Tati cooed about how we all looked so good, and, for once, I felt good.

After our photo op, everyone headed back to Tati's house for some barbecue that she was cooking. I was envious that they all got to go, have fun, and eat that delicious food while I had to go to work and probably have a stale doughnut. Mostly, I enjoyed my job at The Grind. It was easy, and the boss let me do pretty much anything I wanted as long as I was also getting my job done. I only ever really had one or two customers during my shifts because of how they fell in the middle of the day. So, I spent most of that time experimenting with making the perfect latte. It was the most difficult thing I had done all year and required the most brain power.

The bell rang to tell me that a customer had walked in. I stopped fighting with the foam machine and made my way to the counter. A woman with raven-colored hair and fierce gray eyes stood there with a man who looked like he hadn't seen daylight in years. She glared at me.

"You can take a seat wherever you'd like, ma'am. There are menus on all the tables," I said.

"It smells like a wet dog in here," the man with her said. She nodded before taking a seat at one of the booths. He followed close behind her.

They are so creepy. I returned to the kitchen and messed around some more with the foam machine. My phone buzzed. I checked it; I had a text from Tati that said, "URGENT! COME HOME NOW." I slipped my phone back into my pocket and turned to the cook, who was sitting on the counter reading a magazine.

"Hey, there are some customers here right now. Do you think you can take care of them? I have a family emergency." He nodded. I dashed out the back door and jumped into my car.

24

Selene

Tati's house was filled with the scent of smoked meat, and it made my stomach growl. It was bustling with life around the house. Ashlyn and Tati were working the grill. Dean and Aden were on the porch talking, and Pax was with Ben inside the house. I changed out of my dress and into something more comfortable. I smiled at Pax as I headed up the stairs to my room.

I changed into a pair of jeans. I grabbed a black sweater off my dresser and held it in my hands. It had been Jules's, and looking at it brought tears to my eyes. I wiped them away and sat down on my bed. I slipped the sweater on over my head. It still smelt like her, a mix of cinnamon and honey. I sat there for a few minutes just thinking about her and how much I missed her. I went to see her just before graduation.

I could feel the blades of grass crunching under my feet as I stepped on the paved path at the graveyard. Mom's willow creaked in the wind as I approached. I ran my fingers over her rigid bark. I could feel the familiar warmth filling me as I did so. I turned away from Mom's tree to face the freshly planted sapling in a mound of dirt just a couple of yards away. Tears filled my eyes as I walked to the sapling and knelt beside it.

"I am so sorry, Aunt Jules. I'm sorry I wasn't strong enough to save you. I am so lost without you." I crunched a handful of the soil in my hand. "I'm sorry I fought with you so much. I just wanted to protect Tera. If I had listened to you better, maybe this wouldn't have happened." Tears slipped down my cheeks and onto the ground. "Thank you so much for bringing us all together. Thank you for protecting us. I'm going to fix it all now. I'm going to protect everyone. I miss you so much, Aunt Jules."

I could feel the tears forming in my eyes again as I reminisced about visiting the graveyard. There was a knock at my door that drew me back to reality. I wiped my eyes and looked toward the door. Ben poked his head into the room, his eyes locked on me like a lost puppy.

"Selene, can I talk to you?" he asked. Ben always looked scared in those days, but I couldn't blame him. His entire world had been flipped upside down and set on fire.

"Yeah." He took a deep breath and looked into my eyes.

"Selene, I am so, so—"

I cut him off before he could finish. "No, Ben. You don't need to apologize." I grabbed his hand. "I don't blame you for what happened. It wasn't your fault." I knew Ben was in pain. He had lost everyone, and I couldn't hold any animosity toward him. I knew the pain he faced because I was facing it too. No part of me wanted to add to the turmoil he was up against.

"Why? Why are you being so kind to me?" he asked with tears in his eyes.

"Ben, you've lost everyone. I can only imagine the pain you feel. I only know the pain I felt when I lost Aunt Jules. You made mistakes, so have I, and so has everyone else. We could've done a thousand things better, and who knows, maybe everyone would still be alive if we had, but we can't change that now. All we can do now is just be there for each other." I knew Will wasn't dead, but I also knew if he ever heard what had happened to Ben, it wouldn't be a happy reunion. Ben was one of us, and we needed to protect him too.

"Thank you," he said as he hugged me. I grabbed the family grimoire, and we headed back downstairs. Ben joined Pax back in the kitchen to go over more werewolf training. Pax had practically turned the house into doggy daycare.

I walked out of the house and around the back of the porch to discover Dean and Aden sitting side by side on the loveseat. They were laughing until they saw me. They stopped. Aden gave Dean a nod, got up, and headed around to the front of the porch. Dean stood and leaned on the banister beside me. His gaze was locked on the tree line past the greenhouse.

"Thank you," he said softly. The sun made the white streak in his dark hair glisten like a patch of crystals.

"For?" I asked. I hugged the grimoire tighter to my chest.

"Saving my life, accepting me for what I am, not turning me into a roasted 'mallow," he said with a smile.

"Still debating that last one." I followed his gaze and looked out at the tree line.

"Seriously though, thank you," he said. I saw him turn to face me from the corner of my eye. I stayed quiet. I didn't know what to say. "Selene, I—"

"No," I cut him off. I grabbed his hand, which was on the banister between us. I knew what he would say. "Don't. Not right now."

I met his eyes. Their green hue was locked behind a glassy coat. He nodded and turned his gaze back to the tree line. I did the same as I let my hand slip slowly off his.

Ashlyn came around with a tray packed with food. Aden was close behind. Dean didn't even look at the tray. I just stared blankly.

"I hope you're hungry because Tati will kill you if you aren't," she said and put the tray on the table. I sat down in one of the rocking chairs. "Listen, I made sure that everyone has something to eat, children in blankets for the witches and raw T-bones for the dogs."

Ashlyn poked Dean on his side after her joke. He rolled his eyes before sitting beside Aden. We all laughed. I took plates and passed them around to everyone. I made three extra plates of food and brought them inside the house. I gave Ben and Pax a plate each and threw one plate into the microwave for Tera when she arrived home. When I made my way back outside and around the porch, I spotted something. Someone was standing in the center of the lawn about fifty feet from the porch. I froze once I recognized Sevran. He stood there in his sleek burgundy suit with his arms crossed, just staring at me. The others soon spotted him.

"Who the hell is that?" Dean growled as he jumped. Aden dropped a rib from his mouth.

"Get the fuck out of here!" Ashlyn shouted as she frisbeed a plate at Sevran. The plate froze in the air, only an inch from his face. He smirked.

"I like that one," he said. "She's got flare." He waved his hand, and the plate turned to dust.

Everyone else came running, all responding to Ashlyn's shout. Ben was ready to jump off the porch toward Sevran, but Pax held him back. Dean paused at the fear in Tati's face. I shook off my shock and walked down the steps to the grass.

"Selene, wait," Tati called.

I ignored her. I had to do this. I continued until I was just ten feet away from him.

"Why are you here?" I asked.

"I'm here to talk to you," he said. "After all, I still owe you a gift."

"That means I get to ask for something?" I asked.

"Yes," he said. "Are you sure you want to know the answer to your question?"

I glanced back toward Pax. He nodded. I looked back, my eyes narrow and nerves steeled. "I want *The Book of the Damned*."

"Selene, no!" Tati shouted. Sevran's face twisted into a crooked smile.

"I can get you to *The Book of the Damned*, but you won't be strong enough to use it without my help," he said.

"How do I get strong enough?" I asked.

"Selene, stop," Aden yelled. He was still too frozen with fear to move.

"I can help you gain the power you need. All you have to do is come with me," he said.

"And what do you get out of it?" I asked. I knew there had to be a price. There always was.

"You'll just owe me a favor one day," he said. He held his hand out to me.

There was no reason for me not to take his hand. I was closer to curing Tera than ever before. Dean leaped over the balcony and walked toward me.

"Are you crazy?" he shouted. "She's not going anywhere with you, creep."

No one else moved to stop me. They were all too afraid, but I knew everyone wanted to follow Dean. I turned to face him, and he stopped in his tracks.

"You're not seriously considering this, are you?" he asked. "Selene, you're not this dumb. This guy is trying to trick you or something."

"I don't have another choice. This is the only way I can cure Tera, Ben, and even you."

"This isn't worth it. I mean, you can't do this."

"I have to." My vision became blurrier with each second I argued.

"What if I don't want to be cured?" he asked. I felt a pain in my chest. "What if Tera doesn't want to be cured?"

"Then Aunt Jules died for nothing." I wiped away my tears. "I won't let that be true."

"And I won't let you do this," he said. We stared at each other for a moment in absolute silence, waiting for the other to move first.

I felt Sevran tap me on the back. His voice filled my head. *"This is just a taste of what's coming."*

I felt memories flooding my head, memories that weren't mine—hundreds of them, each filled with spells and knowledge from across the world. Decades of studying and practice were burnt into my mind in seconds. Pain filled my entire body.

Dean took that as his opportunity to charge. He sprinted toward me at full speed. He wasn't fast enough, though.

"Codlata domhain," I muttered. I waved my hand as I spoke the Gaelic command for sleep. Dean couldn't even stop his charge before he fell unconscious. His sleeping body slid to my feet.

I turned to face Sevran. "I'll go with you."

Sevran held his hand out to me once more. I placed my hand into his icy palm.

"Let's begin," he said.

About the Author

Randall Lombardi was born and raised on Long Island, NY. He attended SUNY Geneseo for his undergraduate degree in English, creative writing. In 2021 Randall taught 7th Grade English in Clarksdale, Mississippi. He completed his MS in Library and Information Science in May 2024 at the State University of New York at Buffalo. He currently works as a Youth Services Librarian. The Ascension is Randall's debut novel.

You can connect with me on:

🌐 https://randallwrites.org

www.ingramcontent.com/pod-product-compliance
Lightning Source LLC
Chambersburg PA
CBHW061245310726
48971CB00007B/2229